CELG

A Stranger's Secret

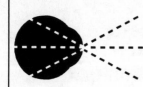

This Large Print Book carries the
Seal of Approval of N.A.V.H.

A STRANGER'S SECRET

LAURIE ALICE EAKES

THORNDIKE PRESS

A part of Gale, Cengage Learning

GALE
CENGAGE Learning·

Farmington Hills, Mich • San Francisco • New York • Waterville, Maine
Meriden, Conn • Mason, Ohio • Chicago

GALE
CENGAGE Learning®

Thorndike Press, a part of Gale, Cengage Learning.

Thorndike Press® Large Print Christian Historical Fiction.
The text of this Large Print edition is unabridged.
Other aspects of the book may vary from the original edition.
Set in 16 pt. Plantin.

LIBRARY OF CONGRESS CATALOGING-IN-PUBLICATION DATA

Eakes, Laurie Alice.
   A stranger's secret : a Cliffs of Cornwall novel / by Laurie Alice Eakes. — Large print edition.
      pages cm. — (Thorndike Press large print Christian historical fiction)
   ISBN 978-1-4104-7942-6 (hardcover) — ISBN 1-4104-7942-0 (hardcover)
   1. Widows—Fiction. 2. Large type books. I. Title.
PS3605.A377S77 2015b
813'.6—dc23   2015008354

Published in 2015 by arrangement with The Zondervan Corporation, LLC, a subsidiary of HarperCollins Christian Publishing, Inc.

Printed in Mexico
1 2 3 4 5 6 7 19 18 17 16 15

*In memory of my mother. The earth
is a poorer place without you,
and I am thankful for how
you enriched my life
with your example of how to
be a godly woman.*

CHAPTER 1

Cornwall, England
March 1813

The storm left more than missing roof tiles and downed tree branches in its wake. A mast, splintered like a twig in the hands of a giant's child and tossed upon the beach, a handful of spars, and masses of tangled rigging bellowed a tale of destruction. That not a box, barrel, or chest floated on the returning tide amidst the skeleton of the wrecked ship testified to destruction well beyond the ravages of the sea.

"Wreckers." Morwenna, Lady Penvenan, spat the single word as she surveyed the wreckage from the top of the cliff, her arms wrapped across her body to stave off the icy blast of wind from the sea and the chill of fear from her heart. For the second time in as many months, the local inhabitants of Penmara village had resurrected the ancient practice of luring ships to their doom upon the rocky shore below her home. She had watched the light bobbing on the cliff top, signaling safe harbor where no safety lay, knowing she couldn't stop the wreckers in the middle of their work without risking her own life and leaving her son unprotected, unable to save the ship and its passengers and crew. But now, if she didn't find out who was leading the men into lawlessness, the whispers of her involvement from the previous wreck would like as not blossom into full-blown accusations. The heaviness of her heart dragging her down as though the skirt of her woolen gown and cloak were soaked with seawater, Morwenna called to the deerhounds, who had been her constant companions since her husband's murder, and descended the cliff path to the beach. By her reckoning, she had another hour to hunt for clues before the tide turned and began to claim what the wreckers had left behind.

The dogs raced ahead, eager for a gallop on the sand after a day's confinement in the house. "Oggy, Pastie, come." She commanded the dogs back to her side.

Their noses deep in a pile of flotsam, they ignored her.

"Do not eat anything rotten."

They emerged with what appeared to be a

hunk of salt beef from beneath the stays of a stove-in barrel. Nothing Morwenna would want and apparently nothing the looters had wanted either, but harmless enough to the canine palate and digestion.

Leaving them to their prize and friendly tussle over who got to gnaw on it first, Morwenna set to her formidable task. She pulled aside sheets of sodden canvas to peer beneath, rolled half-crushed kegs, and lifted one end of what had once been a handsome sea chest to which someone had taken an axe. Not so much as a button remained in the chest. The stench of rum suggested what the keg had once held. Now the barrel lay empty of even seawater. Beneath the canvas, she discovered nothing more significant than wave-pounded sand.

And so the hunt progressed. As though repentant of the damage they wrought during the night, the waves rose and fell with no more force than a lady's blue skirt in a dance, its usual roar more a rumbling hiss. Overhead, the sky glowed ice blue and clear.

Morwenna paused on the edge of the surf. As she feared, nothing of value remained on the shore. Every cask, barrel, and chest lay split open, their contents hauled away. Not even the axes and clubs used to split those containers remained to hint at the owner of

9

the hand that wielded the implement of destruction. Wet sand had captured dozens of footprints, the deep indentation of hobnailed boots.

Every man in the village owned a pair of hobnailed boots. The footprints told no tales. Still Morwenna hunted, occasionally pausing to call to the dogs and keep them close at hand for comfort more than protection. More splintered wood or fragments of fabric, a dislodged button, even strands of hair held the potential for identification of someone.

The flotsam remained void of identifying objects save for lingering odors of rum, salted fish, the stinging stench of tar. Everything with even remote value had been picked clean. Later, men, women, and children would arrive on the beach to haul away whatever was useful to use as firewood or bits of canvas to patch a hole in thatched roofs. When the mines closed as those on Penmara had, families went hungry and cold. If she could find a way to reopen the mines, the villagers wouldn't resort to crime to survive.

She lifted her gaze from the tideline, to the remains of the vessel, one of its two masts sticking out like an accusing finger. No doubt some enterprising souls had waded or taken a boat out to the shattered hull to ensure nothing — nothing and no one — remained aboard. For those sailors who had not drowned . . .

Dead men told no tales.

Morwenna said a prayer for the families of the men who had died by either the hand of nature or the hand of men. She knew all too well the anguish of being left behind.

She trudged the last hundred feet of the beach. Waves swooped in, one or two high enough to dampen her cloak and gown. With each step, her heart grew heavier until it felt like a lump of cold lead in her middle. She reached the end of Penmara land where an outcropping of rock separated the Penmara beach from Halfmoon Cove below Bastion Point, her grandparents' home. The incoming tide nearly blocked the strip of sand that allowed one to enter the cove from the beach and the entrance to a maze of caves beneath. Some of those caves ran beneath Penmara. If anyone grew suspicious about the coincidence of yet one more ship wrecked on her beach, they would likely find goods from the vessel stored in those caves, just enough to ensure she took the blame.

She kicked at a bundle of rags at the edge of the surf and turned away from the sea,

11

calling the dogs to her side. They galloped to her like ponies. Their tongues lolled out of happy puppy grins, and Morwenna braced herself for the impact of a dozen stone worth of dog love.

But they didn't throw themselves at her. At the last moment, they swerved toward the tideline and began to snuffle at the bundle of rags, once-fine wool now water-logged, possibly considered too damaged from salt water to be useful to anyone.

Truly? When men and women stuffed newspapers beneath their shirts for warmth, even water-stiffened wool useless?

Her heart began to thrum like war drums in her chest. "Come away from there, you two."

She clapped her hands at the dogs to get their attention above the rising surf.

A wave foamed over the bundle. The dogs backed up, snorting from snouts full of seawater, then, when the surf receded, they darted right back to poke and sniff at the bundle with muzzles and massive paws.

Suddenly certain of what the bundle of rags contained, Morwenna lunged toward the dogs. "Oggy, Pastie, enough."

Oggy, the male hound, grasped a mouthful of woolen cloak and began to pull.

"Oggy, no. Drop —" The last word choked

in her throat.

The body had just moved without assistance from the dogs.

"Dogs, sit." Morwenna grasped the hounds' leather collars and hauled them away from the body. "I said sit. Now stay."

They obeyed her this time, perhaps sensing an urgency in her tone. Their bodies quivered, but they remained at the head of the tideline while Morwenna returned to the lump of sodden wool and dropped to her knees. Sand and rising seawater soaked through her gown in icy tendrils. She shivered, but ignored the discomfort. She would suffer more if she didn't inspect whether or not the incoming tide had caused the illusion, or if she really had seen a hand emerge from the folds of a cloak.

"Madam?" She scanned the length of the figure, realized it was half submerged beneath a sheet of canvas, and corrected herself. "Sir? Sir, can you hear me?"

Nothing happened. No sound of a response rose above the gentle roar of the surf. The dogs whined from their position at the edge of the tideline.

Morwenna brushed aside a tangle of water-blackened hair and touched the man's face. Skin rough with beard stubble chilled her fingers. Because he'd lain in the cold

for hours, or because he had already suc-
cumbed to weather, water, or a wound she
hadn't yet found?

Shuddering at the notion of inspecting a
dead man, Morwenna slid two fingers to
the soft place beneath his ear. If a pulse
existed, she couldn't feel one. With gentle
pressure, she tugged at his neck cloth. Sodden, it resisted. No way could she untie the
knot. Another wave washed over him and
her legs, prompting her to haste. She worked
her fingers between his skin and the fabric
in search of the pulse at the hollow of his
throat.

She found no pulse, but she found a chain.

For a moment, she gripped the metal
between her fingers, surprised to find a
piece of jewelry around a man's neck, more
surprised the wreckers wouldn't have taken
the jewelry. Most likely in their haste they
hadn't troubled to reach beneath a tight
neck band in search of something no one
would expect to find on a man.

She wanted to tug the chain free, see if it
held a locket or other jewelry that might
identify him. In moments, however, the tide
would rise enough to wash over and drown
him. Already the sand beneath him sucked
away with each receding wave nibbling at
the surface of where he lay. He was twice

her size, but she couldn't wait to move him until she found help.

She took up handfuls of his cloak. With the low heels of her walking boots dug into the sand, she tugged. At the same time, a wave rolled in, sending spray over the man and Morwenna. The sand shifted beneath her feet, and the surf rose higher, high enough to lift the man's body an inch or so off the ground, enough to float him toward her.

"Yes. Yes. Yes," she cried in triumph.

Then the receding wave sucked the sand from beneath her feet, and she landed on her seat. In an instant, Oggy and Pastie leaped toward her, whining and nuzzling against her.

"Back, you beasts." The command held all the affection she felt toward these beloved dogs of her son's father.

They backed away a foot or two and stood, tails swishing, eyes fixed on her face.

"If only you two could pull." She staggered to her feet, turned her face to the water, and watched for the next wave. As it rolled in, raising the level of the tide, she pulled the man toward the dry sand. If she got him above the tideline, she could go for help without fearing he would drown, if he still lived. If he did not . . .

Shivering so hard she could barely hold on to the man's cloak, she planted her feet and tugged again, then again, then again. At last, her feet braced in the rocky sand, she managed to drag the man above the tideline and straightened in preparation to go for help.

Behind her, stones showered from the cliff. She glanced up in the hope someone had come to inspect the wreck and could run for help for her. She saw no one, merely a flitting shadow that might only be a trick of sunlight, wind, and a few shrubs clinging to life on the edge of the rocks.

Disappointed, she turned back to the man. Now that he was in no danger of washing out to sea, she needn't hurry if he no longer lived. She could take the long way, the dry path, to Bastion Point. But if he lived, she needed to make haste and go through the surf.

She stooped and tucked her fingers under his neck band once more. She still felt no pulse. With a heavy heart, she managed to tug the chain free, marveling at the heft of the silver links. A blue and silver medallion swung free. The silver back flashed in the sun, caught a hint of Morwenna's pale face and her own tangled dark hair, and gave her an idea. She wiped the mirrorlike surface

16

on her cloak and held it under the man's nose.

The shining surface clouded. He was breathing. He was alive.

And she knew why no one had taken the medallion even if they had found it. Valuable as the silver might be, the family crest enameled on it warned no one could ever sell it.

Sunlight glinted off the silver and made the blue enamel glow. An azure lion rampant on a field of argent with the inscription *Memor quisnam vos es* — Remember Who You Are. It was a crest she saw painted on the family pew in the village church. Once she had seen it in a book of family history.

The stranger wore a medallion bearing the Trelawny family coat of arms.

Morwenna never believed a body's heart could stop beating as did the hearts of heroines in sensational novels. The instant she comprehended that the unconscious man sprawled on the sand wore a pendant of the Trelawny family crest, Morwenna's heart missed several beats. Her breath snagged in her throat. If a gust of wind hadn't sent spray from a wave crest washing over her, she feared she might have fainted across the stranger's body. The medallion slipped from her fingers to lie against the man's sodden neck cloth.

He must be soaked through. Now that she knew he lived, she realized she must get him some warmth. Her cloak was wet, but not as wet as he. She removed it and spread it across him, then called to the dogs. Their coats were also wet. But they were also thick and warm. She ordered them to lie beside the stranger, one on each side.

"Stay." She patted each of them on their heads. "I'll return as soon as I can."

She gathered her skirts and fled up the beach. Her mind raced over whom she could ask for help. On most days, Henwyn, her son's nursemaid and her maid of all work, was the only other occupant of the house until the outdoor man arrived around noon. She reached the outcropping of rock separating her beach from that of Bastion Point and splashed through knee-deep water to the path that coiled along the cliff to the house. Incoming waves slammed against her, driving her toward the jagged rocks. Sand fell away from her heels as the waves receded. Gripping handholds wherever she found them in the granite, she plunged on through the tide. Going around through trees and over fields would take far too long. Her other hand gripped her dress and petticoat above her knees to keep them from pulling her under.

And all the while, her mind raced around the circular pendant like the letters of the Trelawny family motto. How could a stranger have such a trinket? Morwenna didn't even know such a thing existed. Yet a man who didn't look at all familiar, at least not in his current unconscious and half-drowned state, wore a representation of the family around his neck. To find out why, if not for reasons of simple kindness, she must get this man to warmth and safety and save his life, if it could be saved.

Dead men didn't give answers.

Morwenna hit the cliff path and landed on her hands and knees. For the first few yards, she crawled up the steep incline, then she managed to get to her feet and race to the top of the sixty-foot cliff. To her left, a door led into her grandmother's garden. If it was unlocked, she could get into the house in moments.

She circumvented the garden and then the house, hoping neither grandparent was looking out the windows she passed, and charged for the stables. One or two of the grooms would help her. She had known them all her life, been friendlier with them than the daughter of the family who employed them should have been with servants.

If they were part of the gang that had helped the ship to wreck and left the man to drown, she might be making another mistake in her relationship with the outdoor servants. She didn't care at the moment.

"Miss Morwenna — m'lady," Henry, one of the grooms, called from the stable doorway. "You look half drowned."

"I am, and freezing too, but I need your help. There's a man . . . on the beach."

Henry's eyes widened until the whites shone around irises nearly as dark as Morwenna's own. "He's still alive?"

"He is." Morwenna narrowed her gaze at him but refrained from asking him why this news shocked him.

Of course Henry had been with the wreckers. Who in the village hadn't been? No matter. She needed his help and he would give it, trustworthy so long as she stayed with him and watched every move he made.

Colder than ever, she stepped closer to him. "I need at least two of you to help me get him up to Penmara."

"Not here at Bastion Point, m'lady?" Henry was shaking his head as he spoke. "It ain't right for you to have a man staying up there."

"You can't carry him all the way here. The beach access is blocked by now. Now hurry."

20

"Aye, m'lady." He ducked back into the stable and emerged with another groom. "Go on home, m'lady, and we'll bring him up."

"I must come. The dogs are with him."

The grooms looked grim and gave no argument. They simply set out across country with Morwenna, a brisk trot over open land and then a copse of trees, to more open land above the Penmara cliff. Her path wasn't as steep as the one at Bastion Point, nor as high as the way down to Halfmoon Cove. Chill and urgency lending her power, she managed to keep up with the youths' long-legged strides, then surpassed them on the beach.

She surpassed them because they slowed to drop behind her. When she glanced back, she saw them eyeing the dogs with apprehension as the enormous hounds rose to greet their mistress.

"Good dogs." Morwenna gave them each a scratch behind their ears and then crouched down beside the still unconscious man. She reached for the medallion to test whether or not he still breathed.

But the medallion with the Trelawny family crest enameled upon it no longer hung around the stranger's neck.

CHAPTER 2

All Mama's watercolor paintings were wrong. She portrayed angels as possessing golden curls and sky-blue eyes, white robes and hands tucked up their sleeves or playing a musical instrument, rose-tinted complexions and smiling, soft mouths. But the being David Chastain saw when he opened his eyes to pale sunshine and drab bed hangings only resembled an angel in her slight stature and fine-boned features. Her complexion was as smooth as porcelain and creamy pale. Her hair resembled midnight rather than sunshine and had been anchored on the back of her head too firmly to show whether or not it curled. Likewise, her eyes shone with so deep a brown they were nearly black behind their ruffle of dark lashes, and though her mouth looked soft, even lush, the lips were not curved up, but drooped at the corners as though a smile would stretch them beyond their current ability.

A man could get lost in thinking up ways to make those lips smile. The fullness of those lips, especially the lower one, could give a man notions Mama would scold even her grown sons for thinking. They certainly made him forget that every bone and sinew of his body ached, pounded as though someone had taken hammers to him or burned like a branding iron on the skin.

At least he forgot the misery that had kept him from coming fully awake until he tried to sit up and address the beautiful young woman. Beauty aside, she shouldn't be intimidating in her unangelic gown of grayish purple dotted with threads from the garment she was knitting. Too mundane a task. Hands of an angel should have been playing an instrument whose sweet notes would send him back to oblivion and away from physical anguish. Instead, they were red as though they recently had been plunged into scalding water.

His back felt as though it still rested in scalding water. Pain or not, he remained awake, gaze fixed on the lady. He opened his mouth to speak, but a groan emerged rather than words.

The knitting dropped to the floor as she

sprang out of her chair. She rushed to the bedside and leaned over, surrounding him with the scents of lemon and fresh-baked bread. "You're awake, sir."

Her voice was of a low register and husky. Sultry, like a summer night. The hand she laid on his brow was cool and smooth.

"Would you like some water? Some laudanum?"

"Yes." His voice emerged like that of a frog with a putrid sore throat. "To both."

"He needs broth. Nourishment." This was a speaker out of David's line of sight, an older voice with a thick country accent. "Needs to build up his strength."

"Let him heal first, then worry about his strength." She half turned away. Glass rattled, and she leaned over him again. "Can you lift yourself up, or do you need some assistance?"

He was tempted to say he needed help so this exquisite creature might perhaps slip an arm beneath his shoulders and he could get close to her. But the thought of angels reminded him of his mother, the lady who painted them for the bedchambers of her children and grandchildren. That in turn reminded him of all the manners she insisted her sons practice with females, and he inclined his head to acknowledge that he could raise himself enough to take a few sips of water.

Easier thought than done. He rose on one elbow and reached for the glass she held out to him. Agony shot across his back. A moan escaped his lips, and he collapsed back onto pillows that must have contained red-hot pokers.

Lightning flashed through the lady's dark eyes. "I said we should lay him on his front. The wounds on his back —" She broke off and slid a slim arm beneath his shoulders. "Let me help you."

She was so close her breath, scented with cinnamon, fanned across his mouth. That brought him warmth without the agony of fire, mere regret that such a lovely lady held him close and he wanted nothing more than to drink the elixir that would bring him relief from feeling anything.

"I'll lift you just a little." With surprising strength, she did just that, enough so when she tilted the glass to his lips, the liquid entered his mouth instead of running down his chin. The medicine she gave him first was bitter on his tongue, tainting the freshness of the water that followed. He swallowed with an eagerness that bordered on greedy, hoping this moment of being cradled against softness would last.

25

It didn't last. All too soon, she eased him back onto the red-hot pokers. When he couldn't stifle a throaty exclamation, she smoothed hair off his brow as though he were a child and murmured nonsense sounds that could have been a lullaby.

"Let me call my manservant to turn you over so that your back can heal properly. You took quite a . . . beating in that shipwreck."

"Shipwreck. Yes. Where — ?" He let her guess the rest of the question.

"Penmara."

"Pen—" He couldn't wrap his brain around the unfamiliar name.

"I am Morwenna, Lady Penvenan."

He stared up at her. "Am I in England?"

"You are in Cornwall."

"Barely England." He tried to smile. "Near Falmouth?"

"We're the north coast. Falmouth is in the south."

"I know." Pain deeper than any physical wound shot through him. He tried to move. He clamped his teeth against a moan of pain instead.

"Henwyn, fetch Nicca."

"But, m'lady, I can't be leaving you here alone with a man now that he's awake."

"Go and hasten back. Mihal is about to wake."

"All the more reason why —"

"Henwyn, go."

"You know Sir Petrok and Lady Trelawny aren't happy about you keeping him here."

"What my grandparents think is none of your concern. Now, go."

No words came after the sharp order, but a door slammed, speaking volumes of disapproving remarks. And just as the bang resounded through the chamber, a child's wail rose with it.

Muttering something uncomplimentary, presumably about the woman who had slammed the door, the lady spun away from the bed and strode across the room, heels clicking on a bare floor. Instantly, the crying ceased. The throaty voice did not. It spoke in soothing accents too low for David to understand the words, yet he understood the sentiment of the gentle tones of a mother reassuring her child. He had heard it enough with his sister and her offspring.

She had a child, and she had called herself Lady Penvenan. Alas, his dark angel was somebody's wife. Of course, the good ones always were.

He closed his eyes and allowed the medicine to carry him into a state of not caring

27

so much about the pain — or much of anything. Vaguely he thought of the questions he needed to ask, like the precise location of Penmara, how long he had been unconscious, how he had come to be unconscious in a strange house, and why he hurt everywhere, but especially his back. When the lady returned to his side, he would force the words out.

The next time she came to his side, however, she was with a man, someone with large, strong hands and a soft voice. With the assistance of the two females, this newcomer helped David to sit halfway up and roll onto his chest. The last thing he remembered as his head flopped back onto the pillow was her ladyship exclaiming, then blackness descended.

It ended all too soon, for the pain remained. It was slightly better, and a pang in his belly suggested hunger. Darkness surrounded him save for a lamp to one side. He turned his head in that direction and there she sat, flame drawing blue highlights from the glossy darkness of her hair and gilding one delicate cheekbone. A needle flashed in and out of a bit of wool, and the aroma of coffee permeated the chamber.

"Do you not sleep?" he asked.

She rose. "Sometimes." After setting the

sewing on a table, she moved to the side of the bed. "We haven't been certain you would survive each night, so have taken turns sitting up with you."

"How long?"

"A week."

His chest constricted. "Too long."

"It's why we have been worrying about you. It's dawn now and you are still with us, I'm glad to see."

"Why wouldn't I be?" He raised one hand to his face. His fingers rasped on a week's growth of beard. "Why would you stay here?"

"I found you on my beach more dead than alive. Do you remember why you were there?"

"The ship went aground in the storm." He closed his eyes, trying to recall more. "Then I was here. What happened in between?"

"If you can raise yourself up a bit, I will get you some broth. You must be starved."

"I am, but why — ?"

"Try to drink this first." She crossed the room. Metal rattled. Liquid splashed. Her gown rustled as she returned to his side. "Can you push yourself up just a little?"

He rolled onto his side. The pokers returned to abusing his back, but they had cooled some. Ignoring the discomfort, he reached for the tankard she held out to him. "Beef tea?"

"With a little port mixed in. I'm sorry if you're abstemious, but there's nothing better for restoring the blood."

"My blood needs restored?" That would explain the weakness.

"You seem to have lost a quantity."

"How?"

She clasped her hands at her collarbone. "Your back was cut to ribbons."

He choked on the rich broth. "How? Rocks? Seems all I've seen growing in this county are rocks."

"We grow things well enough. It's still early in spring after all."

A little defensiveness about her land.

David half smiled. "But you do have a surplus of rocks."

She shrugged.

"Was it rocks that hurt me?" he pressed.

"In the hands of men, perhaps it was rocks." If warm custard could hold an edge, then her voice did, perhaps even anger.

David balanced the tankard on the arm that held him half upright and met her gaze. "What are you saying?"

She didn't flinch from his direct gaze. "I'm saying someone beat you. It looks worse

30

than what even a horsewhip can do. Perhaps a truncheon of some sort."

His innards flipped around and over themselves. He sipped more broth, hoping the warmth would settle the activity. He had nothing to fear. He was on his way back to Falmouth to find answers regarding his father's death.

"Why couldn't the battering be just from the sea?" It was a logical question.

"If your injuries were caused by nature, not man, then so was the wreck." She removed the broth from his hand. "I suppose it's possible, but rocks don't usually bruise and bloody a body in a symmetrical pattern."

His ears growing red, David asked, "And how do you know my wounds are symmetrical?"

"Someone needed to tend you, and blood makes Henwyn ill, and Nicca is too hamhanded for treating wounds."

"And your husband allowed it?"

"My husband is . . . gone." Her lush lower lip quivered. "Some wounds are too bad to survive."

"I'm sorry."

No wonder she looked sad.

"Why would someone beat me?" His eyelids drooped, and he forced them up again. "I was merely a passenger on a vessel bound for — for Falmouth."

"From where?" Lady Penvenan asked as she removed the drooping cup from his hand. "If you give me your direction, I'll notify your family."

"Bristol." He could scarcely remember his name, his brain felt so stuffed with lamb's wool. "The Chastain boatyard. Mrs. Chastain."

"Your wife?"

"Mother. Poor Mama." He gave up on his lids and his attempt to keep himself propped upright. "Did you pour laudanum into the broth?"

"No. I will only drug you with your permission, now that you are in your right senses. Your weariness stems from the warmth of the soup and your need for rest."

He didn't believe her. This felt like the dragging fatigue caused by laudanum. Yet doubting her word seemed unkind after all her care of him, so he gave her no challenge.

She drew up the coverlet to beneath his chin, a maternal gesture. Her fingers rasped on his beard stubble.

He flinched. "So sorry for the unkempt state."

"Nicca can help you with that."

"Odd name, that." He swallowed a yawn.

"It's Cornish for Nicholas. We all have odd names to the English."

That made him laugh. Laughing hurt, so he decided to sleep.

Waking again, he found an older woman gazing down at him. "Where's the angel?"

"Lady Penvenan is overseeing the estate — what's left of it." The woman's accent was pure west country and a little harsh. "She's spent too much time nursing you at risk to her reputation."

"Loyalty to one's employer is a fine character to have." He wouldn't rise to the woman's rudeness with his own.

But the word *loyalty* reminded him of something important.

With the pain receding to a dull throbbing except when he moved too quickly, his mind grew clearer. Loyalty to one's employer . . .

Or loyalty to one's family.

Pain, sharper than any dealt him by those who had attacked him, pierced his heart. He did not understand how a loving father and husband could suddenly remove most of the money from the business and family coffers, then disappear in the opposite direction he intended to go. David would swear in a court of law that Father was the most honest man who lived. Who had lived. David wanted to be like dear, sweet Mama, still Father's stalwart supporter even with the sketchy facts laid out before her.

"Return to Cornwall and learn what this is all about," Mama had told him.

With his longing to believe in Father's innocence, David had done so, and someone had tried to kill him. He doubted he was out of danger yet.

Morwenna walked to church alone. Her grandparents would have taken her up in their carriage, or met her on the way if they chose to walk on a fine morning, but Morwenna refused that courtesy from them just as she would refuse to take a farthing of their money. They had shunned her, sent her away from the hallowed halls of Bastion Point when she needed protection. Now they could not bask in the dubious honor of having their younger granddaughter, the widow of a peer of the realm, in their company.

"Your stiff-necked pride is going to catch you a chill and land you in the churchyard," Henwyn predicted as Morwenna kissed Mihal good-bye. The maid preferred to stay behind with the baby on Sunday mornings and attend a gathering of Methodist dissenters during the week. "Then those grandparents of yours will be raisin' him like they raised you."

With a lot of rules and not a lot of affection.

"A little rain won't hurt me." Morwenna flung on her woolen cloak and drew an umbrella from a stand in the entryway.

The former was still stiff from salt water after she had used it to cover Mr. Chastain on the beach, and the latter was so old the shaft was more rust than steel. Together, however, they would keep her warm and dry enough in the light rain.

"I'm more likely to twist an ankle in a hole along the route." She smoothed her hand over Mihal's head.

He grinned at her around the corner of a wooden block he was trying to tuck into his mouth. The block was too big for him to swallow, but Morwenna doubted the flaking paint was good for him, so she removed the block from his hands, set it with its mates on the floor, and beat a hasty retreat before he began to cry and she felt compelled to remain.

For the first half of her two-mile walk into the village, little moisture reached her through the overgrown canopy of trees along the drive. Once she reached the more open passage of the road, the skies released a torrent of water that roared upon the oiled skin of the umbrella, and wind that drove the water beneath the ribs and into her face. Mud caked upon her walking boots and rimmed the bottom of her skirt. By the time she reached the shelter of the church porch, she looked like what she was — an impoverished widow too proud, too angry with how her grandparents had treated her in the past, to ride in dry comfort.

But she was there for the service as she had been every Sunday since her churching a month after Mihal's birth. As had occurred since that Sunday, the local people bobbed curtsies or bowed heads in acknowledgment of her rank of Lady Penvenan, but drew back from her as though the water and mud on her clothes would leap off and soil them. The local gentry had not yet arrived. Morwenna planned her entrance that way. They were friends of her grandparents and most of them preferred to avoid her rather than annoy the Trelawnys.

Morwenna annoyed them enough on her own. At the front of the sanctuary, the Penvenan pew faced that of the Trelawnys. The latter would soon hold her grandparents and Miss Pross, Grandmother's companion, and perhaps a guest or two. Morwenna sat alone in the Penvenan pew.

"You should sit with us," Grandmother had suggested more than once over the past year and a half. "You look so lonely in that big pew all by yourself."

"I am honoring my husband and his family by sitting here." Morwenna thought that sounded better than telling her grandmother that she thought taking advantage of their pew, with its brazier of hot coals to warm the inhabitants, was too hypocritical of her to enact in church of all places.

"I will save Penvenan on my own. I will raise my son on my own. I will not take your guilt money." Behind the closed door of the pew, she mouthed the vow over her *Book of Common Prayer* as though it were a prayer and not the determination that kept her going when she was lonely or sitting stiffly to keep herself from shivering.

She raised her head to see steam issuing from the Trelawny pew, or rather the damp clothing of its occupants — its eight occupants. Grandmother and Grandfather had invited others to join them that morning — Jago Rodda and the Pascoes with their two grown sons. The younger of those sons tried to catch her eye. She returned her attention to her *Book of Common Prayer* and that day's readings. She would not encourage either Tristan Pascoe or Jago

Rodda. Marriage to either of them would solve nothing. They didn't have money, but her grandparents would give them the dowry they hadn't had the opportunity to bestow upon Conan, a dowry Grandfather withheld as a lure to encourage her to marry again.

As though she would ever let herself fall in love, or marry without love.

My faith will sustain me. She hoped those weren't empty words. She clung to them as she clung to her Bible and liturgy — with stiff, cold fingers.

Mrs. Kitto, the vicar's tiny wife, began to pump out the first hymn on the wheezy old barrel organ. Morwenna rose and sang the lines of the hymn from rote. Her voice seemed to echo off the sides of the pew. She squirmed and resorted to merely mouthing the lines. The hymn wasn't important. She came for Mr. Kitto's encouraging homilies, for his prayers. At the end of the service, she rose with renewed strength of mind and spirit and waited for the congregation to depart ahead of her, unlike the Trelawny crowd, who recessed ahead of everyone else. In the event no one wanted to speak to her, Morwenna preferred to exit behind everyone else. On this rainy day, her grandparents and their guests would be long gone before she reached the porch.

But she was wrong. They waited for her along with the Pascoes and the rest of the Roddas.

"Good morning, Morwenna." Grandfather greeted her first.

Grandmother reached out her gloved hands. "You will come home to dinner with us, will you not?"

"Do please come." Tristan Pascoe reached past Grandmother to clasp Morwenna's hand. "It will be ever so dull without you."

Morwenna glanced into his handsome, boyish countenance and wanted to smile. He was so ridiculous.

Behind him, Mrs. Pascoe grimaced, and Morwenna held back her automatic response to a flirtatious male. "I need to return to my son."

"We can carry you to fetch him," Jago Rodda offered.

"Dinner is no place for a child." Mrs. Rodda addressed her son without acknowledging Morwenna.

"You are correct, ma'am." Morwenna smiled at the lady, then turned to Grandmother. "Thank you for the invitation." Though it had been issued like an order. "I must be off home. I have . . . responsibilities there."

"Indeed." Grandfather grasped her elbow and propelled her to the other end of the porch. "We need to talk about that . . . responsibility. You must be rid of it."

"Shall I leave him on the sand for the tide to carry off, as the wreckers intended?" Morwenna spoke through teeth gritted behind a false smile. "Or just dump him off a cliff?"

"Don't be pert with me, young lady. I don't have to let you continue on your own, you know."

Indeed he did not. As a woman, she was neither trustee of her son's inheritance, nor was she his guardian under the law. Grandfather held the latter role and influence over the trustees of Penmara. With a word, they could remove her son and Penmara from her control.

But then Grandfather would remove any hint of power over her.

She inclined her head. "My guest is too ill to move at the moment."

"And your reputation is too fragile to not move him."

"I shattered my reputation at least seven years ago, sir, and marriage to a baron who was murdered for smuggling has not repaired it." She made herself look into Grandfather's obsidian eyes. "Mr. Chastain is not going to hurt it further."

"Do not be so sure of that, my dear." Though he touched her cheek with fingertips so cold she felt it through his glove, Morwenna took the words for what they were — a threat to her freedom, to her determination to succeed without the help of those who wanted to use their money to control her.

The journey to Cornwall had been so horrendous the first time, jouncing over roads not fit for a horse, let alone a post chaise, David had decided to sail.

And ended up in a shipwreck.

He'd been carrying something important. Money? Yes, of course. Necessities in a valise? Most definitely. And . . . ?

In another time of lucidity, he woke to find the disgruntled maidservant in the chamber. Disappointment, sharp as thorns, pricked his chest.

"Where is my lady?"

"Off to church, where any decent soul should be come Sunday morning." The grumbling tones held censure.

David held back a laugh for fear it would hurt his ribs. "I will go straightaway." He sat up as though intending to climb from bed, and realized the pain in his back and side had lessened to a dull ache. Some of his strength had returned.

Not nearly enough. He could sit up without aid, but his head swam at the effort, and he lay back against the pillows. "My things?"

The woman tramped across the room, her footfalls clomping as though she wore wooden clogs. "The vermin left you with nothing."

"What happened? I remember grabbing my luggage and then —" He shook his head. His brainbox swam as though seawater had gotten in and not drained out.

But he knew he had something else. Something important.

His fingers scrabbled at his throat. His bare throat.

"Where is it?" he demanded.

The maid glared at him. "Where is what?"

"Where is the medallion?"

"Don't know nothing of any jewelry."

"I had a medallion around my neck when I went into the sea."

The woman her ladyship had called Henwyn spun from the table and glared at him. "Are you accusing us of thievery?"

"Someone took it."

"Like as not those who attacked you and stole your purse, if you had one, and left you to drown."

Possibly, but the medallion had been securely tucked beneath his neck cloth and shirt so no one would see it. Yet if someone had beaten him, they might have removed his clothes first.

"Was I . . . disrobed when I was found?"

The maidservant sniffed. "You were dressed, though your clothes was cut to ribbons."

"Then how — ?" He decided not to badger the maidservant. Still, he wondered for a moment if the kindness these people were showing him — at least the manservant and her ladyship — stemmed from guilt. But surely not. They would be more likely to take his money, a considerable sum for his travels, nearly all the family could scrape together after Father's disappearance and subsequent death.

"I'll ask her ladyship." If she had found him, she was the most likely person to have it.

Henwyn stomped across the floor. "You do that. Her ladyship said she'll be up after church if you're sensible, though I'm certain you're no such thing." The door closed, not quite a slam this time, but far harder than necessary.

David leaned his head back on the pillows. He didn't fall asleep. With only a minor amount of discomfort, he managed again to push himself to a sitting position against pillows and the elaborately carved headboard. Not until he sat in a more upright position did he realize that he wore a threadbare nightshirt that was a little too small. It pulled across his shoulders and didn't button at the throat. He heard footfalls in the corridor and snatched the coverlet up to his chin. He must have dozed like that, for the next thing he knew, the door opened and the lady glided through.

Though her gown looked dull and a little worn, she could have donned a flour sack and not disguised her natural beauty of porcelain skin, fine bones, and that sad, full-lipped mouth.

With a jerk of his head, he raised his eyes and met her gaze — and held it too long for courtesy. He thought perhaps a crowbar would be necessary to break him away from staring into the fathomless depths of her eyes in an attempt to work out what she might be thinking, why she didn't smile even in a polite pretense of pleasure, why she didn't look away from him at once.

"You look much better." She still gazed at him as she spoke. "Shall I have Nicca in to help you shave?"

He raised one hand to his chin, which must sport a week's growth of beard, and nodded, managing to stop staring at her. "Please. I'm shamed to have a lady see me thus."

"I've seen worse." She glanced down at the coverlet. "I have acquired some clothes that might fit you better than my late husband's."

Ah, yes, the husband who hadn't survived wounds he'd received. No wonder she looked sad. Surely she was too young to be a widow.

"Was he a soldier, my lady?"

She snorted, a sound that would have been unladylike on anyone less delicate and calm. "He was the heir to a barony and inherited this crumbling pile."

Not exactly an answer.

"He was where he shouldn't have been and ran into some evil people." She added the last while turned away from him.

David studied the set of her narrow shoulders, too straight, too rigid. "Seems like you have a lot of those around here."

"Poverty often drives men to perform heinous acts they might otherwise never think to perform. A need to feed one's babies can drive a body to the unthinkable."

And she had a baby to feed.

Unease rippled through David. She had rescued him, but that didn't mean she hadn't robbed him.

He watched her from beneath half-closed lids. She crossed the room to settle on a chair by the window and picked up her needlework. Not needlework as his mother did when seated in the parlor in the evenings. This was more like mending a small garment.

Odd that a lady would need to mend her child's garments. Even his mother, wife of a humble boatbuilder, managed enough servants to do menial tasks like darning. A scan of the room in the light of day, gray though that light was, showed that she either didn't have money for upkeep or had placed him in a shabby room on purpose. The wallpaper was faded blue-and-green stripes, the chair cushions once velvet, now held little nap, and not so much as a small hooked rug lay on the floor. In one corner of the ceiling, a dark spot suggested a leaky roof. But the furniture was all carved mahogany that had once been expensive and was now at least half a century old.

"This room seemed like the best choice, Mr. Chastain." She didn't look up from her work, but must have realized he observed the chamber and found it wanting. "Other than mine, it's the only one in good repair. But my cousin by marriage who lived here for a while restored a few rooms downstairs and put on a new roof. You shan't get rained upon."

"As though I'd complain about a little rain after you have been so kind."

"It's nothing anyone wouldn't do." She bent her face closer to her work. A tendril of glossy hair slid across her cheek, and David wanted to smooth it back for her. She pouched out her lower lip and blew the hair away.

David swallowed and looked out the window. It afforded him a view of woods, barren land, and a tumbledown engine house for a mine.

"So where precisely am I?" he asked to distract himself from that lower lip.

"We are a two-hour ride to the west of Truro." She raised her head for a moment. "And we are on the sea, as you likely guessed, though I don't hear it from here right now. Is that more comfortable for you?"

"You think I've taken a dislike to the sea after being shipwrecked?"

"I would."

"I'd better not." He smiled at her. "I'm a boatbuilder."

"Ah, so that explains why you traveled by sea." She flashed him a quick glance. "I wondered."

"Have you ever ridden overland from Bristol to Falmouth?"

"I've never been farther east than Exeter."

"I have." He shifted on the bed and the ropes squeaked. The pain returned with a vengeance at the memory of that frantic cross-country ride, days of worry and wonder, anger and apprehension.

He gripped the coverlet so hard some of the stitching around the edge came loose. "The first time I went to Falmouth."

She said nothing, simply continued to look at him.

"I went to claim my father's body. I took it home by sea, then set out to sail back to conclude my business I couldn't take time for then."

"How curious." She didn't ask what that business was.

He wanted to ask her about the medallion, but fatigue washed over him as had the sea the night of the shipwreck, consuming, chilling, brutal. Pounding. Pounding. Pounding. Darkness tumbling him over and over, then the pain, waves, then nothing like he'd ever experienced. He closed his eyes, unable to think how to politely accuse her

48

of taking the pendant he shouldn't have been wearing.

Fabric rustled. "I will leave you to sleep, Mr. Chastain. Nicca will be up in a few hours to tend your wounds and do anything else for you." The door handle rattled.

"My lady?" He had to know, force the words out. "What happened to my purse?"

"If you had one, then the wreckers stole it."

"Wreckers?"

"Men and women who lure ships to the rocks for easy pickings."

"That's barbaric."

"And illegal. Transportation or hanging if caught and convicted."

He lay still for several moments, absorbing this terrible news, then, figuring he knew the answer, asked, "My medallion?"

"The one with the family crest on it?"

Shock shoved the fatigue away like the waters of the Red Sea. He straightened, eyes flying open. "You saw it? You have it?"

Slowly she approached him, her dark eyes intense. "I saw it when I hauled you onto the shore. I saw it that once. But I made the mistake of leaving it around your neck in my haste to fetch help. While I fetched that help, the medallion disappeared."

"Indeed." He let all his skepticism ring in

his voice. "Who else was tramping over the beach when you were . . . on your way to fetch help, you say?"

"I'd like to know that myself. I would also like to know" — she leaned forward so her face loomed within a foot of him — "from whom did you take it?"

He met her challenge. "Why should it matter to you?"

"Because —" She stopped. "Why do you have that crest if your name is Chastain from Bristol and you are a m— a boat-builder?"

Certain she had been about to say "mere boatbuilder," David stiffened, ignoring the sudden stab of a dozen pokers in his back. "I cannot see how that is any concern of yours."

"I do." The other corner of her mouth turned up, yet he couldn't think of the stiff curve that didn't reach her eyes as a smile. It was more a bitter twist. "My name is Morwenna Trelawny Penvenan, and that is the Trelawny family crest."

"Then what," David asked, his heart pounding like a sledgehammer driving home a spike into solid wood, "was it doing on my dead father's body?"

CHAPTER 3

Morwenna rocked back with the impact of Chastain's words. "How could your father have been in possession of that medallion? I never knew it existed." She broke off to change her rambling speech to one that made sense. "When and where and how did your father die?"

"He died in Falmouth three weeks ago. I don't know how." His face twisted. "Or why he was even there."

Morwenna gazed into his eyes to discern whether or not he spoke the truth. They were rather fine eyes, gray-green like the sea before a storm, and direct, as she had noticed before. They went well with his longish dark hair spread out against the pillow slip like a cloud and the dark beard stubble that gave him a rather piratical visage.

She remembered brushing her hand against the rasp of that stubble, and her fingers tingled with other memories, those few mornings she had awakened to find her husband still there beside her . . .

Her chest tightened with a longing for what could never be, thanks to Conan's own lawlessness. She stiffened her spine and tossed her mending into the basket she had lugged into the invalid room while she watched over the stranger, David Chastain. "What can you tell me?"

"Why should I tell you anything?" No belligerence tinged his voice, deep and thick with the musical cadence of Somerset, the *s*'s almost sounding like *z*'s, the *r*'s as thick as clotted cream. "I don't know you or anything about you."

"You know nothing of the Trelawnys or Penvenans?" She arched her brows in disbelief.

He shrugged, winced, and shook his head. "Should I?"

"I . . . don't know." Morwenna wished she still held her needlework so she would have a reason to duck her head and hide the heat she felt climbing into her cheeks. "I thought everyone knew about the Trelawnys at the least."

But then, why would a boatbuilder from Bristol? To her knowledge, none of them had ever been to Bristol and only in Somerset to perhaps visit Bath or on their way to London from Cornwall.

"If they are the sort of people I should have heard of, then I don't move in the types of places where I would have heard of them." He flicked his gaze over her in a way too impersonal to be rude. "I suppose that refers to you as well, Lady Penvenan." He emphasized the "lady" as though it were a barricade he were erecting. Then he grinned and tore the barrier down again. "Mama might have heard of your family, though, if you have family in London. She reads the gossip rags from there."

"My uncle is a member of Parliament. And a year and a half ago" — Morwenna rose and began to stride around the room — "my husband's murder would have garnered some space even in London papers. He was, after all, a peer of the realm, even if he never did take his seat in Parliament. He couldn't afford to stay in London for weeks on end."

But if he had, he might have made the sort of connections she wished she had, men with money to invest in two derelict mines whose flooding had put them out of business and dozens of men and women out of work. All they needed were mine engines to pump the water out. Engines that cost more than the sale of all the other lands could provide.

She paused at the window and gazed upon the distant engine houses. The storm had blown off the rest of one roof, leaving the rusting and broken engine, one of Newcomen's first built in the previous century, exposed to the sunshine and sea air. The rest of her son's inheritance was crumbling before Morwenna's eyes.

She would halt the destruction spread out before her. She would stop it with her own efforts, not by taking her grandparents' money or marrying one of the two men courting her.

With that determination uppermost in her mind, she decided to tell this stranger the truth. Perhaps if she spoke, he would do so as well.

She faced him again. "A vessel outbound from Bristol wrecks on my beach during a storm when they never should have been this close to land, and I find you battered by nature and man and left to drown on the sand at high tide. I need to know why."

"So do I." He touched his neck where the chain should have lain but didn't take his eyes from her. "That medallion was the last thing I had from my father, except for a letter that is likely now at the bottom of the sea."

"No, it's in the library, though I doubt you can read it. I found it in your coat pocket and set it in the sun to dry."

He leaned forward, his hair swinging across his shoulder and catching a current of sunlight to show a hint of cinnamon blended with the coffee. "May I see it? Will you fetch it for me?"

"Of course." She left Mr. Chastain alone.

Down the corridor, in the dressing room she used as a nursery because the rooms intended for children were just below where part of the roof had blown away years earlier and water had ruined all the furnishings and damaged the plaster, Mihal, Lord Penvenan, began to cry. She sprinted down the threadbare runner to snatch him out of his bed.

She lifted the baby into her arms. He had grown so much in the past three months, growing nearly too heavy for Morwenna to carry far or for long. She figured she would do so as long as she could manage at all. Hugging him to her, wet diaper and all, she pressed her cheek against his dark curls. "I've got to make you prosperous, my little one. No way will you grow up to live and die as did your father."

"Ma." He squirmed in her hold. "Go."

"All right. Let me change you." She set him on the table she had set up for such a purpose. "Will you lie still for me?"

"Go." Which was as good as saying he would not.

He was too much like his father, too much like her — dissatisfied with sitting still. And if she were honest, rebellious. If she told him to sit still, he would wiggle about like a hooked fish. If she told him to be quiet, he would yell at the top of his lungs. If she asked for a hug, he would push her away.

She hugged him anyway. He would not grow up with parents — a mother — he saw when convenient for her. With her own parents, that had been every three to five years. Now she hadn't seen them for six. They were probably dead in some South American jungle, killed by nature or strange peoples, while they pursued their dream of unearthing a hidden gem mine.

The instant she let Mihal go on the table to reach for the supplies she needed to wash him, he rose on hands and knees and headed for the wall. From experience, she knew he intended to use the wall to pull himself up. She caught him around the middle, flipped him onto his back, and began to tickle him by way of a distraction. He convulsed with giggles, wriggling and flopping and forgetting he would rather be ambulatory than lying on his back.

One accidental jab with a pin had taught him to lie still as she gave him fresh cloths and a dry petticoat. His stockings were all right, and she pulled on the little shoes she had commissioned for him in Truro at a shocking expense. Then she lifted him down and took his hand. "Let's go visit Henwyn in the kitchen and get you something to eat."

"Eat." He used another favorite word. "Eat. Eat. Eat." He yelled the word past Chastain's room.

Morwenna considered taking food up for him, then decided to send Nicca up with a dinner tray. Nicca wouldn't talk much and would be in a hurry to get to his own dinner. Being left alone now that he seemed more awake would incline David Chastain to talk.

Morwenna hoped.

David Chastain with a Trelawny medallion and the wrath of the wreckers upon him. He claimed to be a boatbuilder and was built like a man who could carry the strakes for a ship-of-the-line all by himself, step masts without assistance, and hold them while others rigged the ship . . . All right, so she might be exaggerating, but he was certainly on the side of large and muscular. She wasn't certain of height, not yet having seen him standing. Next to her, anyone was tall. She hadn't even reached Conan's shoulder, and he wasn't more than a whisker above average in height, strong, but not overly so. He'd been so gentle . . .

David Chastain seemed gentle enough, but his will seemed formidable. Despite his pain and days of mostly unconsciousness, he managed to guard his tongue. She knew all too well when a man was lying by omission, and David Chastain was certainly not telling her everything he knew.

"I'll worm it out of you, sirrah." She lifted baby Mihal to carry him down the steep back staircase. "Mmm. What's Henny cooking for dinner?"

"Ma." Mihal patted her cheek where a tear had escaped to slip over her lower lid.

"Silly Mama." She tipped her head to wipe the wetness onto the collar of her dress.

Too late. Mihal had puckered up, eyes squeezed shut in that grimace portending his own vociferous tears. "Tears are pointless. You'll learn that when you get older."

Mihal wailed, the sound magnified in the stairwell.

"Soon, we'll get you some dinner soon." Morwenna pitched her voice loudly enough to rise over the sobs, more for Henwyn's sake than Mihal's. She didn't want her maidservant to think she had set the child to weeping. From the day of his birth, she had sought to be joyful for him, only show her delight in his presence and life. Most of the time she succeeded. He was the joy in her life, the remaining part of his father, and easy to distract with tickles and kisses, a toy or a song.

But not always. Sometimes the tears flowed without warning, and he had learned they meant Mama was unhappy.

"Not with you." She paused on the landing to cradle his head against her shoulder. "Never you."

She squeezed back more tears and descended the second flight to the kitchen passage. Whiffs of fish stew and onions drifted over the flagstones. Morwenna's stomach cramped. If she never saw another pilchard preserved in salt it would be too soon, but the preserved seafood was cheap and a quantity had been stored in the cellar. She couldn't waste what little income she possessed buying bacon or beef. Any beef they procured, usually dried and tasteless as leather, they saved for broth for when a body was ill.

Of course, her grandparents would give

her all the food she, her miniscule staff, and any number of guests — especially Jago Rodda and Tristan Pascoe, suitors for her hand — could eat. All she had to do was ask them.

She would not ask them. The last time she asked them for help, they said only if she compromised her principles, a promise to her husband. Though the need for that silence had changed, her grandparents had not. They would have more conditions for her to meet. Cousin Elizabeth had faced that. If she could stand strong against their form of loving dictatorship, then Morwenna could stand stronger.

Lack of sleep was robbing her of strength. For too many nights she had sat up watching over David Chastain, spooning laudanum and broth down his throat, listening to him cry out and moan in pain every time he moved. Yet he never said anything as people often did when under the power of an opiate and spirituous medicines, though she had been weaning him off of those for the past few days. He didn't rave. He told her nothing.

Waking, he told her nearly as little.

Her son suddenly too heavy for her to hold, Morwenna let him down. At once, his crying ceased, and he raced ahead in that side-to-side gait, rolling like a drunken sailor on a heavy sea. His palms slapped the kitchen door and shoved it open. "Ma!" He shouted the name as though practicing to announce someone of importance.

Henwyn jumped and dropped her spoon into the stew pot. "Don't be doing that." She glared over her shoulder at Morwenna. "One of these days I'm going to — what have you been weeping about?" Her face changed from annoyed to concerned. "Has that man been upsetting you?"

"Not at all. He's polite."

Except he had a rather bold glance from time to time.

"Weariness is all." Morwenna dashed her sleeve across her eyes.

"And hunger," Henwyn added.

"No, just some bread —"

Henwyn used another spoon to fish the first one out of the pot, then scoop some of the thick broth into a bowl. "You'll eat this whether you like it or not. Many a miner's wife would be happy to have half so much."

"Then take it to them." Morwenna took the bowl to set on the deal table scrubbed so often it was nearly white. "Come, little one." She scooped up Mihal and set him on her lap. Spoons lay on the table and she retrieved the smallest one, a half-sized spoon made of silver that had fed Penvenan heirs for at least a century. "Let's eat up all the fishies."

Mihal was happy to gobble up the stew thick with turnips, onion, and bits of salted pilchards. Despite Henwyn glaring at her from across the table, Morwenna managed a mouthful or two, but her stomach contracted around each bite and each thought of what the man upstairs had to do with her family.

A Trelawny medallion.

Were she inclined toward superstition, as most Cornish natives were, she might think it had found its way home, but from where? Bristol? Nonsense. Bristol was not the sort of town to which Trelawnys ventured. It wasn't picturesque like Falmouth or important to the navy like Plymouth. It was not on the way to anywhere important —

"Go." A hunk of bread in one hand, Mihal struggled to have her release him.

Morwenna set him on his feet and rose, brushing crumbs from her skirt. "Henwyn, I'm leaving him for you to watch. I need to get Nicca —"

"Nicca has already gone up to see that man." Henwyn opened the lid to a box of toys Morwenna had rescued from the schoolroom — blocks and tin soldiers, their paint faded — that her husband must have played with. "You go to your estate work. And you, little man, come help me build a house."

Mihal was more likely to build towers he could knock down, but the blocks kept him occupied for long stretches, enough for Henwyn to knead bread or roll out dough for pasties.

Morwenna headed for the one room in the house that was well-appointed — the library. Paneling had been polished, the floors covered with a fine Axminster carpet in burgundy red and blue, and the furnishings were new. During the rare occasions she entertained callers, she was grateful to have this one chamber that didn't put her to shame.

She opened the door and started back. A man crouched before the hearth coaxing a tongue of flame into a full-blown fire. He glanced up at Morwenna's entrance, then returned to his fire.

"What are you doing here?" she demanded of Jago Rodda.

And why hadn't the dogs barked a greeting and alerted her to the presence of a visitor?

Because they lay in the corner of the room behind the massive desk, each gnawing on a bone. Looking at the canines gnawing away set off an alarm in her head, something she should remember. But it eluded her, and she focused her attention on Jago.

"You bribed my dogs to be quiet and not notify me of your arrival?" Morwenna heard the shrillness in her query and took a breath to calm herself. At the same time she glanced at the desk.

Good. She hadn't left papers pertaining to the mines laid out. Since wind off the sea had made the chamber chilly, she doubted he had been there long enough to open drawers.

"I didn't want them to bark and wake up the baby." Jago gave one more puff of the bellows and rose, one hand extended. "Or perhaps you. You look as though you should be asleep."

"At least you're not flattering me unnecessarily."

"No flattery of you would be unnecessary, my lady. Surely your mirror tells you that."

"I don't bother with mirrors." Rather glad she must look a frump in her gray dress and sloppily knotted hair, Morwenna rounded the desk but did not sit, forcing Jago to stay standing. "To what do I owe this honor?" She didn't bother to keep the irony of the word *honor* out of her tone.

A tightening of the corners of Jago's smile told her he noticed, but he forced the smile even wider. "To see you, of course. You've been scarce for days."

"You saw me in church. Other than that, I've been preoccupied." Morwenna moved one foot over to give the nearest hound an affectionate rub. He responded with a thump of his tail, his jaws never ceasing their chewing.

Jago's smile slipped off his face. "I heard. You're taking care of some derelict stranger from the wreck."

"I wouldn't call him derelict. His clothes were fine enough. But he lost everything."

"Then how will he pay you for your care?"

In information, she hoped. She shrugged. "If he does, he does. If he does not, it's charity." She leaned down and scratched Pastie behind one ear. "And what may I do for you?"

"Do I need a reason to call?"

"To make it proper, yes."

"If you're concerned about proper, you shouldn't be keeping a man in your house."

Morwenna shot upright, banging her hip on the corner of the desk. She glared at Jago. "What was I supposed to do with him? Leave him on the beach to drown?"

"You should have had him carried to Bastion Point."

"And lose more blood than he did coming up here? I think not." She folded her arms across her bosom. "And if that is your only reason for coming to call, then you may take your leave. I have work to —"

The dogs sprang up and raced for the door. Morwenna headed after them, reaching the front hall just as the knocker sounded on the great door. Jago hadn't followed. When she opened the door to see her grandparents, she understood why.

"This was planned." Not a polite greeting, so she held out her hands.

The dogs, wagging their tails, shouldered their way in between, their welcome far warmer than had been their mistress's.

"They're hoping you brought them more meaty bones." Morwenna clasped her grandparents' hands. Grandpapa's was still strong, but Grandmama's felt frail, the bones fragile, and her conscience pricked her for not being more gracious.

She tried again. "Come in from the cold. The sunshine is deceiving." She stepped back so Sir Petrok and Lady Trelawny could enter the house, the dogs nudging them forward over the threshold as though they were sheep and the dogs, collies.

"Go on with you." Grandpapa bent to

scratch Oggy under the chin.

Pastie sat before him, her own chin raised in expectation.

Despite herself, Morwenna chuckled. "Bribing my dogs won't help them guard us very well." She sobered and glanced from grandparent to grandparent, her lips thinning. "To what do I owe this honor of three guests in one afternoon?"

"Ah, Jago is here already." Grandpapa nodded.

"Shall I go to the kitchen and help Henwyn make us some tea?" Hefting a substantial-looking basket, Grandmama headed in that direction before Morwenna could speak.

Grandmama would be happy to find Mihal there. Indeed, she likely expected him to be there, and her desire to play parlor maid stemmed more from a desire to see her great-grandson than a cup of tea.

Glancing back, she noted Grandpapa's eyes fixed on her, and realized Grandmama had absented herself to leave Morwenna to him.

She sighed. "What is it?"

"Your guest." Grandpapa was not a man to prevaricate. "We think you should move him to our house now."

67

Morwenna planted her hands on her hips. "No."

"Morwenna, Jago wants to ask you to marry him —"

"He knows better. Conan —"

"Is nearly two years in his grave. It's past time you considered his son's future."

"I am. I'm speaking with investors —"

"Who won't touch those mines if you sully your reputation again."

Morwenna moved her hands from her hips to grasp her upper arms. The hall was freezing, and she had left her shawl somewhere. The flame inside her was sure to heat her well enough, and she wouldn't air this disagreement in front of Jago. Not that he wasn't probably listening from the library.

She took a step closer to Grandpapa and lowered her voice so it wouldn't carry fifty feet down the corridor. "I'd rather sully my reputation than see an injured man suffer as Mr. Chastain would with a move."

"Would you?" One of Grandpapa's silvery eyebrows formed a question mark. "And will he thank you with enough to buy mine engines?"

"I doubt he has that much." Morwenna tapped her toe and sought arguments without speaking of the wreck or the medallion.

"You're already in danger with this second

wreck on your beach," Grandpapa said before she formed her words. "There's talk, and with this man off the ship at your house . . ."

"What? They think I saved him from the wreck I caused and nursed him back to health? That makes no sense."

"It does if you want to ensure he doesn't talk."

CHAPTER 4

As Nicca entered the chamber, voices rose from the foot of the great staircase, Morwenna's throaty voice and the basso of a man past his prime, but nonetheless still powerful in his speech, an oddly familiar voice, though David could not have heard it before. He knew no one in this part of Cornwall, unless one counted his unwilling acquaintance with those who had attacked him and left him to die.

With that in mind, wondering if perhaps he could identify them, David motioned for Nicca to leave the door open, then he slid from the bed onto a floor that could have served as an icehouse beneath his bare feet and padded to the opening into the corridor. Clean neglect in the form of faded wallpaper and a threadbare carpet runner met his gaze. Those voices met his ears as clearly as though they were being spoken into a speaking trumpet.

They might as well have been. The staircase was wide but not open. As an engineer, David knew about how sound could funnel upward or outward with the shape of construction. This staircase had been designed in such a manner, possibly by accident, probably on purpose so that anyone upstairs could hear what was going on in the hall below as a form of protection or warning.

The words he heard told David he had been given a warning. Oh, Lady Penvenan denied the accusation that she was keeping David to protect herself. But of course she would. Any sensible person would deny such a claim. But the possibility that the accusers were right lay heavily upon David's shoulders. It simply made too much sense to deny.

When a second lady's voice joined those of the other two and the three moved away, David trudged back into the bedchamber past the stolid Nicca. Instead of crawling into the bed, despite his body aching in every limb, David sank onto the rag rug before the fire. Cold seeped into him from the skin to his marrow.

You're not a prisoner, he told himself. *You can leave anytime you like.*

Except his money had been stolen and her ladyship had gotten rid of his clothes; he was as weak as a newborn cat, and Nicca stood between him and the exit. David wasn't a small man. A lifetime of working in the boatyard had developed his muscles, and he was taller than most men. Nicca, however, was bigger and around David's own twenty-five years. In a bout of Cornish wrestling, David wouldn't bet on himself, were he a betting man. His best option was to stay and regain his strength, accept the lady's kindness, even if she held ulterior motives, and learn what she was about.

He tried to rise on his own to return to the comfort of the bed. His back protested, and he slumped onto the hearth again.

"Let me help you, sir." Nicca picked him up beneath the arms as though David weighed no more than the sleeping child her ladyship sometimes brought into the room with her, a sure sign he could in no way leave here.

"I got you some fish stew," Nicca said. "It'll help set you right."

David didn't care much for fish stew, but it wasn't so bad. The bits of pilchard floating in the thick broth, along with potatoes and turnips and onions, tasted better than the thin gruel they had been feeding him. He felt stronger afterward, strong enough to shave himself as Nicca held the mirror and balanced the basin. He donned a clean shirt and then his limited strength departed, and he fell into a deep sleep from which he didn't wake until morning light poured through the window. Considering the time of year, he guessed the time must be near eight of the clock. He had slept nearly sixteen hours.

He had been drugged. He must have been to sleep like that. The stew. Someone had dropped laudanum in the stew, where the strong flavor of fish and onion would drown the bitterness of the drug.

And her ladyship stood by his bed bearing another tray of food.

David fixed his gaze on her face, met and held eyes so dark he could scarcely make out the pupils nor read any of the thoughts behind them. "Why?" He tried to ask the question, but his throat was so dry he couldn't manage more than a croak.

"Why?" Her already wide eyes widened farther, the lashes just about touching her eyebrows. "Why what?"

"Laudanum? Another opiate in the stew?" That came out better.

She set the tray on a table beside the bed. "I put nothing in your food or drink, Mr. Chastain. Nor did I order it done."

Then her servants had acted on their own?

73

Either that or she was lying.

Proceed with caution, Chastain.

"You slept well, though." Morwenna fussed with the items on the tray. "Perhaps that means you'll be up and about soon."

"I hope so." He did feel a bit stronger today.

"You look better." She drew something from her pocket. "This is your letter. I opened it in an effort to preserve it, but I assure you I could not have read it." She handed him a wrinkled and splotchy sheet of foolscap. "Would you like a cup of tea first? It's strong. My husband was a smuggler, and the cellars still hold a keg or two of leaves, so this is a luxury we can still afford." Her tone was breezy, too breezy, as though she didn't want to show any emotion regarding her poverty.

Poverty, a good reason to wreck ships for their cargo. If smuggling had proven too dangerous, wrecking or stealing ore from mines were substitutes.

David took the letter, smudged and wrinkled, maybe with a word or two showing, and set it aside as though its contents didn't matter. He reached for the teacup she held out to him, heavy earthenware crockery that didn't go with her slender hand.

74

Nor did the redness of her skin, a redness that came from lye soap and hot water, as though she had been doing laundry or scrubbing floors. He considered the cleanliness of his room and the corridor beyond, and his heart twisted.

Those red hands were a good reason for her to lure ships to their doom on her rocky beach. She must carry a heavy burden.

"How old are you?" He blurted out the question without thinking of its rudeness, but once out, he didn't bother to take it back.

She laughed, more a snort than a bubble of humor. "I am two and twenty. I look older, do I not?"

"Oh yes, ma'am, at least three and twenty." He smiled at her over the rim of the thick, white mug.

Her lower lip quivered and for a moment, he thought she would smile. Then she turned away. "You look at least three and twenty yourself, now that I can see your face."

"Add two years." He sipped the tea, hot, strong, and sweetened with honey. The very smell gave him strength. The warmth going down his throat felt like an elixir of life. "I'm the youngest."

"Youngest? You have siblings?"

"Two brothers and a sister."

"But they sent you out after your father?" She shot him a dubious glance.

"I'm the only one left at home who can get away. One brother is at sea, one is running the boatyard, and my sister is . . . er . . . expecting an interesting event any day now."

"And your mother?" Lady Penvenan removed the teacup from his hand and replaced it with a tray across his legs. It held a bowl of porridge and a slice of toasted bread spread with bramble jelly. "I wrote to her."

"Thank you." The sweet, tangy aroma of the dark berry jelly reached his nose, and he closed his eyes, seeing Mama standing at the stove in their big, sunny kitchen, stirring and stirring and stirring and telling them all they needed to do to help or they would get none of her preserves. "Don't be surprised if she arrives instead of a letter."

"She's welcome, although —" A hint of pink touched her cheeks. "There's nowhere here for her to stay. The roof leaked and most of the rooms are uninhabitable. But my grandparents have more than enough space." She turned toward the door. "Grandfather sent over some clothes for you. You may wish to start getting dressed so you can regain your strength."

Not the words of a woman who wanted to keep him close. And yet, he was certain she had drugged him the day before. Or someone had.

He glanced at the cup of tea. He had swallowed half of it. If it had been tainted, he had already ingested a drug. Or maybe it was in the porridge. He could refuse to eat it, and yet it was nourishment he badly needed.

He had to risk it.

He ate the porridge and finished the tea. When the overwhelming fatigue didn't come over him, he considered he had gone without anything unnatural in the food and climbed from the bed. With the coverlet wrapped around him for warmth and modesty, he made himself pace across the room, then back again. The chill of the floorboards kept him alert, kept him moving. The bedposts, a wardrobe, a desk gave him support on his perambulations when his head swam. The pain from his back felt more like stiffness than screaming pain now. The quiet felt like his upper-floor room was a dungeon despite daylight coming through the window. He only needed to open that door to remind himself he wasn't truly a prisoner. If her grandfather had sent over clothes, they were somewhere in the house. He could find them. And be gone.

But she had brought the letter, not his purse.

He had forgotten about the letter in his need to regain his strength. He snatched it from amid the bedclothes and moved to the hearth and the chair her ladyship occupied when watching over him — or guarding him.

As if a lady who couldn't weigh more than eight stone could guard him. In another day or two, he could simply pick her up and move her out of his way if she tried to stop him from going anywhere and the massive Nicca wasn't around. The notion of her keeping him prisoner was ludicrous. He could tell her nothing of the wreck. She hadn't even asked him what he might remember.

"So what will you tell her if she does?" He asked the question of the polished reflection of himself in the grate.

Nothing. He would tell her nothing.

He lifted the poker and coaxed the fire into a greater blaze, for the room held no warmth in the dampness of the house. The blaze was still small, the coal supply minimal. The flames were enough to warm his ice blocks of feet, though, and he leaned back to hold the letter to the light.

He had read it before. He had read it half

a dozen times. He even remembered whole sentences from it. Still, it made no sense then, the words sounding more like the ramblings of a man out of his head with drink. Except Papa didn't drink spirits. The illness must have been upon him. One thing that was clear in the letter was that Papa knew he was dying. The word "dying" had shown up at least four times.

Now, it didn't show up at all. Most of the ink had run or been washed away. David tried to recall the words that fit into the random letters still clear on the cheap paper.

D G S R B V F Y g Y N and, finally, the word that had been protected by the seal of wax: *Trelawny.*

The name had meant no more to David than the family crest on the missing pendant. But now it meant a great deal. The lady who had rescued him was a Trelawny. This was Trelawny territory, she had explained. Everyone in Cornwall knew the family and apparently farther afield. But the name hadn't been unfamiliar to his father. It was important enough for Papa to have written it in his last message to the family, a ramble of regrets, predictions of his imminent death, and an explanation of something that was no explanation at all beneath the pen of a feverish man.

David let the letter slip from his fingers. It fluttered to the floor. His head drooped, but he beat his fist on the arm of the chair. "Why? Why? Why?"

Father had disappeared a month ago with every penny in the boatyard safe. He had told them he was going after a possible commission from a company in Edinburgh, Scotland. A week later, they received word of his death in Falmouth, Cornwall.

Scotland had been rare, but not unheard of. They had never done business in Falmouth. They had never done business with the Trelawny family.

Except his father must have, or at least intended to. But if that were the situation, why not Truro or even this village instead of the other side of the county?

David rose and began to walk again. Shuffle was more like it, but he was moving upright, blood flowing to his limbs, his brain. With it came a chill deeper than the cold rising from the floor and into his bare feet.

Morwenna, Lady Penvenan, was a Trelawny. Maybe her interest in him lay beyond his potential information about the wreck. He didn't believe for a moment she hadn't read what was left of his letter. She would have seen the Trelawny name. She had seen the pendant. She might hold the medallion in her possession. That first day, she had been far more interested in why he possessed it than she had about his being a survivor of the wreck . . .

His head began to spin and he considered returning to the bed, but as he turned toward the four-poster, a knock sounded on the door and it opened to show the lady herself, a small boy clinging to one of her hands and her other arm cradling a pile of worn leather-bound books.

The child spoke first. "Eat." He grinned, released his mother's hand, and ran forward. "Go."

"His favorite words." Lady Penvenan glanced down at the child, her face softening, becoming even more beautiful, if that were possible. "*Dog* completes the list."

"You have —" The boy slammed into David's legs and clung to the coverlet for balance. David scooped him up beneath the arms and held him dangling in the air.

The boy giggled and kicked his legs.

David leaned back against a bedpost for balance. "You're a sturdy lad, aren't you?" He grinned at the glowing dark eyes so like his mother's, including the lashes. "Looks like you've had plenty to eat."

"Go. Eat."

"How about *please*?" David spoke the word with exaggerated care. "Please."

"Puh-lee," the boy parroted.

David laughed and set him down. "It's a good start. Remember to say that to your mama."

He straightened with a wince to meet the surprise on her ladyship's face.

He shrugged. "I have nieces and nephews. We all live in the same house."

"I think I'd probably go mad if I lived with my family." She held out the books. "I heard you pacing and thought perhaps you are bored up here and might like some books. It's a selection . . . I didn't know what you would like or if — um — well, there's no obligation to read any of them. I don't have a great deal of time for reading and was a terrible student, so I understand if . . ." She turned off, this time her face turning positively strawberry in hue.

David's stomach hurt from trying not to laugh at her fumbling way of trying not to say she didn't know if he could read. He cleared his throat twice before he knew he could speak without his amusement shaking his voice. "I was much better at mathematics and geometry, but have read a novel or two." He took the books. "My mother was a schoolmistress before she met my father.

She taught us our letters, and my father taught us our maths."

"I wouldn't have learned anything if not for my cousin Drake and my husband." She bent to scoop up her son as he headed toward the hearth. "We all grew up together, the Penvenans, my two cousins . . ." She spun toward the door so fast her skirt swung out and revealed tiny feet in knitted booties rather than proper shoes. "Nicca will be up shortly with the clothes and a bath." She left, not even shutting the door behind her in her haste to depart.

Regretting telling him too much about herself? Cousins and Penvenans suggested at least four other people. Her husband was dead, but where were the rest? Deceased as well?

Each encounter with the lady brought more questions than answers, including why clothes and a bath in late afternoon . . .

He'd put the question to Nicca when he arrived within the half hour. David spent the intervening time perusing the books. They were a motley selection of sermons, poetry, and one entertaining novel satirizing a previously published popular novel of nauseating virtue. He started to read *Joseph Andrews,* and then Nicca arrived with clothes flung over one shoulder and a bucket of steaming water in each hamlike hand.

"Be back with the tub." He set the buckets down, tossed the clothes onto the bed, and departed. With two more trips the bath was ready and Nicca started to leave. "Get your dinner."

"Why?" David asked.

Nicca cocked his head. "You might be hungry."

"No, why the new clothes and bath now?"

"The squire's coming." Nicca departed before David could ask more questions.

So he availed himself of the luxury of a bath. The soap stung his still healing cuts and scrapes, but he didn't mind. Being clean was too delightful to concern himself with a little discomfort.

The clothes were a surprisingly good fit, sober garb, though the silver buttons proclaimed the clothes were not intended for mourning, and the fineness of the linen shirt and wool coat and breeches had surely been bespoken for a gentleman of means. He would have preferred boots to the thin leather shoes, but boots would have been more difficult to size. The soft leather, fit for dancing, stretched around his larger feet. They, too, sported silver hardware in the form of buckles large enough to have been costly, but small enough not to be ostentatious, just like the buttons on the coat. The clothes of a gentleman indeed.

No one had thought to provide a ribbon for his hair, so he employed the brush left for him to make it as neat as possible and, a little shaky, returned to the armchair by the fire a moment before Nicca burst into the room and began to drag the tub away. "Squire's coming."

The open door allowed the rumble of voices to drift into the room, the murmur growing to a rumble of distinct voices — Lady Penvenan's and that familiar, yet not familiar, man's rich timbre.

"You should allow the man to have his dinner, Grandfather." Lady Penvenan sounded agitated. "This is unkind to confront him on an empty stomach."

"It's already dark out. I don't want to stay out much later." So the man was her grandfather, not someone David would have met before. Not someone he had heard of before this unwanted sojourn onto the north coast of Cornwall.

He rose to meet the man standing, hoping he would be taller to give himself some advantage.

When the man strode into the chamber, the only advantage David felt was his youth.

The Trelawny patriarch was at least David's height, despite a slight stoop of age, and still vigorous in build. No question as to whose clothes David wore. Trelawny wore similar garb — with fine Hessian boots.

"You're looking well, Mr. Chastain." Her ladyship nodded to him, then turned to her grandfather. "David Chastain."

No "Mr." Neatly put in his place.

David bowed, though he felt like perhaps he should tug at his forelock like a scullion. "Honored," he murmured.

"Hmph." Trelawny swept a glance up and down. "You didn't tell me he was so young, Morwenna. All the more reason to get him out of here."

"He isn't strong enough to travel." Her firm, round chin was set. "And now his mother might be on her way here. I know I would be."

"I expect she is, if she's gotten your letter." David flicked his gaze back to Trelawny. "To what do I owe the . . . privilege of this call, sir?"

"Sit down before you fall down, and we'll talk." Trelawny stalked to a chair, sat, and pulled out a pipe.

"You're not smoking that in my house." Lady Penvenan reached for the pipe.

Trelawny snatched it out of her grasp. "I

won't light it, but let an old man have his indulgence." He stuck the stem between his teeth, then removed it and pointed it at David. "I said sit."

"I'm perfectly all right standing, thank you." David couldn't take his eyes off that pipe. Surely he had seen it before, if not this pipe, then one similar, the stem a pointer, the bowl scattering ash as a man talked . . .

Her ladyship snorted. "As long as Mihal doesn't find his way in here and run into you. You'd go over like a tree in a storm, from the look of you."

"No room for pride when you're beaten to a pulp." Trelawny stuck the stem between his teeth again.

"If her ladyship sits . . ." He needed to show these people that just because he grew up handling an adz when this man probably handled a silver rattle, didn't mean he didn't have manners. Father had been the third son of a country squire and Mama the sixth daughter of a baronet. She knew manners and insisted her children used them.

Her ladyship's lashes swept up for a second, then dropped. She ducked her head and flopped onto the edge of a chair. "I-I'm sorry. I wasn't thinking."

"A bad habit of yours, Morwenna. You

don't think." Trelawny rapped the bowl of his unlit pipe on the wooden arm of his chair as though calling a courtroom to order.

Her face hardened to that of a marble statue. "I think we need to get this interview over with so Mr. Chastain can have his dinner and rest. He looks worn to a thread."

He felt worn to a thread and gladly released enough pride to sink onto a chair. "Your servant, sir."

"Hmph." Trelawny narrowed his eyes, intensifying their dark stare. "You are either an excellent actor or have no idea who I am."

"No, sir, I do not."

"Sir Petrok Trelawny."

David chose his response with care. "Until I learned of my father's death in Falmouth, I had never even heard the name Trelawny."

"Well, you are going to hear a great deal more of it, as we are moving you to our family seat at Bastion Point."

"No, Grandfather, you are not." Lady Penvenan glared at her grandsire. "As you see, the man can barely sit upright for more than a quarter hour. How do you expect him to endure the drive over to Bastion Point?" She turned to David, her expression gentling. "The distance isn't great on foot or by horseback, especially at low tide, but you can't ride or walk, so would have to take a carriage around to the house. That is a five-mile drive over our road, which is in appalling condition."

"You cannot stay here, lad." Trelawny ignored Morwenna and addressed David. "Her reputation cannot bear having a single young man staying here."

"Then I'll manage the drive." David inclined his head. "My mother would take a strop to me if she thought I willfully compromised a lady's reputation."

Trelawny gave him an approving nod. "Glad to hear you are more sensible than my granddaughter."

"But, Grandfather, I have been waiting until he was stronger before I questioned him about the wreckers. If he's at Bastion Point, I can't do that."

"You can come visit. That would please your grandmother."

"I don't recall anything about the wreckers, my lady."

If he was removed to Bastion Point, might he not put himself in worse danger than he might be here with her ladyship, a child, and two servants? After all, Bastion Point sounded like a fortress. At the same time, he couldn't harm a lady's reputation no matter how nefarious her actions toward him.

"You may remove your household to Bastion Point if you like, Morwenna," Sir Petrok suggested. "We've been wanting you to do so since those unfortunate events. It would calm the gossip."

"Or make it worse."

"It's your heritage."

"And Penmara is Mihal's heritage." Her face worked as though she was about to burst into tears.

David raised one hand, aching to reach out to her, take her hand, and comfort her. Only as he would have done for his sister or mother. As he had done for them when they received the news of Papa's death.

"I must stop these men to preserve it," she added.

Trelawny reached out his hand, spotted with age, but large and still strong-looking. He covered her hand where it gripped the arm of her chair. "My granddaughter, you won't stop these men by compromising yourself more than you already have. Come to Bastion Point and . . ."

What she could do once there, David didn't hear. Trelawny's words kept repeating themselves in his head as though he were in a cave with the phrases echoing off the walls again and again. "These men . . . These men . . ."

David had heard those words spoken before in that voice, yet not that voice. A younger version of this voice and speaking to a lady. And in that moment, he knew that, although he may never have met Sir Petrok Trelawny, the patriarch of the family, or any Trelawny, he had heard them in the boatyard office.

One night when he stayed late in the workshop to complete a boat design, he heard voices in the office, then a light shone beneath the connecting door. More curious than concerned that Father would entertain midnight visitors, David moved to the door and lifted the latch. By the light of the ship's lantern on Father's desk, David caught a glimpse of a middle-aged couple, both the man and the woman with sun-bronzed skin. The man toyed with an unlit pipe. The woman wore several woolen shawls. They must have heard him, for they ceased talking. Not wanting anyone to see him in a day's worth of sweat and grime, David slipped away and exited the workshop through the boatyard door. Two days later, Papa had departed, saying he was headed for Scotland, and a week after that, he was dead.

"I believe," David said, "I would prefer to remove myself to Bastion Point on the morrow."

CHAPTER 5

This would never do.

Morwenna yanked one of her three dresses off its hook in her armoire and flung it in the vague direction of the bed. She could not go live with her grandparents. She was a woman grown, a widow, a mother, the mistress of a derelict estate. She must not look as though she were abandoning Penmara, or the men who considered investing in her mines might withdraw their support.

Yet if she did not retreat to Bastion Point, she couldn't learn anything from David should he remember.

Should he choose to remember.

He remembered something. While Grandfather spoke, she had watched David's face from the corner of her eye and seen his expression change, grow cold and remote. That was the sort of expression a man took on when he acquired knowledge that was not good news for someone.

Her or himself? Or intertwined.

Yes, their lives were intertwined. She didn't know why, but she suspected from the moment she rescued him from drowning in the surf, she needed to keep him close.

So she would submit to Grandfather's authority and return to Bastion Point.

"Ridiculous." She yanked a hat off the top shelf of the armoire.

Grandmother insisted she wear a hat to church. Grandmother would likely insist she have new clothes. More than once she said that going on two years was more than enough time for mourning a husband. She didn't seem to understand that Morwenna's continued mourning bore as much to financial restraints as it did respect for her deceased spouse.

"You could become a wealthy woman if you remarry." Grandmother had spoken the words more than once in the past six months since official mourning ended.

Lately, she had been adding, "If you married Jago Rodda or Tristan Pascoe. You know we would love that."

Morwenna should love it too. The Roddas and Pascoes were wealthy. Tristan was handsome and educated, but he was a second son, not the heir to anything. Despite his intelligence and charm, he seemed to have no purpose in life besides visiting friends from university and flirting with Morwenna. Jago was the Roddas' only child. Jago was handsome and intelligent as well, and looked at her as though she were a meaty bone and him a hungry hound.

"The hounds!" Morwenna flung open the bedchamber door and raced down the corridor to the back steps, calling for Henwyn or Nicca. They should be in the kitchen having their breakfast with Mihal, as they would be staying at the house to keep it from being empty.

"The dogs." Morwenna shoved open the kitchen door. "I can't leave the dogs here." She glanced around. "Where are they? Where are Mihal and Nicca?"

"All of them are in the garden." Henwyn set a newly washed cup on the sideboard. "With Mr. Chastain." She gave Morwenna a sidelong glance. "He cleans up right nice, don't he?"

"I hadn't noticed." Morwenna tried to avoid Henwyn's eyes, failed, and shrugged. "All right, yes, he is a fine specimen of a man on the outside. Who knows what he is on the inside."

Henwyn nodded and smiled. "Good to hear you haven't had your head turned.

You're needing better than the likes of him, being a ladyship and all."

"I didn't deserve to be a ladyship."

She hadn't deserved Conan. With Conan, everything changed except for her past behavior, and she would pay for that for the rest of her life. Good girls like her cousin Elizabeth got what they wanted. Morwenna got what she deserved.

She would never live up to the standards her grandparents expected. Jago Rodda and Tristan Pascoe might want to marry her, but it was only for her looks — and her dowry. It had always been her looks with Jago. He had lusted after her since she was fifteen and he somewhere around twenty fresh back from university. Many would say she wasn't good enough for Jago even if she was a Trelawny and now a Penvenan. As for Tristan? Tristan was too young to take seriously as a suitor, let alone consider as a husband.

But saying any of this aloud, even what she had admitted, was inappropriate to speak of with a servant.

She refocused her mind on the dogs. "I can't leave the dogs here with you and Nicca, and I can't take them to Bastion Point."

"You can leave them here with us." Nicca

pushed through the back door, carrying Mihal. He set the child inside a pen made of chairs. "I'll take fine care of them, you know."

"And they'll be protection for me alone in this pile of a house." Henwyn began to dry the washed dishes.

"Dog." Mihal spoke from the far end of the kitchen where he had settled himself amid a sea of tumbled blocks. "Dog."

"He'll miss them." Morwenna looked at her son.

She would miss the hounds as well. They had been such a comfort to her when she was *incent* and exiled to a cottage in the woods. In those achingly lonely days, days of terror, she longed for her grandparents to allow her to move back to Bastion Point for the safety of her unborn child, yet she dared not break her word and give them the information they insisted she divulge, if she wanted them to accept her back into the fold.

Anger and bitterness over that time twisted in her belly, an acidic roil.

"Could you bring them over for visits?" She crossed the room to join Mihal on the floor, a much better activity, building up the blocks, than packing to return to Bastion Point. "I know you are occupied here keeping things clean and trying to keep the roof on."

"And I'm working on plowing up more land for the garden by planting time." Nicca grinned, proud of his work.

"I think I should go with you," Henwyn said. "You need someone loyal to you, and who'll be watching the boy?"

"Grandmama has twenty servants. If I am occupied —"

"Which you will be, if I know Lady Trelawny," Henwyn broke in.

"Then one of them can see to him. Miss Pross will adore having him about."

Miss Pross was her cousin Elizabeth's former companion, chaperone, lady's maid, but hadn't wanted to leave with Elizabeth when she married. Grandmother had offered the middle-aged spinster a position as her companion, and Pross had stayed, quiet, efficient, and good at listening, offering insight when appropriate.

Unlike Henwyn, who had grown outspoken in the two years she had served as Morwenna's maid of all work and, for much of that time, only companion.

"I don't like you there alone with all those people." Henwyn slammed a copper pot onto the table. "And that man there like he's an honored guest. Don't know why you can't stay here."

"I need to be near him in the event he talks. I need to know — something. If one more wreck happens on my beach . . ." Morwenna turned her attention to Nicca. "We'll arrange to have you bring the dogs over every day, weather permitting. Perhaps a run on the beach during low tide. The Bastion Point beach is so much better than ours."

Not nearly as rocky and inhospitable. Ships didn't go aground accidentally or on purpose in Halfmoon Cove.

"I'll send a note —" Morwenna broke off, remembering that neither Nicca nor Henwyn could read. "I'll send a servant over." She picked up Mihal, much to his objections, kissed him on the cheeks, then set him amid his blocks again. "I'll pack now."

"You'd best be about it then. The carriage is coming in a quarter hour." Henwyn stomped across the room to where a kettle of hot water perpetually simmered on the hearth when the fire was lit. "Will you be taking some tea up to Mr. Chastain?"

"He's gone on up to his room to rest," Nicca said.

Henwyn sniffed. "He shouldn't be doing all that climbing. He still looks as weak as a kitten for all his size."

"He'll eat better at Bastion Point." Morwenna couldn't help the disloyal thought that so would she. No fish stew. No fish at all if she said she didn't want it.

For a moment, her heart rebelled against taking anything from her grandparents. Doing so felt like treachery. Thirty pieces of silver in exchange for her pride, her dignity, her promise to her husband. She stacked up one more tower of blocks for Mihal, replaced the chair that kept him from crawling toward the fire when no one was looking, and crossed the kitchen to fetch a tray from a hook on the wall. "I expect Grandmother has real sugar."

"Honey's as good as all that," Nicca muttered. "Proud of my bees."

"And thankful we are to have them." Morwenna spread a worn and mended serviette onto the tray. She had embroidered over the darns to give it some elegance for when she had callers, but her needlework, other than knitting, was rather awful.

"It'll give him strength for the journey." Henwyn ducked into the pantry and returned with a pot of honeycomb. She tapped a generous portion into the steaming mug, then set cup and spoon onto the tray. "Come back down, m'lady, and I'll fix you a cup for yourself."

"I'll take mine now, too, and I must finish packing my things. Mihal's are all ready."

"You need to be sitting down when you drink it, not sipping here and there while it grows cold." Despite her grumbling, Henwyn prepared a second cup of tea, this one in one of the few pieces of china left to the household. "So you don't forget that you are a lady of your own manor while you're over there."

"As if I could."

She would be writing letters from Bastion Point, asking a few more gentlemen of means in Cornwall if they would consider investing in the Penmara mines. If only she could afford to hire a mine engineer to inspect them and estimate how much ore might be there below the floodwater. The miners, now out of work because the engines stopped pumping out the water years ago and no money remained for repairs, claimed that the mines held wealth in copper and tin.

She didn't want the tin. It had to be inspected and stamped with a government seal. This cut into profits. But copper — in Cornwall, copper was gold, especially with two wars raging. The navy needed copper to coat the bottoms of their ships.

She picked up the tray and Nicca sprang

forward to open the door. As he was about to pull it closed behind her, no doubt anxious for his own cup of midmorning tea, she turned back to ask, "Why are the dogs with Mr. Chastain?"

"He asked for them. Said he owed them or sommit of the like."

"And so he does." Morwenna headed up the back staircase balancing the tray with care, then halted so abruptly halfway up that she slopped tea over the rims of the cups.

She hadn't told Chastain about the dogs finding him, nor how they looked over him. She doubted either Nicca or Henwyn — especially not Henwyn — had said anything to him.

As fast as she dared with the teacups, Morwenna sped up the steps and balanced the tray on one hip while she knocked on his door. A scrabble of paws and a yip or two of greeting preceded a slow, steady tread across the floor. Then the door opened and Mr. David Chastain stood in the opening.

Morwenna caught her breath. By daylight, he looked even better than he had in the flickering glow of candles the previous afternoon. Her grandfather's sober garb suited Chastain's looks, emphasizing the glossiness of his dark hair, the hints of copper and cinnamon amidst the coffee-brown strands, and making the green lights in his eyes a little brighter than the gray. He towered over her, her head perhaps reaching the center of his chest, and he was broad, far broader than her husband had been. Truth be told, he was better looking than Conan, and the smile he gave her —

She swallowed against a dry throat, pushed down a sense of guilt for looking upon another man with favor. "Tea," was all she managed.

Oggy and Pastie sat beyond Chastain, their tails wagging as though they expected cups of tea as well.

"The tea is welcome." His voice, that hint of Somerset, broke the spell.

Fine feathers did not make a fine bird.

She thrust the tray into his hands, then snatched up her cup. "I need to pack my things. We leave in a quarter hour." She spun away, sloshing hot tea onto her fingers.

"My lady —"

She ignored him and traversed the hall to her chamber. Not until she heard doggy toenails on the floor behind her did she remember she had intended to ask Chastain how he knew he owed the dogs something. Too late now. She could scarcely return.

When she turned around, though, she saw

him standing in the doorway still watching her.

She ducked into her chamber, the dogs with her. Once her door closed behind her, she sank to her knees and hugged both hounds, Conan's beloved hounds. "How could I do that? How could I compare him to Conan and find my husband wanting?"

Conan wasn't wanting. He had been kind, loving, and as honest as a man engaged in illegal activities dare be. He had been completely open with her. She knew of his hopes and dreams, how he wanted to marry off his sister for her sake and reopen the mines for the sakes of the villagers barely managing to survive. He wanted to restore the house and fill it with a dozen children. He wanted to take his seat in Parliament and carry her off to London to dress her in fine silks and jewels . . .

Pastie squirmed out of Morwenna's hold and trotted across the room to inspect a dress that had slid from the pile on the bed to the floor. Oggy remained and licked Morwenna's face where some tears ran.

"I should stay here away from him." She released Oggy and rose. "You cannot lie on that dress. It's the best one I own."

She wore it to church and Grandmother frowned at it every Sunday, then reminded

Morwenna of Miss Pross's skill with a needle and how Elizabeth had left behind an entire room full of gowns.

Because she had purchased new ones for her new life.

Morwenna snatched up the gown and began to fold it while talking to the dogs. "I can't take you with me, but Nicca will bring you over to visit." She set the dress into the small leather trunk Nicca had found somewhere in the attics. "You'll be all right here without me?"

Their big dark eyes gazed at her with sorrow.

"Don't do that. I feel guilty leaving Penmara as it is. But this is for Penmara's sake."

They sighed and slumped to the floor.

"Mr. Chastain remembers more than he is saying, and I must find out what it is for all our sakes. You do understand —"

Carriage wheels sounded on the drive, and the dogs sprang toward the window, barking.

"Quiet." Morwenna shoved the last two gowns into the trunk and slammed the lid.

The dogs stood on their hind legs, paws on the sill, and whined with their noses against the glass. Mist formed where their breath fanned across the panes. That wouldn't happen at Bastion Point. No occupied room would dare get so cold.

Morwenna buckled one of the straps on the trunk and picked up the second just as Nicca knocked on the door. Distracted from the carriage outside, the dogs charged for the portal and the distraction inside.

"Sit," Morwenna commanded.

The dogs sat, wagging and quivering as they had when guarding David Chastain on the beach while she ran for help.

While she was gone . . .

Something else niggled at her mind, some point she was missing, something important.

The knock sounded again, interrupting her concentration on the missing memory piece.

"Come in," Morwenna called.

Nicca opened the door. "I'll get that for you, m'lady." He patted each hound as he passed. "This be aught you have?"

"And Mihal's things." Morwenna nodded toward the makeshift nursery.

She knew she should call him by his title, or at the least Master Mihal, but that was so much to hang upon the fragile neck of a baby not yet two years old. She wasn't formal to her two servants. Her grandparents would insist on it, though.

"Penvenan," she corrected herself for practice.

Nicca shouldered her trunk, then headed over to the other one she had packed for Mihal. When he picked it up to balance on his other shoulder, the dogs took on worried expressions and slunk over to Morwenna, tails drooping.

"Nicca will take good care of you." She hugged each of them. "Be good."

She left the room, the dogs trailing behind, and found David Chastain in his doorway with two footmen from Bastion Point.

"But Sir Petrok said we must carry you, sir," one of the footmen was saying. "It's not worth our jobs to not do so."

"I think carrying me —" David broke off and shot Morwenna a pleading glance over the footmen's heads. "My lady, do please tell them I can walk to the carriage."

She wasn't certain he could. He stood upright, but one hand braced against the door frame. A close inspection showed the slightest tremor in his forearm, and his face was too pale for good health. Worse, a sheen of perspiration beaded across his brow just below the hairline.

But she understood the man's need for dignity and addressed the footmen. "If he wants to walk, let him walk. Just be prepared to catch him if he tumbles face-first down the steps."

David shot her a grateful glance. "I won't go tumbling down the steps."

The two footmen stalked ahead, their faces set. Morwenna followed, one dog on either side of her. Nicca took the back steps with the trunks. He would take them around the side of the house, and Henwyn would meet them in the front with Mihal. Even without the servants and baby, they made a strange cavalcade. Morwenna tried to get the dogs to stay in the house for fear they would follow the carriage, but, for once, they ignored her command and stuck to her as though glued to her skirts. Ahead of them, David Chastain descended one tread at a time, a hand on either railing. His hands gripped those railings with white-knuckled tension, and his movements were stiff. More than once, he emitted a grunt as though he stepped too hard and jarred his battered body. Each time, one of the footmen shot him a "We told you so" look. They made it safely to the entry hall. One footman sprang forward to open the front door. Only two more steps and a dozen feet to the carriage remained. David managed those well enough, but lifting his foot for the first high step into the vehicle defeated him. Twice his shoe slipped off the tread. The third time, he slumped against the side of the carriage and might have slid to the ground if Morwenna hadn't sprung forward and wrapped her arms around him.

"Pride goeth before a fall," he murmured.

"And we're both going to fall." Morwenna swayed beneath his weight. "John. Joseph." They were laughing, with their faces red from trying not to do so aloud, but stepped forward to help.

And Oggy leaped between them. He didn't growl or bare his teeth. A dog his size didn't need to, especially not when Pastie joined him.

"Oggy, Pastie, sit." Morwenna dared not release David to pull the dogs away, but she was growing flushed with mortification for standing in front of her grandparents' servants with her arms around a near stranger and his arm around her shoulders. It was just too intimate, whatever the reason.

"Oggy." She heard the strain in her voice, then when the dogs continued to ignore her, she made herself look up at David.

His face was too close to hers, close enough for her to catch green sparks in the sea storm of his eyes. Green sparks because he, too, was laughing and trying to keep it inside.

"I should let go of you." She spoke through gritted teeth. "But I spent too many hours nursing you to let it all go for naught because of my pride."

"I beg your pardon, my lady." He cleared his throat. "I've thought up better ways to get a lady's arms around me than risking cracking my head on the side of a carriage."

"If you've had to think up ways, then they aren't initially willing."

Which was probably untrue. Before Conan, she would have been more than willing to put her arms around a man who looked like David Chastain. Her cheeks heating, she returned her attention to the footmen still held at bay. "Go fetch Nicca. The dogs will listen to him."

As though the hounds were nipping at their heels, the footmen sprinted around the side of the house. The instant they were out of sight, the dogs began to wag their tails and rushed over to lick David's hand.

"What's wrong with you beasts?" He grasped Pastie's collar, then moved his arm from around Morwenna's shoulders and bent enough to rest his other hand on Oggy's back. "You can release me now, my lady, not that I minded in the least. I just think maybe you'd prefer some privacy."

"Some pri— you were about to —" Morwenna caught a faint snicker and glanced up to find the coachman leaning down to watch from the safety of the box. She released her hold on David and backed away so fast she caught her heel in the hem of her gown. The arrival of Nicca with the footmen and Henwyn with Mihal drowned out the ripping of Morwenna's hem, but she felt the stitches go. "You'd better be worth this trouble, David Chastain," she grumbled beneath her breath.

Then the cacophony of Nicca getting the dogs under control, the footmen loading luggage into the boot, and Mihal wailing over leaving Henwyn, Nicca, and the dogs behind overcame anything but Morwenna's need to see David safely tucked up in the coach and herself settled with Mihal on her lap. It seemed to take half of an hour, but at last the door slammed, and the footmen climbed onto the box with the coachman.

Mihal still wailed. Then David began to distract the boy with silly faces and mimicking the voices of various animals. While the carriage dipped and bounced over the rutted road, David persuaded Mihal to speak the names of different animals according to the sounds they made. By the time they reached the public road and turned left toward Bastion Point, Mihal had fallen asleep in Morwenna's arms.

She lifted her eyes to David's, only to find him gazing down at her, that heart-stopping smile on his lips. She swallowed and flicked her gaze away. "Thank you."

"I miss my family."

"I expect they miss you, especially after your father . . ." She trailed off, leaving space for him to say something.

But the carriage dropped into a rut in the drive, jostling them forward. David grunted and grabbed for the overhead strap. Morwenna braced her feet and clutched Mihal too tightly, waking him up.

"Dog," he bellowed.

"You'll see the dogs tomorrow." A ridiculous thing to say. He didn't know what that meant.

Morwenna closed her eyes, suddenly too tired to face another quarter hour or more of jouncing along the Cornish lanes barely fit for horses, let alone a carriage.

"Allow me?" David took Mihal from her. This time he distracted him with one of the buttons off his coat. It was too big to harm the child, who put everything into his mouth, and Morwenna decided to say nothing about how unkempt they would arrive with David less one button on his coat and her hem dragging like an uneven train.

Grandmother would certainly use it all for an excuse to take over their wardrobes, if not their comings and goings. At the same time as she worried about that, she admired a man who considered the needs of a small child for entertaining over the impression he made upon the arrival at a fine country estate — and more. He recognized her weariness, much of it due to nursing him, and, without saying a word, helped to alleviate her discomfort.

"So you spend a great deal of time with your nieces and nephews?" she asked.

"Most evenings we are all together with the children." He glanced up at her. "We have a nursemaid who helps out with the little ones, but my sister and sister-in-law usually see to the care of their own children."

A criticism of her? It wasn't deserved. She was trying to run what was left of Penmara and save the rest, once the work of the lord of the manor, but Morwenna's responsibility with Mihal three months shy of two years old. She looked at David. "You remembered the dogs from the beach." She made it a statement.

"I think I may have regained consciousness long enough to remember them lying beside me. When I heard them baying outside at Penmara, I asked Nicca to bring them up to me." He snatched the button before it fell to the floor. "I like dogs." He wiped the button on his sleeve, then tilted it toward Mihal. "Look at that. You can see yourself."

"They like you — the dogs, that is."

"Dogs and children." He cupped Mihal's hand in his and placed the button between the delicate fingers. "See, if you hold it like this . . ."

Mihal stared at his miniature reflection in the shining silver. "See."

"Another word." Morwenna wanted to hug her child. She felt odd without him on her lap, but he seemed so content where he was, she dared not remove him.

And they were almost there. The carriage turned between the pillars with their crouching lions, and the drive grew smoother, the rumbling of the wheels quieter. On either side of them, trees marched with well-tended shrubbery beneath.

David glanced out the window, and his eyebrows arched. "This is where you grew up? Or did you live elsewhere with your parents?"

"I lived here with my parents and then here with my grandparents." She clutched her hands together on her lap and did not look out the window. "My parents left for some adventure when I was near Mihal's age. They have only come home three times since."

"They haven't wanted to meet their grandson?"

"They don't know they have a grandson." Morwenna's throat closed. "They haven't been home in five or six years."

"How sad to not have your parents around. My father . . ." He leaned his head back against the squabs and closed his eyes. The action didn't disguise the pain etched on his features.

Mihal threw the button across the carriage and began to wail. Morwenna took him back onto her lap and held him close, murmuring what she thought was nonsense to him, words she often crooned, a lullaby of declarations. "We have each other. We are our family. We aren't alone when we're together." And on and on she spoke to him when he was tired or hungry or frightened until the carriage rolled to a halt before the fan-shaped steps of Bastion Point and she found David's hand on her arm.

"My lady?"

Morwenna jumped and looked at him.

He was staring out the window past her.

"There's a military officer of some sort here."

Morwenna followed his gaze to where three men in uniform filled the doorway to her grandparents' house. But they weren't military precisely. They were riding officers, revenue men, the sort who would be investigating a suspicious wreck of a ship.

CHAPTER 6

David had never before seen anyone's face lose color in a heartbeat. Morwenna was so fair he wouldn't have thought she could grow even whiter, but the instant she glanced out the window, the delicate pink across her cheekbones leeched away and her breathing ceased.

"My lady?" He wanted to take her hand. The baby decided to squirm down at that moment, and all David's attention centered on stopping the boy without hurting himself. Mihal fought him, his gaze intent upon the shining button lodged between the other seat and the wall. From the corner of his eye, David saw that the lad's mother was focused on the riding officers, and she was frightened.

Guilty?

"My lady —"

The carriage door opened and a footman dropped the steps before David could ask

117

her anything. She started to rise, stopped, looked at Mihal. "I . . . need to get him inside."

"I'll hold him until you're on the ground." Though the action strained the healing wounds on his back, David reached for the button, then scooped the child back onto his knee.

"Miss Pross is here to take him," one of the footmen said.

Beyond him, a petite lady of late middle years swerved around the officers and descended the shallow steps of the great house. She would have been plain if not for the brilliance of her smile.

"Lady Penvenan." She clasped Morwenna's hand. "I have missed this boy." She gave David a glance with brows arched in query. "You are the mysterious stranger."

"Not at all mysterious, ma'am. I have a name and address and family fully disclosed."

What he thought he knew about the Trelawny family and his father's mysterious death, his father's odd behavior toward his own family, was what made David a mystery.

Miss Pross snorted and reached for Mihal. "I held this little one when he was mere hours old. Quite an adventure we had." She hefted him onto her hip. "And not so little now."

David ignored her chatter, focusing on Morwenna, who crossed the smooth gravel between the carriage and the officers and Sir Petrok. Despite the obvious tear in her hem trailing the ugly black skirt behind her, she moved with a gliding grace that displayed confidence and elegance with each stride. If he hadn't seen her pale at the sight of the officers, David would have thought she didn't have a care in the world except to ensure these gentlemen of the law were welcome at Bastion Point.

"Sir?" The footman at the steps was staring at David. "Are you staying here?"

David snapped his attention to what he needed to do. "I was gathering my strength for the arrival."

Entirely the truth. The renewal of strength he had experienced before leaving Penmara had abandoned him somewhere on the rough Cornish roads. Rising seemed far too much of an effort. With the aid of the overhead strap, he hauled himself to his feet, then stood, stooping to accommodate for his height and the low roof of the vehicle. He was waiting for his legs to steady before he attempted a descent.

The footman held out a gloved hand. "Allow me to help you, sir." The servant's face flashed to compassion before resuming its stony expression.

His own face stiff with mortification, David accepted the help and managed to reach the ground without falling on his face. "I'll wait here a moment until the Trelawnys finish conducting their business with the officers." David leaned against the coach side, remembering doing so at Penmara, Morwenna's slender arms around him, pressing her cheek against his chest. He had smelled her hair, sweet and tangy like lemonade, a refreshing scent. He'd never been so close to a female not related to him. He wanted to do so again — with this female.

Except she might be responsible for him being on the other side of the county he needed to be on.

At the foot of the front steps, the revenue officers seemed to think much the same as David — that Morwenna Penvenan was involved with some nefarious dealings. "We don't need your permission, ma'am."

"My lady." Her spine stiffened. "I am Lady Penvenan."

The officer reddened. "Er, my lady."

"We have a warrant," another officer said.

"If you had come to me sooner" — Sir Petrok spoke from his superior height both endowed by nature and from the upper step on which he stood — "I would have given you permission without you making this so public by seeking a warrant."

"You have no right —" Morwenna began, then her shoulders shimmied inside her cloak, too small a motion for a shrug of resignation, too powerful for anything like a sob. More like someone shaking off spiders.

"I am the boy's legal guardian and the estate is his." Sir Petrok's expression was kind.

"The trustees." Morwenna's voice had faded, making her sound very young and vulnerable.

David took two steps forward before he remembered he was an outsider with no right to lend her support.

No one noticed him, as Sir Petrok shook his head. "The trustees don't need to agree to a warrant or a search."

"But my servants . . . The dogs . . ." Morwenna raised a hand to her cheek, then let it fall limply at her side. "I should go with you."

"We'd rather you did not," the officer with lieutenant's bars on his blue coat said.

"I'll go, child." Sir Petrok descended the steps and laid one hand on Morwenna's shoulder. "The dogs will listen to me."

David suspected they wouldn't dare not listen to him.

"You go inside and let your grandmother spoil you." Sir Petrok fixed his gaze on David. "And you get inside and sit down before you fall down, Mr. Chastain."

"Yes, sir." David took another step toward the house and the double front doors.

"Halt." The lieutenant raised one hand. "Who are you?"

"David Chastain."

"What business —"

"Mr. Chastain is our guest." Sir Petrok's voice cut across the lieutenant's question with the whip crack of authority. "You have seen to it that we cannot stop you from searching Penmara, but this is my land and questioning my guests you cannot do."

The lesser officer smirked behind the lieutenant's back. The young man flushed. Gravel crunched beneath his boot heels. "We'll be about our business then." He executed an about-face and strode to the rest of his men and the waiting horses.

"Grandfather —" Morwenna turned to Sir Petrok, her face still washed of color, her eyes bigger and darker than usual against the pallor. "Why do they wish to search Penmara?"

"We'll discuss it later." Sir Petrok glanced

at the officers mounting their horses. "Go inside and make yourself presentable for dinner."

"Make myself — revenue officers want to search my home and you're concerned about me looking presentable?" Color flooded into her face and her hands fisted at her sides. "This is the outside of enough."

"Unacceptable and not unexpected. Now get inside." Sir Petrok turned toward the carriage David had just vacated, spoke to the driver, and climbed inside.

David reached Morwenna. "Allow me." He held out his arm.

Fortunately — or perhaps not — they stood in full daylight with a dozen windows looking down upon them, or he might have kissed her. The panic in her eyes, the way she turned her face up to his with such relief for his presence, and, above all, that trembling strawberry lip, provided pure temptation, all the worse for him not expecting it to wash through him.

He wrenched his gaze away. "We'd best go inside."

She offered him her arm without a word and, still in silence, David leaning on her surprising strength, they climbed the steps. No one opened the door for them, so David lifted the handle and stepped back to allow

Morwenna to enter first. As he waited for her to pass, he caught the *sotto voce* words of one footman, "Beware. Her ladyship is among us again."

"Friends of yours?" David asked.

Morwenna's face grew rigid. "Youths from the village."

He could not — should not — press the matter further. Her past was none of his business. Being a gentleman in behavior, if not birth to these people, was his business in light of the lady who was crossing the flowered carpet toward them.

She could have been any age between fifty and seventy with a blue lace cap adorning her snowy locks and eyes, the sparkling green eyes still clear and sharp. The few lines that marred her creamy complexion denoted more laughter than sadness, and she had maintained a trim figure that lent elegance to her height.

"Grandmother." Morwenna took David's hand and drew him forward. "David Chastain."

"How do you do, Lady Trelawny?" He bowed.

Lady Trelawny held out her hand to him. "I do well, especially to have my grand-daughter here to stay as well as you. This house is too big for Petrok and the servants

124

and me."

"Thank you." He shook the proffered hand.

"With our grandson gone and other granddaughter no longer in England, we had hoped Morwenna would live here with the baby, but, alas —"

"Penmara will tumble down around our ears if I don't stay there," Morwenna said. "You have rooms for us? Mr. Chastain is probably dropping."

"He doesn't look well. You must rest before dinner, Mr. — oh, dear, what happened to your coat?"

"An inconsequential sacrifice for Lord Penvenan's entertainment." David pulled the button from his pocket.

"I will have someone make repairs while you rest." Lady Trelawny looked at Morwenna again. "And I have a different gown for you to wear to dinner. That one isn't fit for the dustbin."

"But it's my second best." Morwenna sounded too sweet.

"We won't discuss your wardrobe in front of a guest. Would you prefer tea first, or tea in your chamber, Mr. Chastain?"

"Whichever —"

"His chamber," Morwenna broke in. "Can you not see he's falling down?"

"Morwenna, your manners." Lady Trelawny's brows drew together, but she smoothed her forehead at once and gave a brisk nod. "All right. Morwenna, you're in your old room. Mr. Chastain is in the opposite wing."

She swept from the room, her lavender gown floating around her like a cloud.

David followed, not sure he dared do anything else. Morwenna stalked behind until they reached the top of the steps and Lady Trelawny turned left and started down a side corridor. Then Morwenna darted forward, tripping on the torn hem of her gown. "You're placing him in Elizabeth's room? Grandmother, this house has at least thirty bedchambers and you're putting him in hers?"

Thirty bedchambers for two old people and a companion? David's family home didn't have thirty rooms, and nine adults and six children lived there.

Eight adults.

The reminder slammed into his middle, the physical pain of his father's death, the loss of his wise counsel, an absence, a lack in his life so strong he didn't catch more of the sniping between grandmother and granddaughter — more from the granddaughter than grandmother. Something about the remoteness of the room from the rest of the house. Lady Penvenan's objections didn't move her grandmother, who stopped in front of a door at the end of the corridor.

"This faces the garden on the one side and sea on the other." Lady Trelawny opened the portal to a spacious chamber with two leaded paned windows affording considerable light. "Our other granddaughter married in '11 and, with this terrible war with America now, won't be back for many years, I expect, if ever, so I give this chamber to guests."

"And Drake's room?" Morwenna asked. She looked to David. "He's Elizabeth's brother, but we pretend he doesn't exist."

Lady Trelawny looked surprised. "We don't pretend he doesn't exist. We receive letters from him as regularly as we can with this war on. He might even come home."

"Grandfather would welcome him?" Morwenna laughed. "Now that Elizabeth has gotten out of the Trelawny clutch —"

"That's enough, Morwenna." Lady Trelawny turned her back on her granddaughter.

One Trelawny flown from the nest, another who didn't want to be there, and one who had gone for reasons unknown. And that didn't include a son of the house who preferred wandering the world to home, and another preferring London and politics to this beautiful house and land. What a peculiar family. Perhaps it was normal for these wealthy members of the upper classes. The boatyard did business with wealthy men, but David preferred to design and build. He left the selling to Papa. He did well with clients.

With the Trelawnys, despite their claims of never hearing of him? If they denied knowing him or his family, he needed to learn why, preferably before Mama arrived. And Mama would arrive. *When* was the key there, not *if.*

She would be amused to find him in a chamber of a palace with a view that took his breath away.

"How high up are we?" he couldn't help but ask as he looked out the seaward window to a panorama of foaming water and blue sky etched with a ruffle of darkening cloud on the horizon.

"Sixty feet plus the ground floor." Lady Trelawny joined him. "Seventy-five feet from the sand. Elizabeth loves the sea. I hope you don't mind it after your ordeal."

He offered the grandmother a smile. "I don't mind at all. I am a boatbuilder and designer, after all."

"And you do business in Falmouth as well as Bristol?"

"My father handled the business side of things. My brother some too. I'm the brawn."

Her ladyship laughed, a surprisingly musical sound for an old lady. "I expect you are and more." She patted his arm. "Let me have that coat and I'll send up Petrok's man to make it good as new before you rise. I'll send you some tea. Dinner is early here, as we keep country hours. Two hours."

She waited while he removed the coat, wincing as he drew his arms from the sleeves. With more promises of tea, she departed. David toed off the shoes and stretched out on the bed. A fire crackled on the hearth, warming the chamber along with shafts of sunlight streaming through the westward window. He drew the coverlet over himself anyway. Somewhere in the recesses of his head, he recalled the shocking cold of the water when the ship began to turn turtle. He'd dived into the water and headed for shore so he wouldn't get sucked down when the ship capsized and sank. He remembered wanting to save others with his strong swimming ability, but couldn't find them in the dark. All around him was dark with a hint of lighter black to the east. That was all. Cold, cold water. Waves higher than a man's head. One of them catching him and . . . nothing.

He fell asleep to the sound of the surf far below. When he awoke, he found fresh linens, his pressed and mended coat, and a cup of tea that had been brought into the room. The tea in the cup was cold, but water steamed from a pitcher on the nightstand, where a bar of finely milled soap lay with shaving gear and towels. Not one thing in that chamber belonged to him. He had lost everything, as well as the money the family scraped together to send him on this journey of finding answers.

Send him to look for Trelawnys in Falmouth when they weren't there at all, but living on this coast where a storm had tossed him ashore like flotsam.

Not a coincidence. That was the stuff of epic poems by persons like Sir Walter Scott. This wasn't a romantic's poem; this was cold reality.

He wasn't here at the Trelawnys by accident.

CHAPTER 7

The revenue officers were searching Penmara. The idea made Morwenna sick to her stomach. Hands pressed to her roiling middle, she leaned her brow against the glass and wished the windows of her bedchamber looked upon Penmara, even if it were too far away to be seen. But that was Elizabeth's old chamber where David had been placed. Morwenna's room was on the opposite corner of the floor, facing north to the sea and east toward the Rodda estate. She couldn't bear the sight of the sea with its reminder of treachery as deep as the bottom, as cold as the roaring waves. Out the other windows, she saw nothing but the rough landscape, grazing cows, some fields, trees, and the distant plumes of smoke from the Trelawny mines.

Those mines worked, producing the valuable copper ore to add to the Trelawnys' already overflowing coffers.

She could possess a quantity of that wealth. All she needed to do was humble herself and ask for help and prove she had reformed her wayward spirits. All she had to do was turn Penmara over to her grandfather.

"But I want to make Penmara prosperous myself. It's the least I can do for Conan.

"God, what am I going to do?" She beat her brow against the cold glass. "What, what, what?"

She was innocent of misdeeds. She had always been innocent of misdeeds since Conan came into her life. But her escapades before that, if not illegal, were too close to immoral for anyone to believe her now. She wasn't altogether certain moving David and herself to Bastion Point would help much. She wasn't even certain her grandparents believed her innocent.

Wanting to see her son, now installed in the nursery a floor above her, with Miss Pross spoiling him with some trinket Morwenna couldn't provide, she turned from the window. Her heel caught in the torn hem of her gown. She stumbled, catching herself on the corner of a table just as Grandmother walked into the chamber without knocking.

"That gown is a disgrace, child." Grandmother's gaze dropped to the torn hem.

"It just needs a few stitches. I didn't have time to repair it before we came here."

"It needs more than stitches. Look."

Morwenna looked and winced. Her heel had gone right through the fabric worn from too many washings. "Perhaps I can embroider —"

"Rather like putting a new patch on an old garment. It will only pull away and make things worse." Grandmother crossed the room and opened the dressing room door. "That's why I had Miss Pross adjust some of the gowns Elizabeth left behind. Of course, I would love to take you to Truro or even Falmouth for new dresses, but since you won't do that, these will have to do."

Morwenna glared at the half dozen or more gowns Elizabeth had brought from London and then left behind. They were sewn of the finest muslin, merino, and even silk fabrics, soft feminine gowns with lace and ruffles and fancy embroidery, the like of which Morwenna hadn't worn since her secret marriage produced fruit. When her condition had begun to show, her grandparents had exiled her to a cottage in a remote corner of the estate, where she lived with Henwyn and the dogs until Mihal was born. She had missed the prettiness. If these dresses hadn't belonged to Elizabeth once upon a time, Morwenna might have, at least in secret, been happy to don one and look pretty again.

An image of David looking at her with admiration flashed into her mind's eye, and she winced away from such a thought, then turned her back on the treasure trove of dresses. "I will darn this dress."

"We are having guests for dinner — the Pascoes, the Kittos, and the Roddas."

"All of whom have seen me dressed as I am."

"And Mrs. Kitto has suggested the church take up a collection so you can dress better and perhaps catch a husband." Grandmother smiled, her eyes twinkling. "I suspect she means to bring one of the young men in the parish up to scratch."

Morwenna laughed at Grandmother using slang and joined her in the dressing room and stared at the gowns. "If Mrs. Kitto wants to take up a collection, it should be to clothe some of the miners' children. Some of those families are desperately poor."

"We do, my dear. You aren't charging them rent, and we provide enough to feed them. But the men drink up what little money they acquire."

"It's difficult for a man to see others supporting his family. I think they drink to drown their shame." Morwenna sought for the soberest dress.

Clever Grandmother hadn't picked anything sober. She had chosen sky blue and pomona green, begonia pink and primrose yellow. Morwenna sought for lavender, a color for half mourning. The closest she found was a delicate violet silk with gold threadwork around the neck, sleeves, and hem. A gold cord sash snugged beneath the bust, and a gold gauze shawl would keep her from freezing.

"I have no shoes." She released the gown with a little too much care and stalked back into the bedchamber.

"I know." Grandmother's voice grew soft. "Morwenna, we —"

"I need to find my baby. He fusses if he doesn't see me often enough, and I . . . need him."

Her arms ached with emptiness when she was away from him.

"Your old slippers will do. You left most of them behind."

"I left my gowns behind as well."

"Yes, but those cannot be let out enough to accommodate your . . . increased proportions."

Morwenna snorted at Grandmother's attempt to be delicate. Unable to pay for a wet nurse and not wanting one anyway, Morwenna had nursed Mihal herself. Hard work had given her back a small waist, but her hips and bust had expanded with motherhood. Elizabeth was more a Trelawny in build — tall and full-bosomed; thus, her gowns could be cut down while Morwenna's old dresses could not be expanded.

"I'll look presentable for your guests," Morwenna said.

Grandmother went to the hallway door. "Dinner is in two hours. Mr. Chastain is resting, poor lad. He looked like he was in pain."

"I expect he is. You should see his back and ribs."

Grandmother's eyebrows arched. "And you have?"

"Someone had to patch him."

"You could have called the apothecary."

"He doesn't give me credit, ma'am." Morwenna reached past Grandmother and opened the door. "And David Chastain is not the first man whose chest I've seen."

She caught Grandmother's expression, a blend of pain and regret, and her heart seized with a clench of guilt for the reminder that they had failed to give their second granddaughter a moral compass, unlike her ice queen of an older cousin.

Except Elizabeth wasn't an ice queen when she was around Rowan Curnow. And if anything made Morwenna jealous of Elizabeth — the favored, the obedient, the biddable until Rowan came along — it was the love those two had shared and their life together. Respectably married or not, Morwenna never enjoyed true togetherness with Conan, the ordinary day-to-day of sharing meals, evenings, a house with her spouse. Too rarely had they shared a bed before Conan's life was cut short. And she wouldn't — couldn't — risk it again, loving and losing. She could love her son. She took the steps up two at a time. She needed to hold Mihal if only for a few minutes.

But Mihal held a velvet animal as though it was his best friend.

"Dog." He held it out to her.

"He's beautiful." Morwenna crouched before him and held out her arms. "May I have a hug?"

He hugged the dog. "Dog."

Morwenna glanced at Miss Pross, who sat in a rocking chair by the window, her face aglow with joy. "He should go down for a nap soon."

"I was about to do that when I heard you

coming."

"Then let me." As though she needed someone else's permission to put her own child in his cot.

Morwenna scooped boy and stuffed dog into her arms, at which he proceeded to yell in protest, "No, no, no, no."

"Don't you say no to me, young man." Morwenna balanced him on her hip and headed for the cot with its railed sides padded with linen someone had once upon a time embroidered with a menagerie of foreign animals like tigers and elephants, as though that were restful. Probably her cousin Drake's cot brought down from the attics. She set Mihal onto the mattress, where his objections grew to a bellow, loud enough to wake Mr. Chastain on the other side of the house and a floor below.

"Dog. Dog. Dog."

"You have your dog." Morwenna laid him down and drew the coverlet over him.

"No. Dog." He kicked off the covers.

Morwenna pulled them up again, wondering if she should smack his diapered bottom. The nanny whom Drake, Elizabeth, and she had shared was free with her smacks, but Morwenna thought Mihal too young.

"He wants this, I believe." Miss Pross set

138

a second stuffed dog, this one black and white with golden eyes, beside the boy.

"Dog." This was said with cooing affection, as he cuddled the toy close beneath his chin and settled onto his bed.

"Wonderful." Morwenna caressed Mihal's cheek and blinked against a burning in her eyes.

Mihal wanted a stuffed toy rather than her. She hadn't thought she would lose him like this until he was old enough to go away to school.

"Sleep well, Mihal. I'll be back as soon as I can." She headed for the door.

"No hurry about getting back. I know there are guests tonight."

"I will return." Morwenna spoke through clenched teeth.

No one would take over care of her son. Just because she had agreed to come to Bastion Point for a while didn't mean they could take over command of her comings and goings.

But of course they could. She might be the blackest of the Trelawnys' more than fair share of ebony ovines, and too much of her genteel upbringing reminded her not to make a scene in front of others not in the family. That included Miss Pross. So she left the nursery without protest. She dressed in the purple gown and pinned her hair into a chignon with the help of Grandmother's maid. She then made her way from her wing to the main block of the house to present herself in the drawing room in time to greet the first of the guests.

And David.

Morwenna started at the sight of him on the other side of the great room with one shoulder propped against the carved marble mantel, one hand holding a glass containing a dark red liquid, firelight gleaming off the silver buttons on his coat and buckles on his shoes. If not for the fact he wore no gloves and a myriad of nicks and scars peppered his hands — signs of a man who labored with tools — his old-fashioned hair and simple but elegant garb would have proclaimed him a country gentleman. Even his hair, clubbed with a black satin ribbon, wasn't unusual in the country. Though he was still pale, the dark circles of fatigue had faded from beneath his eyes, and he didn't look the least ill at ease conversing with Grandfather, one of the wealthiest men in England and certainly the most powerful man in Cornwall.

At Morwenna's entrance, he straightened from his lounging posture, and for a moment, shock widened his eyes. Then he bowed, and when he straightened, his face held no more expression than bland courtesy.

"Good evening, Morwenna." Grandfather spoke. "You are looking well."

"Thank you, sir." Morwenna glanced at David, then back to her grandfather. "Have you, um, heard anything from . . . Penmara?"

"They intended to search the caves below Penmara before they search the house." Grandfather chuckled. "Why they need daylight to search those caves is beyond my comprehension, but it's their decision."

Knees suddenly weak, Morwenna sank onto a chair. "The caves. Of course they're searching the caves." She was going to be sick right there on the rug.

"My lady?" David closed the distance between them and pressed his glass into her hand. "You've gone pale."

She lifted the glass to her lips. Cherry cordial, sweet and rich. She sipped, and its warmth dissolved some of the cold fear inside her.

"Thank you." She returned the glass to him.

Grandfather studied her with speculation in his narrowed eyes. "Will they find —"

The ringing of the doorbell stopped

141

Grandfather's inquiry. The three of them fell silent until the butler ushered the vicar, Mr. Kitto, and his birdlike wife into the room.

Grandfather presented David to them, and the vicar began to pepper him with questions. "Where are you from? How did you manage to survive the wreck? Do you have family?" and so it went. David gave polite but short responses, mostly yes and no, his speech slow and rhythmic in comparison with that of the Cambridge-educated vicar.

One corner of his mouth twitching, Grandfather seated himself beside Morwenna. "What has you worried, child?"

The kindness of his tone closed Morwenna's throat, and she stiffened her spine against trusting this softer Grandfather after a lifetime of his authoritarian treatment. "I don't like strangers pawing over my property."

"Will they find something they shouldn't?" Grandfather persisted.

"Of course not." Morwenna made each word a whiplash.

"Then don't concern yourself." He looked about to say something more, then rose at another ring of the bell. "We will discuss this and much more later."

Grandmother entered right ahead of the Pascoes, the Roddas, and then the Polking-horns. They were all polite to David, their glances curious, their questions numerous. He seemed to hold his own with quiet calm, though he had surely never been a guest in a house like Bastion Point. He had said even his married siblings shared the family home. Morwenna couldn't imagine it, having grown up with a house too quiet most of the time, so much of the time she made her own trouble so as not to be alone.

Then Jago broke away from Mr. Kitto and headed for Morwenna. He placed a glass of cherry cordial in her hand and then took the chair beside her that Grandfather had vacated to greet his guests. "You are looking fetching, my lady." His eyes flicked down her person, then up to linger far too long at the décolletage of the gown.

She wrapped the scarf more tightly around her shoulders. "How good of you to come."

"I wouldn't stay away once I knew you were here." He took her hand in his. "I can see you more easily now that you're here, though I see you haven't gotten rid of your unwanted guest yet."

"He is neither a guest nor unwanted." Morwenna reclaimed her hand. "I doubt he wants to be here any more than —" She

143

couldn't say he wasn't wanted there; he was.

"Let's not talk about him. It's bad enough we have to dine with him," Jago said.

"His manners are impeccable."

Not a half dozen feet away now, David was discussing ship construction with Mr. Pascoe and his elder son, Caswyn. "We've never built anything larger than a sloop," David was saying, "but I'd like to do so one day. Of course, we would have to expand . . ." He trailed off and shrugged, his face growing stiff.

"Excuse me." Morwenna rose and glided forward. "Mr. Chastain, perhaps you should be sitting. You are not even a day out of your sickbed."

"Forgive us for keeping you standing." Pascoe inclined his head to a group of chairs. "We could sit there and continue this delightful discussion."

"If this war weren't on," Caswyn said, "I would love a leisure boat simply for sailing. I miss sailing."

"The war with America makes matters worse." David seemed to recover with aplomb from whatever had distressed him moments earlier. "I scarcely remember a time when England wasn't at war and venturing far off the coast became dangerous." He lowered himself onto an upright chair upholstered in gold damask, a new acquisition of Grandmother's. The rich fabric framed him, glowing fabric against his dark hair and clothing, a portrait one could have called *Stranger at Ease.* He was probably in some discomfort, if not outright pain. He had just met a half dozen strangers, and he sat in the drawing room of someone well above his social class, possibly for the first time, yet he appeared at ease. His shoulders were broad and straight against the high back of the chair, his hands rested on the arms without any fidgets of tapping fingers or the like, and no more tension lined his chiseled features.

Laborer or not, he was a fine figure of a man, a man with a calm self-assurance, and Morwenna experienced a frisson of interest — perhaps something more — ripple through her. She shivered and wished for a cashmere shawl instead of the silk scarf around her shoulders. She shouldn't be cold. The room was warm, far warmer than any room ever managed to be at Penmara. Yet gooseflesh prickled along her arms.

She didn't seat herself near David nor return to her seat near Jago. She crossed the room to the hearth and held her hands out to the blaze.

"I'm so happy to see you residing here,

my dear." Mrs. Kitto popped up beside Morwenna, as though conjured from the marble fireplace surround. "A pretty young lady like you shouldn't be living alone at that tumbledown old house."

Morwenna stiffened. "That tumbledown old house is my son's inheritance."

"Of course it is." Mrs. Kitto patted Morwenna's arm. "And we can trust in the Lord to see it restored by the time he cares. Meanwhile, you are safer here. And besides, you are more likely to meet eligible young men here." She cast a sidelong glance toward Caswyn then Jago.

The latter caught Mrs. Kitto's glance and rose to join them. Tristan, arriving late, followed in Jago's wake.

"I don't wish to remarry." Morwenna made certain the young men heard her. "At least I would prefer to restore Penmara before taking on the responsibility of a husband and perhaps more children."

"I should think marrying well would help restore Penmara faster than . . ." Mrs. Kitto trailed off, as though she didn't want to say how Morwenna was trying to restore the Penvenan wealth.

"I am close to having investors," Morwenna began. "The mines —"

A thunderous knocking boomed against

the front door. Conversation stopped. Everyone turned toward the drawing room entrance. No guest would pound on the door. That sort of racket meant trouble. And only one kind of trouble had arrived at Bastion Point of late.

Morwenna pressed her hand to her mouth. When one of the revenue officers pushed past the butler to enter the room before being announced, bile rose in her throat, burning while the rest of her may as well have been standing next to an iceberg rather than a fire. As though rehearsed, Grandfather, Tristan, and Jago closed ranks around her, then, oddly, so did David, rising stiffly from his chair and striding to her side as though she were a great lady in a carriage and they were outriders.

The officer tramped across the carpet, parting the guests with the sheer force of his presence, and halted in front of Morwenna with her entourage. "Lady Penvenan, you are under arrest."

CHAPTER 8

Morwenna swayed. David raised his arms, ready to catch her in the event she fainted. She was stronger than that, this pocket Venus of a lady, all creamy skin and luxuriant hair over a frame of pure steel.

Something inside David's chest twisted, tightened, stabbed him through the heart. Despite his own suspicions regarding the lady's conduct where he was concerned, he wanted to draw the military man's cork. Back at his sides again, David's hands fisted. Beside him, so did Rodda's.

Jago Rodda, the son of family friends, wealthy and probably attractive to women, the perfect suitor for the beautiful widow. He was the man to defend her.

David shoved his rough and scarred hands into his pockets and waited for someone to defend her ladyship.

But she stepped forward, chin raised, and addressed the revenue officer on her own.

"Why do you need to arrest me?"

"She has contraband on her property, Sir Petrok." The lieutenant spoke as though Morwenna weren't there.

Her grandfather made no effort to intervene. A lack of respect for his granddaughter or indifference? His face gave nothing away.

"What contraband?" Morwenna asked.

The lieutenant continued to look at Sir Petrok. "We found a barrel of Lancashire wool and a crate of knives from a Sheffield ironworks in a cave directly below Penmara." He shot a glare at Morwenna. "That cave has a door leading into the Penmara cellars. She will have to explain that to the magistrate."

"I am the magistrate." Sir Petrok's voice was as cold as the Irish Sea. "We can settle this right now."

"Er, well . . ." The young officer's face reddened. "This is highly irregular. We will have to take her to a different parish."

Sir Petrok drew himself to his impressive height. "Are you questioning my integrity, young man?"

"No, sir." The officer drew his shoulders back and puffed out his chest in a way that had David's fists clenching again. "It is your granddaughter's integrity that is at question."

"If you weren't in uniform, sirrah," Rodda said through clenched teeth, "I would call you out for that. You are speaking of my future wife."

Morwenna shot Jago an unfriendly glance, then focused on the lieutenant. "Anyone can walk into those caves. You have no evidence that I am involved in any illegal activity."

A few barrels of contraband might prove nothing, but David might be able to — eventually.

The notion didn't please him. He wanted to shout that she had saved his life, not tried to harm him when she could have with no one the wiser.

Except for whoever had taken his pendant — her family's pendant.

He clasped his hands behind his back and watched the scene unfold with the same rapt attention as the rest of the assembly.

The lieutenant smiled, seeming to grow taller, fuller of chest, a man ready to declare victory against all odds. "But your house isn't easily accessible to everyone, and we also found a smuggler's lantern in the room used as a nursery. It was tucked beneath a pile of folded diapers that weren't in the least disturbed." The officer smiled at Sir Petrok, then Morwenna. "Can you explain that away?"

A moment of silence told its own tale —
no one could give an explanation as to how
the sort of lantern smugglers used to signal
one another and to get about at night ended
up in a child's nursery. The lanterns consisted of a long tube that allowed the user
to direct the beam without being seen from
the sides or behind. From the top of a cliff,
it would be perfect for suggesting the lights
of safe harbor to a ship in a storm.

The lieutenant looked smug. His men
looked proud of their officer. All the guests'
faces were set, and the elder Trelawnys aged,
their faces lined with fatigue.

Her lips bloodless, her eyes dilated, Morwenna swayed as though too heavy a burden
had been thrown upon her shoulders. She
began to crumple. David's arm encircled
her tiny waist without a thought, and he
nestled her against his ribs as close as those
battered bones could bear. Over her head,
Jago Rodda glared at him. Tristan merely
looked disgusted and turned away. Beside
him, Morwenna tucked her head against his
shoulder, shivering as though she suffered
an ague. She was such a little thing, he
suspected he could pick her up despite his
weakened state. Her looks, her delicacy of
form, her state as an impoverished widow

of a murdered man, urged David to protect her as he would his sister or any female in his family.

But she's not in your family. The admonition wasn't much use. He might believe the evidence condemned her as part of the wreckers, perhaps even the leader, but that suspicion didn't stop him from wanting to shelter her.

"You can unhand her, Chastain." Jago spoke softly between his teeth. "Sir Petrok will see to all this."

David didn't move. Neither did Morwenna.

Sir Petrok stepped forward so less than a yard separated him from the lieutenant. "Anyone could walk into Penmara and plant that lantern. It's scarcely habited."

"Or habitable," Jago muttered.

Morwenna stiffened, then sagged farther.

"The servants say no one has been about who shouldn't be," the officer said.

"Servants with family in the village involved in the trade." Sir Petrok curled his upper lip. "You are naïve to believe them."

"And you are hindering me from the performance of my duty." The lieutenant took a step closer to Morwenna. "I must take her into custody."

A violent shudder raced through Morwenna. "My baby." It was a breathless whimper.

Sir Petrok stepped forward and barred the officer's path to Morwenna. "No, you do not. Trelawnys do not go to jail with common criminals."

"They do if they are common criminals," one of the men muttered.

Sir Petrok shot him a withering glance, then turned back to the lieutenant. "I will see that my granddaughter does not leave the parish."

"But, sir —" The young officer's face reddened.

Sir Petrok's face hardened. "Do you doubt my word?"

Morwenna's breathing quickened.

David increased his hold. "Are you going to faint?"

She shook her head against his shoulder but made no move to straighten.

"Would you like me to help you to a chair?" David shifted, bracing himself to half carry her to the nearest chair.

Jago saw to it no need remained. He brought a chair to the hearth, and David eased Morwenna onto the cushion. It was the chair David had been sitting in a few moments earlier. He'd felt like some sort of specimen on an entomologist's display cloth. Now, Morwenna, her dark beauty smoldering against the gold brocade, looked like some exotic jewel, a pearl beyond price.

A pearl that might have come too close to costing him the price of his life. She was a Trelawny, and the evidence of his father's connection to the family had disappeared.

He lived because of her. But of course. She needed information from him, needed to know how much he knew. He should despise her, fear her. He did distrust her, and yet . . .

The sight of the revenue officer stalking from the room, his spine too rigid, drew David's attention away from Morwenna to Sir Petrok. His mouth was set in a hard, thin line, and his eyes blazed. "The idea that my granddaughter was involved with that wreck, with murder —" He looked at David. "And here's evidence of her kindness to the only survivor. Did my granddaughter ever seem to have a murderous nature to you, Mr. Chastain?"

"No, sir." But she had drugged him, or ordered him to be drugged, whatever she claimed.

"Did she take so much as a farthing from you?"

"No, sir."

Not as far as he knew.

Sir Petrok looked back to his guests. "Let us proceed down to dinner and put this behind us."

"I would like to go to my room." Morwenna's contralto voice shook ever so slightly. "No, the nursery."

"I'll take you." Rodda held out his hands to her. She placed hers in them and stood. "You are kind, but go down to your dinner."

"And so should you," David pointed out.

"She doesn't need company right now," Rodda said.

David shot him a look of exasperation. "Don't you know those who hide look guilty?"

And those who are fools help their potential enemies.

"She needs to lie down," Rodda insisted. "To suggest she spend hours in company is cruel. To suggest such a lady can be guilty of anything is worse."

"I am not a fair maiden for knights to joust over." Morwenna surged to her feet. "I believe Mr. Chastain is correct, and I should go down to dinner."

Not in the running for Morwenna's hand in marriage, David didn't join Pascoe and Rodda's squabbling about who would escort Morwenna down to dinner; he trailed behind her and the other men, admiring the way the fine gown flowed around her, shifting from light to shadow like water rippling through sunshine and clouds. Instinct strained toward the notion that no lady so beautiful could be guilty of a crime so great as causing a ship to wreck. He might think that her grandfather believed her not innocent — were he not her grandfather. But no doubt a Trelawny defended another regardless of his personal doubts.

Or perhaps he was also involved and such doings were a part of his vast wealth? On the other hand, could not the materials have been planted for the revenue men to find?

Deep in thought, David sauntered into the dining room and took the only seat left — one to Lady Trelawny's left, the least important seat at the table, he suspected. She smiled at him graciously, for Lady Penvenan sat to her grandfather's right. The grandmother nodded to her husband, and he bowed his head to ask a blessing over the food. From what David knew of the upper classes, this wasn't the usual practice. It surprised him. It disconcerted him. The gentry might attend church for appearance's sake, but Mama complained how the country was being led by hypocrites, godless men who only pretended to have faith. Trelawny's prayer wasn't for form, as he hadn't asked the vicar to say it.

Less at ease now than before the blessing, David merely stared at the bowl of white soup set before him, though Lady Trelawny had dipped her spoon into her bowl, signaling that everyone else could eat.

"Is it not to your liking, Mr. Chastain?" Mrs. Kitto asked.

David started, then picked up the soup spoon. "Not at all. My mother makes it often."

"His mother doesn't have a cook?" Mrs. Rodda spoke loudly enough for David to hear, as he suspected she intended, since she couldn't address him directly from her seat across the table.

David pursed his lips to stop himself from responding.

Lady Trelawny shot him a quick smile. "Does your mother enjoy trying her hand at cooking?"

"On the cook housekeeper's day off, yes." He tasted the thick soup made with milk and veal broth.

Mama's was better, so much better that he ached for a bowlful. He ached for his family, for his father . . .

He wanted to set his spoon down and excuse himself. Every bone in his body ached. Every muscle in his face ached from smiling and making polite conversation.

"Do you have brothers and sisters, Mr. Chastain?" Mrs. Kitto spoke from his other side.

He gave her the same answer he had given Morwenna. Conversations flowed around the table, only an occasional phrase or sentence reaching him with clarity, as he exchanged pleasantries with Mrs. Kitto, then more so with Lady Trelawny, as fish replaced the soup and fowl replaced the fish, then a haunch of venison appeared, all accompanied by sides of vegetables usually not available in late winter and early spring. David chose sparingly from the dishes, spooning out the fine fare with as careful a hand as he dealt out answers to the questions with which the two ladies peppered him. He feared if he said too much he might slip up and admit he knew the allegedly missing Trelawnys had been in England in the past month, and he suspected them of having something to do with his father's demise.

By the time the butler carried in a trifle, David was certain he would collapse face-first into the fruit, cream, and cake confection. He clenched his jaws against a yawn, but he had to taste it. Mama loved trifle.

No one made better trifle than she did. And if they didn't find the missing money, she wouldn't be able to afford the ingredients in the height of summer when cream was more plentiful and thus less expensive, let alone this time of year when most cows were still carrying young.

This trifle was good, thick and rich, dissolving on the tongue like ambrosia. Mama would approve. Papa would tease her . . .

Not again.

The smooth pudding stuck in his throat. He swallowed, but a lump had formed, and he set his fork across his plate.

"Do not tell me you dislike trifle, Mr. Chastain." Lady Trelawny shook her head of golden-white curls. "I won't believe you."

"Probably not used to such rich fare," Mr. Rodda murmured from the other side of Mrs. Kitto.

"It's very good." David swallowed again. "I believe I'm fatigued is all."

"Of course you are." Mrs. Kitto patted his arm. "I'm sure Phoebe will release you to your bed if you ask her."

"Of course." Lady Trelawny inclined her head. "If you are unwell, we never hold a guest against his will."

David hoped he wouldn't have to test that claim. For now, he intended to stay to the conclusion of the meal, until the last guest departed. Guests sometimes talked, especially men without ladies present. Once Lady Penvenan was gone, perhaps they would talk about the accusations against her.

The ladies rose and departed for the drawing room and coffee. The butler carried in pots of steaming coffee, set them on the dining table, then withdrew, leaving the seven men alone, five of whom turned to David.

"So what do you recall of the wreck?" the elder Rodda inquired.

David shrugged. "Very little. I was asleep when we struck. I was thrown from my berth, realized what had happened, and got myself dressed before going on deck as fast as I could. We were already taking on water far too quickly. I thought we might capsize, so I went into the sea. The next thing I remember with any clarity was waking up at Penmara."

"Did you not think it odd Lady Penvenan was nursing you?" asked the younger Rodda.

Sir Petrok scowled at him. "What are you implying, Jago?"

"I didn't particularly care who was nursing me." David answered the question, then thought perhaps it wasn't the truth. He had cared. What man wouldn't want an angel looking down upon him when he woke in pain and confusion?

"I was just thinking that he must have suspected her ladyship's involvement," the younger Rodda said to Sir Petrok.

"If I had any suspicions toward her ladyship," David said, "I wouldn't express them to you or a dinner party at large." Realizing how rude he might sound, he glanced to Sir Petrok, ready to apologize.

He met an approving glance and affirming nod from Sir Petrok. "I would hope you would come to me, lad."

"Or maybe he went to the revenue officers," Tristan Pascoe suggested.

"That's enough." The man's father looked from Sir Petrok to David. "Please forgive my son. He has been dangling after Morwenna — er — her ladyship since coming down from university. And he's jealous of any man who so much as speaks to her."

David laughed with the first genuine amusement he had experienced since learning of Papa's treachery. "I am hardly in her ladyship's league." He held up his hands, callused and scarred. "I design and build vessels, none large enough to sail farther than Dieppe."

Pascoe turned red.

"And where would our fishing folk and coastal merchants be without work like yours?" Mr. Pascoe smiled upon David.

"Or our smugglers," the elder Rodda murmured.

"Please, please." Mr. Kitto raised his hands. "Let us cease this sparring. Will we be seeing you at services next Sunday, Mr. Chastain?"

"If you wonder if I attend church regularly, yes, sir."

"I doubt he is well enough recovered for the trek into the village." Sir Petrok rose. "Let us join the ladies. Perhaps they will civilize our conversation." He didn't lead the way, but stood aside and allowed the others to pass. When David trod into the corridor, Sir Petrok fell into step beside him. "If you wish to return to your room, no one will blame you."

"A not so subtle hint, sir?"

Sir Petrok laughed. "Not at all. You simply look done in. If you wish for some reading material, the library is here." He paused at a set of carved double doors. "You are always free to come here at any time. If I am there and wish not to be disturbed, I post a footman outside here in the hall."

"Thank you, sir." Gratitude rushed through David. None of the books from

Penmara had come with him. "May I —
that is — perhaps I could acquire some
writing materials in the village?"

"The library is well stocked with ink,
quills, and paper of whatever quality your
writing requires. Feel free to write in the
library or take supplies to your room. I will
frank any letters for you." With a nod, Sir
Petrok opened one of the doors, then
climbed the steps to the first-floor drawing
room.

David entered a treasure trove of books,
fine furnishings, and *objets d'art,* all glowing
with the patina of age and care by the light
of a fire and several lamps. Such luxury,
such waste, to burn coal and oil in a room
no one was using. Unless Sir Petrok had
planned this side excursion for David and
the room had been readied for him. No
doubt the boatbuilder was only given so
much access to the guests.

"For which I am grateful."

More of Jago Rodda and Tristan Pascoe,
and David might have forgotten himself and
planted one of them a facer.

He raised his right hand. It was easily half
again the size of one of Pascoe's, and nearly
as much of Rodda's, as was David himself.
Striking him would not only be against
everything he believed in, it would likely

land him in a prison cell. But the men's comments were beyond acceptable, jealous or not.

As he began to peruse the shelves for a copy of *Joseph Andrews,* the book he'd been reading at Penmara, David admitted that the ground wasn't thick with ladies as beautiful as Morwenna Trelawny. If only she would smile, she would probably slay everyone in sight. Not that she frowned. Her mouth simply showed no emotion whatsoever except for an occasional quiver of that lower lip that gave him ideas he shouldn't have for a lady whom he didn't know.

Perhaps Papa had been right. In one of their last conversations he said David should find a wife. If he was thinking of kissing ladies he barely knew and certainly didn't trust, he shouldn't remain single.

But now they didn't have the money for David to marry, unless they acquired several good commissions, customers willing to advance payment so they could buy building materials.

Oh, Papa, why did you do it?

Suddenly too weary to stand any longer, he sank onto the chair behind the desk. As Sir Petrok told him, a shelf to the side of the desk held stacks of paper, and the top of the desk held a tray with bottles of ink and quill pens with tips neatly trimmed. The paper wasn't large enough for him to set down any of the designs forever running through his head, but he could write a letter.

He selected plain foolscap, ink, and a pen and began to write to his oldest brother, Martin, to ask after the state of the boatyard. He was just about to write, *I have no intention of leaving Cornwall yet,* when the door opened and someone gasped.

Morwenna stood framed in the opening, her hand to her heart.

"Am I that frightening?" He offered her a smile.

She closed the door. "You looked like my cousin Drake sitting there."

"And that startles you?"

"Grandfather banished him nearly two years ago for coming close to getting caught smuggling once too often."

David's eyes widened. "A lawless bunch, you Cornish gentry."

The corners of her mouth pinched. "Drake thought it a lark. My husband did it to survive."

"And where did he get banished?" David picked up the sander and dusted his letter without the comment regarding when he would leave. Just because he sealed the missive didn't mean it would remain that way.

"Barbados or Jamaica. I forget which. We have plantations at both."

"And slaves?" David shook the sand into a tray set for that purpose, then folded the parchment with care.

Morwenna shook her head. "Not now. The last time we heard from Drake, he said he had managed to free the last of them." She ventured farther into the chamber. "That was a year ago. We haven't heard from him since."

"And you haven't heard from your parents since . . . ?"

"A little longer."

"Indeed." David picked up the wax jack and pressed out a lozenge. "You seem to misplace relatives with abandon."

"Two wars rather get in the way." She brought him a candle. "This works better than the lamps."

David accepted the candle, held the flame close enough to soften the wax, but not near enough to burn it. When the wax glistened, he pressed his thumb onto the softened surface to seal the letter. "It's been good for shipbuilding. We've made several cutters for naval captains." He set the letter on another tray where others already lay waiting for the post. "Where do you expect all these relatives have gone?"

"Drake is likely still in the West Indies. Elizabeth is in Virginia, and my parents?" Morwenna shrugged and spun away with the candle, trailing flame and smoke behind her. "I've accepted that they are probably dead."

"Why?"

"They've never been away so long without at least writing, war or not. I wanted them to know of their grandson —" She jammed the candle into its holder, then stood facing the mantel as though studying the frieze of vines and flowers across the front of the piece. Her shoulders shook ever so slightly.

"My lady?" David rose, needing one hand on the desktop to do so, and paced across the room to join her. He rested one hand on her shoulder. "Are you all right?"

"Oh, of course. I'm simply *in alt.*" Sarcasm dripped from each word, and her lip curled. "My husband is dead, my son's inheritance is tumbling down around our ears, and my friends and family are vanishing one after the other. And now I've been arrested for wrecking, which could turn into an arrest for murder."

"It was a stupid question, wasn't it?"

Her shoulders heaved and a bark of laughter emerged. "A man who recognizes his lack of wisdom. How refreshing."

"I would never lay claim to wisdom. I don't lay claim to much knowledge except when it comes to boats and wood. I'm not very well educated except in maths. I need math to do my work. But I haven't read philosophers or even much literature that is supposed to enlighten the mind. I'm just a simple laborer."

She looked up at him, and he wanted to add, "A simple laborer who can scarcely bear not to kiss you right now." He wouldn't. That would disrespect her and his host. But those unsmiling corners of her mouth had softened, increasing the lushness of her lips, and she looked on the verge of smiling. He settled on smoothing his fingers over a strand of her hair tumbling from her chignon. Silky hair that urged the most self-controlled man to tug it from its pins and send it spilling through his fingers.

He wasn't the most self-controlled man. Nor was he wise. He had enough of both wisdom and self-control to pull his hand away from her and shove it into the pocket of his coat. "I was writing to my brother to see how the yard is doing without me."

"Are you vital to the works?"

"I was. I hope to be so again."

His tongue burned with the need to tell

someone of his father's peculiar behavior, perhaps something as serious as treachery against the family, as hard as he found believing that to be true, a way to release the anguish inside him. But he would be telling the very person who might somehow be connected to that theft.

He took a step back, carrying himself out of touching range. "So your cousin smuggled with your husband, your parents are explorers, and your other cousin married a foreigner. I can't imagine a family scattering like that."

"In this family, staying in one place is the unusual."

"Your grandparents have."

"They didn't in their youth. My grandfather was a bit of a pirate."

"Indeed, a lawless family."

"Which condemns me." Her chin quivered. "I was the one who stayed here and lived a law-abiding life." She lifted a china ornament from the mantelshelf, a delicate figurine of exquisite detail and delicate color, but only a shepherdess for all its artistry in the design. "Grandfather may have persuaded that revenue officer that anyone could have placed those barrels in the caves or even hidden that smuggler's lantern in my son's room, but did you notice no one was surprised to learn of their existence?"

"I was more concerned about you than the reactions of others."

"And Grandfather was concerned about preserving the family reputation."

"I think he cares —"

She shot the hand holding the figurine into the air. "No, no, don't deny lack of defense of my innocence. Nor did anyone else." She began to twirl the statuette between her palms. "They've all been waiting for me to succumb to the allure of easy wealth." The shepherdess shook in Morwenna's hand enough to make the porcelain folds of the girl's skirt appear as though they moved in a stiff breeze. "I'm a Trelawny who was once the black sheep, so now I must be guilty. So much for the safety of giving up my independence to come here under Grandfather's thumb."

David rested his hand on her wrist, felt the tension. "I believe that thumb protected you tonight."

"It's not worth it. He thinks me guilty as well. I'll never get my investors now." With that pronouncement she hurled the figurine across the room.

It struck the edge of a bookshelf and shattered. Fragments of ruined china tinkled to the floor like pattering rain. Morwenna followed the figurine across the room and beyond to the door, the corridor, somewhere out of David's sight, then his hearing. He caught the rumble of laughter from the drawing room on the floor above, but no nearby whisper of silk. Yet he did not move. He kept his gaze on the fragments of china, feeling the residual anger behind the destruction, his heart torn between certainty that her ladyship was innocent after all, and wondering if his certainty stemmed from feelings that had nothing to do with wisdom, with her innocence or guilt, but wholly focused on a new apprehension in his life.

His interest in Morwenna, Lady Penvenan, cut far more deeply than a need to learn how her family was involved with his family.

If he wasn't careful, he would tumble head over heels for her ladyship.

The thought was enough to keep him awake most of the night. With the coverlet wrapped around him like some kind of oversized mantle, David sat by the window facing the sea. Waves higher than he was tall swooped in and crashed upon the sand below, their roar reaching through distance and glass. Wind rattled the windows in buffeting blasts, and the only light shimmered from the white crests of the surf. Somewhere out to sea, a storm raged, heading their way.

David shivered despite the covering and blazing fire, and prayed for those ships to stay away from the shore in the event the wreckers took a chance on luring another vessel to its doom upon the rocky sands below. Surely they wouldn't, and yet . . .

He tossed off the coverlet and reclaimed his shoes. No harm came from looking, from assuring himself no one else would suffer, or worse, die. And while he was below stairs, he could collect foolscap and ink, perhaps even find a pencil or two, and bring them to his room. He needed to work, to put the designs in his head to paper. When he returned home, perhaps he could build the pleasure craft he saw by his mind's eye.

If Chastain's still existed. If his brother had been unable to procure more commissions and credit, or if his other brother hadn't come home successful from his last trading voyage, David's designs would never be built.

What would he do without his work? How would the family support itself?

The Bible said God would provide all their needs, but David didn't see how. Maybe he could work for someone else . . .

Despair washed through him. He gripped

the door handle so hard his hand shook. He leaned his head against the panels and took several deep breaths, welcoming the pain in his ribs and back that accompanied each inhalation.

I will not blame my father. I. Will. Not. blame him without proof of betrayal.

No matter what Papa had done. He needed to have Mama's loyalty and belief in his father's goodness. But he wasn't sure he would ever again believe in anyone's goodness and loyalty.

He opened the door. It moved silently on its hinges and his leather-soled shoes made no sound on the polished floorboards of the corridor, nor the thick carpet runner down the center. Still, a figure detached itself from a niche down the way and glided toward him.

"May I assist you, sir?" The voice and form, dim by the light of a candle in a glass globe, belonged to one of the footmen who had come to Penmara.

David closed the door with a decisive click that echoed off plastered walls. "Why are you lurking outside my bedchamber door?" Even to his own ears, his voice sounded harsh.

The footman bowed. "Not lurking, sir. I or another footman are always here when we have guests or family in this wing."

"Then when do you sleep?" Now David was merely curious, not accustomed to such service.

"I will be relieved at two of the clock and allowed to sleep later." He bowed. "The Trelawnys are most generous employers."

And hosts — unless this man's job was to guard David. A quick look noted a horse pistol in the man's belt. To keep potential intruders out, or keep David in?

Time to test it.

"I am headed for the library." David started forward.

The footman fell into step beside him. "I can fetch what you need."

At which time, David could escape — if he intended to do so.

"No need." He increased his stride, but the effort cost him. By the time they reached the head of the steps, his ribs ached anew.

And the footman hadn't left his side.

David gripped the top of the banister. "On second thought, I would like you to fetch me some foolscap, as large as available, and pencils, if you have them."

"Sir Petrok will have them." The man sounded offended that David would suggest the Trelawnys were not in possession of something.

David grinned. "Very good then. I need larger sheets for design, if possible. I didn't see any in the library, so perhaps Sir Petrok doesn't have anything larger, but perhaps you know of somewhere —"

"I can find some as yet uncut." The footman stalked down the steps, his shoes also silent without a step creaking.

David waited until the man was around the corner and into the library before he sped down the steps with as much haste as he could manage and moved in the opposite direction. The night before, he had noticed small parlors and anterooms along this way. After procuring a candle from one of the wall sconces, he ducked into one of these rooms and found his way to long, multipaned windows so tall and low-set that they served as doors. A convenient design onto the terrace beyond. Perhaps he could make such a change to Mama's sitting room, so she could walk directly into her garden instead of having to walk around. She could sit inside that way and watch the grandchildren playing in the garden while she worked at her needlework.

If they could keep the house and she had a garden come later in the spring.

The thought shot him into action. He unlatched one of the windows and stepped over the low sill onto flagstones. The wind wasn't so high here, not like the sight of the waves had suggested. When he had crossed the terrace, he realized why. He was in the walled garden his room overlooked, but nothing paltry of mere yards in width like Mama's. This was almost the size of the boatyard and contained at least a score of trees.

Difficult not to be envious of such opulence. Mama would adore this. If he could build a truly seaworthy vessel, one capable of crossing the ocean, and his brother could captain it for higher profits instead of having to serve other men as mate, they could one day purchase such a family home.

If . . . The enormous *if* in their lives.

Heartsick, David began to pace along the nearest path in search of an exit. He heard the surf pounding the cliff. The sea couldn't be far.

He found a door at the far end of the garden. An iron bar served as the lock, a barricade easily lifted and set aside. He did so and stepped onto the cliff beyond.

The wind nearly knocked him back into the garden. His candle extinguished, yet enough light shone from the surf below and flashes of lightning in the distance to limn the diminutive figure of a woman at the top of the cliff.

Morwenna, Lady Penvenan, of course. Who else would it be standing there in the wind and the first splashes of rain, her shawl and hair whipping out behind her.

David closed the distance between them and rested one hand on her shoulder. She screamed and jerked away from him, spinning with one fist aiming for his face.

He caught her wrist, his fingers encircling the delicate bones without having to place any pressure on them. "It's me, my lady."

She didn't relax. "What are you doing here?"

"Watching the storm." He released her wrist then leaned down so he spoke into her ear. "Watching the cliff like you." His breath stirred her hair. It tickled his nose with the scent of lemons.

She started and turned her head so her damp hair slapped across his cheek. Her right arm shot out to the west where a headland jutted into the sea. "Then look your fill and see my fate."

He followed her pointing finger. At first he saw nothing but lightning streaking and magnified through approaching sheets of rain. Then the lightning vanished, and in the ensuing darkness, he caught a flash, two flashes, three of light reflecting off the rainy curtain.

CHAPTER 9

David's hands came down on Morwenna's shoulders, gripping them hard enough to hold her near, gentle enough to feel like comfort. "Is that Penmara?"

"It is." Morwenna resisted the urge to lean back against his broad chest. Earlier in the evening, his strength had sheltered her from the horror of what the lieutenant had told them all. She had wished away everyone in the room so she could be held.

No one had held her with such tenderness in far too long.

You're frightened, vulnerable, lonely. You. Do. Not. Care. About. Him.

But that was a lie, the part about not caring. She liked him, but how much was because of the person he was, and how much was her empty heart and arms, she didn't know. What she did know was that caring was dangerous. Yet she didn't move away from him.

"How long will the wreckers stay there?" David asked.

She shrugged. "Until morning. Until — until a ship wrecks." She shuddered with a violence that knocked her teeth together.

He moved his hands from her shoulders to her waist and drew her back against his chest. "You're cold. We need to go in."

"I need to watch."

Not until the words flew from her lips did she realize how they could be understood. And he understood them that way. She felt it in the sudden tension of his body.

No sense in denying it. Denial would make her sound defensive, as though she did have something to hide. Now she must go inside where she could not see across the headland to the cliffs above Penmara.

She stepped out of David's hold, instantly freezing to her marrow, and turned toward the house. "Let us be on our way before we catch our death." Because the night was so dark between flashes of lightning, she took his hand and led him back to the garden. "How did you find your way out here?"

"I had a candle." He lifted the iron bar into place to secure the door.

"Then why did you come out here?"

"Perhaps the same reason as you."

Morwenna gritted her teeth. "Do you

mean if my coming out here is innocent, you came out for the same reason?" Her hands fisted around the edges of her shawl. "But you say 'perhaps' in the event I have other reasons for being out here, as in waiting to see if my gang is successful this time?"

"I haven't made any accusations, my lady." He took her hand this time, as they traversed the path toward the house. "I was concerned."

And wanted to stop her or anyone else?

Weakened from his wounds or not, he was a powerful man. The hand holding hers was surely broad enough and long enough of fingers to capture both her wrists at once. The roughness of calluses told a tale of labor that explained his strength.

Conan's hands had been callused as well, but not so much. They weren't nearly as strong. David's were more like Sam Carn's, honed in the mines.

Dear Sam, her first flirtation, then her friend, now a married man who wouldn't so much as look at her for fear of enraging his wife. Another abandonment, another loss. In days, perhaps as long as weeks, David would leave. Everyone went away, leaving her with the broken pieces to try to fit back together again. Each time, another sliver went missing, leaving an aching hole.

She removed her hand from David's and gathered anger around her like a half dozen shields. "You may as well outright accuse me of being in league with these men. The lieutenant didn't hesitate to do so."

"And it got him nowhere. His evidence was poor at best."

"He could get a conviction from a jury at the assizes, men who don't know me."

"But they know your grandfather, which seems to be enough."

They reached the steps to the terrace, and Morwenna slammed her booted foot onto the bottom tread. "Of course. Think badly of the widow with the tarnished reputation, but don't dare offend the richest man in Cornwall. I tell you, if I'd been alone at Penmara, I'd be in chains right now."

"Like as not your grandfather would have gotten you freed by now." Was that a hint of contempt in his voice? Perhaps mere scorn?

"He might think me legitimately innocent." Her tone lacked conviction.

Grandfather knew she wanted to save Penmara on her own. She wanted Mihal to have a mother he could be proud of when he grew old enough to hear the tales of her past and perhaps even be taunted about them despite his rank. If he wasn't proud of her then, he, too, might despise her for her misbehavior as a youth and remove her from his home and life.

Her throat closed, but she mustn't drown in self-pity. She couldn't change the past. She could only work hard to change the future. She would do so on her own instead of relying on those who never believed her capable of anything good and right.

She stomped up the next two steps and swept across the terrace. "Don't follow me in right away. The footmen will think we had a rendezvous." She closed the window behind her, resisted the urge to latch it so he had to find another way in. He was barely out of his sickbed and the rain had come ashore in earnest.

One of the footmen stood at the foot of the steps, a sheaf of rolled paper under one arm and a handful of pencils in the other hand. He looked puzzled until he saw her. "My lady, have you seen Mr. Chastain? I was getting materials for him, but now he's gone."

"I don't know where he is." Strictly speaking, that was the truth. "But he's a man grown. He'll find his way back here." Without waiting for the footman to respond or David to return, Morwenna swept into the library and closed the doors behind her.

The lamps had been extinguished for the

night and only embers remained of the banked fire, giving the merest glow of light to the chamber. Morwenna drew a candle from its holder, noticed how the wax taper was broken, held together by its wick alone, and realized it was the one she had jammed into the candelabra earlier that night. Until that moment, she hadn't realized how much anger still raged in her heart. Or perhaps she realized it when she smashed the Dresden shepherdess, a ridiculous piece of bric-a-brac if ever there was one.

Still, she should not have allowed her temper to get the best of her simply because she knew the only reason the lieutenant had not walked away with her in shackles was because she was Sir Petrok's granddaughter. For all Grandfather had no formal education, he knew the law, and he knew power and was never afraid to apply both regardless of the accused's social rank. She'd been freed by his power, not because anyone believed in her innocence.

She used the candle to gather a flame from the hearth, then used the flame to light one of the lamps. The glowing wicks swam and blurred her vision. Her lids grew hot. She tossed the broken candle into the fireplace and pressed the heels of her hands against her eyes.

She would not weep. She was strong. If she did nothing else well, she excelled at controlling her emotions. That she had lost her temper even for a moment there with David sent a flush rushing through her body and up to her hairline. She didn't want this anger. She wanted peace and calm and respect. Once upon a time, she wanted love. She had satisfied it with poor substitutes, flaunted her wantonness until Conan came along and showed her something different — true caring from the heart despite her past indiscretions. Then, suddenly, he was gone.

"Why, God? Why?"

The urge to smash something swept over her, and she snatched a book from the nearest shelf, extinguished the lamp, then left the library before she damaged anything else.

The footman was nowhere in sight. Neither was David. Inside, the house lay still save for the normal creaks and snaps of a house built nearly two hundred years earlier. Outside, the storm buffeted the stone walls, howling around the corners and lashing rain against the windows.

"No ships. Please, God, no ships."

If another vessel wrecked tonight, nothing Grandfather said would keep her from being carried off to another parish, another magistrate's jurisdiction, to be arraigned and held in jail until the assizes. Not the best barrister in England would keep her out of prison. Book in hand, Morwenna climbed the steps, nodded to the footman stationed in her wing, then climbed another flight to the nursery. She wanted to hold her baby. She settled for opening the door and gazing upon him by the light of a rush burning inside a pierced canister. He lay on his back, his limbs flung in four directions, a half smile curving his lips. He had kicked off his covers. She ventured far enough into the chamber to draw them up again.

His eyes opened and the smile widened. "Mama."

"Mihal." She bent and kissed his chubby cheek, then such love for this child, this one right and good thing she had accomplished in her life, overwhelmed her, and she sank to her knees. "Sleep, my baby."

"Mmm." He rolled onto his side and nestled beneath the blanket.

"Please, don't let me lose him too." She mouthed the prayer, then rose and left the nursery, drawing the door silently closed behind her.

But there was Miss Pross in a pink wrapper, her gray hair in curling papers. "My lady, you shouldn't risk waking him."

Morwenna curled her hands as though literally reining in her indignation. "Miss Pross, I will look at my son when I like. If he wakes, I will take care of the matter. I have been doing so for nearly two years. I expect I'll be doing so for the foreseeable future. Just because —" She broke off and spun away before she said something she would regret.

She regretted too many things she had said in her twenty-two years.

In her chamber, she lit a candle and looked at the book she had collected at random, thinking perhaps she needed to make up for the lessons in literature and history she had neglected when a schoolgirl. She had chosen a copy of *The Tempest,* a play by William Shakespeare.

She laughed at the irony, then settled down to read it until her eyes burned with fatigue, then closed in sleep.

She slept until a maid brought her hot chocolate and offered to help her dress.

"I can dress myself."

She had constructed her dresses to lace up the front so she didn't have to concern herself with getting assistance, which was rarely available.

The maid shifted from foot to foot, her

face paling as though she expected Morwenna to throw something at her head if she spoke.

Morwenna sighed. "What is it — Rowena, right? You're a Carn."

"Yes, m'lady." The girl relaxed. "I be the youngest."

"Do you disapprove of my peasant's garb?"

"No, m'lady. It's that, um, Lady Trelawny, she . . . um . . ."

"Never you mind. I can guess. She had you remove all my blacks and now I must dress in my cousin's castoffs."

"They are ever so pretty." Rowena darted into the dressing room and returned with a gown of pale pink muslin. "This will look ever so nice with your dark hair."

"Except for last night, I haven't worn colors in nearly two years."

"Then it's time you did." The girl blushed. "Begging your pardon for being so bold, m'lady. Sam's always telling me my tongue will get me in trouble."

Morwenna snorted. "He's a one to talk." She sipped at the hot chocolate, thick and rich as she had not tasted in far too long.

It was one of the seductive lures of staying with her grandparents. But she had overcome the temptation after Mihal's birth.

She would overcome it again.

Feeling like each sip was a pomegranate seed that would hold her to Bastion Point, she drank more of the hot liquid and inspected the dress. "It'll do if there's a shawl and perhaps a woolen petticoat to wear beneath."

"I have the shawl, m'lady."

Certain she would freeze the instant she stepped into the unheated corridor, Morwenna allowed herself to be buttoned into the frothy pink dress, then wrapped in a shawl of warm but light cashmere. All the while, a question burned on her tongue. Rowena's cheerfulness suggested the answer. The fact that Morwenna had been allowed to sleep in and then dressed in frivolity proclaimed the answer to be the one she wanted, yet she ached to ask.

She kept her tongue behind her teeth and waited until she stepped into the breakfast parlor on the ground floor. Grandmama had decorated the chamber in Chinese wallpaper painted with bright-yellow chrysanthemums and commissioned a weaver to design fabric to match to cover the chair cushions. With the golden oak floors polished to a gloss, the room appeared bright and cheerful even on days as foggy gray as this one, especially with several lamps and a crackling fire turned high to make up for the lack of sun.

Morwenna was the last to arrive. David and Grandfather rose at Morwenna's entrance.

David pulled out a chair for her. "May I fetch you coffee or tea, my lady?"

As she had the night before during dinner, taking surreptitious glances at him, Morwenna marveled at his fine manners and proper way of speaking despite the Somerset accent. She felt her lips quiver as though she might actually want to smile his way.

"Coffee, please." She slid into the drawn chair and nodded to her grandparents. "All was well last night?"

"No one wrecked a ship, if that's what you're asking," Grandfather said.

"You know it is."

"You are going to have more than coffee, are you not, Morwenna?" Grandmother spoke with too much haste. "You're too thin, though you do look lovely in that gown."

David set a cup and saucer before her. "I am happy to get you anything you like, my lady."

"No need." Morwenna looked up at him in time to catch an expression in his face she had seldom seen directed her way —

admiration. Lust, hunger, yearning, yes. Admiration — all too rare. Her insides quivered, and she spoke more sharply than she intended. "Sit down, Mr. Chastain. I can serve myself when I want to eat."

For a moment, his eyes widened, but he said nothing, merely returned to his seat.

Morwenna sipped her coffee, another luxury for her, and addressed Grandfather. "There were lights. I went out to the cliff and saw lights."

"It could have been the riding officers," Grandmother suggested.

Morwenna started. "I hadn't thought of that. Did the lieutenant say anything, Grandfather?"

"I don't think he would have told me if those were his intentions, but it's highly unlikely." Grandfather's dark eyes fixed Morwenna with a glare as hard as obsidian. "The good lieutenant and his men were set upon on their way back to their quarters last night."

"Oh no. No, no, no, no, no." Morwenna shot to her feet, the back of her hand to her mouth. She was going to be sick. Bile clogged her throat, burning away anything else she might have said.

Across the table, David had gone pale and his hands gripped the edge of the table.

"When?" Morwenna managed to squeeze the single word past her constricted throat.

"Immediately upon leaving Bastion Point." Grandfather rose, coffee cup in hand. "You were in front of half a dozen people all the while and could not have given any messages commanding anyone to do so, which lends credence to your innocence. Unless . . ." He sighed and glanced at David then back to Morwenna. "I could have given such an order."

Morwenna caught her breath. Her heart had plummeted with enough force to crush her insides. She folded her cold hands around her coffee cup for the warmth, for something to hold on to in a world spinning out of control.

Across the table from her, David's face had turned to stone, his eyes more gray than green, his lips compressed into a hard, thin line.

"No one would suspect you of anything, Petrok." Grandmama rose, her skirts whispering. "We need fresh coffee. This is getting cold." She swept from the room, elegant and straight even at seventy.

Grandfather's gaze followed her from the room, the jet eyes softening, his lips curved in a gentle smile. Love. He gazed upon his wife of fifty years with love and adoration.

And Morwenna wanted to weep. In the midst of distress having to do with his youngest grandchild — again — he took a moment to admire his wife. Not for the first time, Morwenna wondered if Conan and she would have been able to hold on to their love that long. During their brief marriage, she thought so. Conan had saved her from destroying her life with her rebellious spirit. Now that he was gone, she had only her fledgling faith and her will to save her.

Though her coffee had grown cold, she now clung to the coffee cup as though it were the familiar ache and anger that sustained her through the grief of losing Conan. "I should return to Penmara. It will separate you from suspicions against me."

"You shouldn't be over there alone except for Henwyn and Nicca." Grandfather patted her arm. "I don't think you're safe if these people are willing to place evidence in your house." He turned to David. "I am sorry you are dragged into our family crisis."

"I think tossed into it is more the point, sir." David's face relaxed, and he smiled, the green returning to his eyes.

A shiver ran through Morwenna and she rose to stand by the fire, except the heat of the flames didn't make that kind of gooseflesh go away, the kind that warned her she longed for the warmth of arms around her. She needed to return to Penmara to be away from this man, this stranger, who so disturbed her with a simple smile, a light touch on her shoulders, a rich-timbred voice with an accent that was barely tolerable among the country gentry, let alone anywhere else.

"I should go to Mihal." She turned toward the door, but Grandmother had opened it.

"You have had no breakfast, child." She stepped aside. "Here is more coffee and the mail."

Two servants entered, one bearing a coffeepot with steam issuing from the spout, and the other bearing a tray upon which resided several newspapers and a handful of letters. The coffeepot went to Grandmother, the letters to Grandfather.

Morwenna returned to her seat and watched Grandfather sort through the mail as one of the footmen took away her cold coffee and replaced it with a clean cup.

"Shall I fill a plate for you, m'lady?" the man asked in an undertone.

"Yes, George, do that." Grandmother spoke up before Morwenna could refuse.

"There's a letter here for you, Mr. Chastain." Grandfather slid a thick packet of paper to their guest.

David picked it up, hefted it, and glanced

at Grandfather, a faint flush on his cheeks. "You didn't have to pay the extra postage on this, did you, sir?"

Grandfather shrugged. "I have no idea. My steward takes care of such minutia."

Grandfather didn't care about an extra penny or two on a letter over the penny post rate. David apparently did. That spoke of the same sort of poverty Morwenna suffered. All the more reason why she should steer clear of her growing attraction to the man. She couldn't afford to involve herself with another penniless man if she wanted to save Mihal's future.

She peeked at him from beneath her lashes as the footman slid a plate of eggs, bacon, and toast before her. David still gripped his letter, his thumb braced over the seal as though anxious to open his missive, but too polite to do so in front of everyone. His face bore such a look of anticipation and longing, Morwenna felt like laughing in true amusement for the first time since she could remember.

"Go ahead, Mr. Chastain," Grandmother said. "As you see, Petrok is reading his mail. You may also read any of the newspapers you like."

"Thank you, my lady. I, um, perhaps should be excused."

"Nonsense." Grandfather spoke without looking up from his letter. "We all eat while we read our mail. Phoebe, I believe I see your latest issue of *The Ladies' Monthly Museum* here." He slid a rolled periodical across the table.

Grandmother picked it up and began to scan the contents.

Morwenna forked up a mouthful of bacon and watched David break the seal on his letter and unfold the sheets. Other than love notes secreted to her by various means, Morwenna had never received a letter in her life, unless bills counted. In the short time she had spent at school, she hadn't made friends with her classmates. Other females rarely interested her. Her cousin and Conan's sister had been enough in the way of female friends. Now they were both gone.

Looking down at her plate, she tasted the eggs. Oh, they were good. She must buy chickens for Penmara in the spring. If they produced more than her small household could eat, she could sell them or trade them for things like milk. Mihal needed milk to grow —

"You should read this, Morwenna." Grandfather interrupted her musings to hand her the letter he'd been reading.

Surprised, she dropped her fork with a clatter. Grandmother glanced up. David's gaze never lifted from his letter.

Morwenna took Grandfather's post and began to read with growing excitement. When finished, she glanced at Grandfather, her eyes wide, her lips parted. "I know I should be angry that they wrote to you instead of answering me, but this is wonderful that they are willing to invest."

"I am one of the trustees of the estate, child." Grandfather rescued the letter from dropping onto Morwenna's eggs. "I have given you free rein because I believe females are capable of managing estates on their own, but few men see things that way."

"More fool them," Grandmother said from the other side of the table.

Grandfather laughed. "I will make arrangements to go to Falmouth to meet with these men."

"Falmouth?" David's head shot up. "Begging your pardon, did you say something about going to Falmouth?"

"We did." Morwenna arched her brows at him. "Do you wish to go?"

"I . . . must." David laid his hand on his letter, the long fingers and broad palm nearly covering the page. "Soon."

"Can you ride?" Grandfather asked. "We

can take a carriage, but riding is faster."

"Not with the way he's bruised." Morwenna spoke before thinking how inappropriate such a remark was, not to mention how inappropriate her having seen the extent of his bruising was.

And if he couldn't ride, it only emphasized his poverty.

"I can," he said. "My mother finds carriage travel . . . uncomfortable, so we all learned to ride for traveling to Bath to see her family."

"Then as soon as you feel well enough for the travel, we will go." Grandfather gathered up his newspapers and rose. "I will be in the library reading. The papers will be there when anyone wants them." He excused himself and departed.

David gathered up his letter's pages and looked to Grandmother. "If it's all right, my lady, I would like to go to my room."

"Of course. Would you like me to send up tea or coffee?"

He hesitated, then inclined his head. "Coffee would not go amiss."

Morwenna wanted to go see Mihal, but Grandmother seemed inclined to linger. Leaving her would be too rude.

But they were, and Grandmother fixed her eyes upon Morwenna. "He seems to be a fine young man."

"He has nice manners."

"And a beautiful face and form." Grand-mother smiled. "Don't tell me you didn't notice."

"I noticed." Morwenna toyed with the eggs she no longer wanted to eat.

"Has he told you about his family?"

"Some about his family. He seems to hold them in high regard."

High regard? She did him an injustice. He adored his family and likely they felt the same about him.

A twinge something akin to jealousy pinched her.

"He asked for drawing materials." She changed the subject away from families.

"He designs boats. And does the building, from the look of his hands. I expect he misses working."

"So do I." Morwenna pushed back her chair, rude or not. "I need to see my son. If the weather clears, Nicca is bringing the dogs over next low tide."

"And Jago will call. So will Tristan Pascoe."

Morwenna groaned. "Grandmother, I do not want suitors."

"Not even to save Penmara? You will get

your dowry if you marry well, and perhaps more."

"You mean more as in Bastion Point now that Elizabeth and Drake are gone and you have to leave the lands to someone?"

"Morwenna." Grandmother looked pained. "We would leave you Bastion Point because we love you and admire the woman you have grown into."

"Oh. Well. Um . . ." Morwenna didn't know how to respond to that kind of compliment. "I wouldn't know what to do with it all. Perhaps you should simply divide it between the three of us."

"We would like to do so now. But if you marry appropriately, we would have great pleasure in seeing the land go to you."

Conan had been an appropriate husband with his ancient lands and title. But their marriage had been secret, with no dowry forthcoming. By the time her grandparents knew the truth and offered her a home and financial support — if she moved to Bastion Point — she was too hurt, too angry to accept their largesse.

"It would be your money to spend on Penmara then, since you won't take it from us now," Grandmother continued.

"It would be my husband's money, which he may or may not spend on Penmara."

Morwenna opened the door. "But I will receive the gentlemen. If I'm not on the beach. They could potentially both invest in the mines."

She left the dining room, nodded to the two footmen in the front hall because she could not bear to ignore servants as though they were invisible, and climbed the flight of stairs to the first floor.

Where she found David leaning against the corner leading to his chamber, his face as white as the plaster behind him, his letter crushed in his hand.

Chapter 10

David didn't notice that Morwenna had come up the steps until he smelled her sweet lemony scent and felt the warmth of her hand on his arm. He started and looked down at her, read the concern on her face, and scrambled to focus his mind on her, not his brother's letter.

Except his brother's letter might affect her.

"Are you all right?" Her warm, husky voice washing over him.

He managed a smile. "I am well enough, my lady."

"It wasn't bad news from home, was it?"

For the most part, it was terrible news.

He focused on her lovely face and the good news in the letter. "We have new work, if I can fix my mind on creating a design."

"I'm pleased to hear that." She narrowed her eyes. "So you think you can't design?"

"I can. It's naught that I haven't done before."

"Then why" — her hand gripped his arm — "did I find you looking about to crumple to the floor? Unless, of course, you are ill."

"My lady." He covered her hand with his, cupping her slender fingers between his palm and the sleeve of his coat. "Do not trouble yourself about my family dealings. They will work themselves out."

"I see." She snatched her hand free. "Then I shall leave you to yourself." She spun on her heel and stalked away fast enough the frill at the bottom of her dress swung out behind her.

If a footman didn't stand around the corner, David might have pounded his head against the wall in frustration, or until he knew the right course of action to take. He would rather walk out on a spar in a gale than continue the balance between gratitude and too much caring for Morwenna, and wondering what game her parents were playing and if she was involved.

He slapped his palm to his brow, then drew his fingers down his face as though he could wipe away confusion and the flash of hurt on Morwenna's face. He didn't even know how to tell her that he wasn't saying anything because he didn't want to bring her pain unnecessarily — or at all. He wanted to follow her. He wanted —

He cut off that line of thinking and continued to his room.

He entered his chamber, then stood before the desk, too restless to sit as he reread his brother's letter. It began with common news from home. The boatyard had one simple commission that would stave off creditors for another few weeks if they were careful. Mama still determined that Papa was innocent of wrongdoing, and Rebecca, their sister, was increasing again and sure to make everyone crazed with her demeanor soaring from excitement one minute and dropping to bouts of weeping the next.

That bit made David smile. Rebecca was normally the sunniest of creatures with a smile for everyone and rarely a harsh word — until she began to expect an interesting event. She then turned into a creature none of them knew for at least three months.

Still smiling, though he knew what lay on the next sheet, David turned the page of the letter.

A middle-aged couple came to call at the office yesterday, right after we received your letter. They wouldn't leave their name and grew agitated when they learned our father was not there. When I told them he was deceased, the woman burst into tears and ran back to their carriage. The gentle-man (for they were prosperous looking) looked ready to commit murder. I thought he, too, might break down and weep. I of-fered to help them with whatever I could, but they left as though the hounds of Hades chased them. Do you know what this might be about?

David knew. Or at least he thought he knew who the couple was — the Trelawnys, Morwenna's parents she claimed she hadn't seen in six years.

And why would she lie about that? Mar-tin's letter spoke of a couple who knew nothing of Papa's death, so they could not have had anything to do with it. In that event, why would Morwenna lie about her parents being in England? Because her parents were good enough actors to pay a call on the dead man's business and family and pretend no knowledge?

What if Morwenna knew of her parents' visit to Bristol? She could be lying to him about knowing nothing of their where-abouts. He didn't want her to be. He wanted her to be as honest as the day was long and then some. And yet, he had landed on her beach, in her house, drugged without his knowledge by her or her servants.

He didn't know how to find the answers other than time and proximity to the Trelawnys. Time — something of which his family might be in short supply if they were to save the family business.

After folding the letter with care, David slipped it into a drawer of the desk. Thinking better of such an obvious place to keep it, he retrieved it and slipped it behind a stack of boxes on a high shelf in the dressing room. With the boxes aligned just so, he would know if anyone went searching his room.

Drawing materials lay on the desk from the night before. He spread out a sheet of the foolscap, weighed down each corner with inkpot, book, and two china figurines, and picked up a pencil. Designing, calculating ratios of length to beam, deck to keel always helped to clear his mind. He could lose himself in the numbers and lines on the paper and let nothing else intrude. When finished, he often found the answer waiting for him the instant he put his mind back to it. From the time he began to work in the boatyard, his family learned to leave him alone when he bent over a drawing. Even when Papa saw him making a mistake, he waited until David finished to point it out so they could discuss the error in relationship to the whole.

Who would check his work now? Martin was no good at design.

He shut his mind to that as well and concentrated on planning the project Martin mentioned in his letter. He didn't know how long he had been working when the sound of barking dogs penetrated his concentration and carried him to the window facing the sea. From that height, he could only catch the merest glimpse of the beach because the tide was out. He opened the casement. Wind blasted into his face, sharp and cold, clearing his head of remnants of sums, and he leaned into it, out over the stone sill to view the dizzying drop to the sand —

And the sight of a Morwenna, Lady Penvenan, he didn't know existed.

She was cavorting with the deerhounds. Holding a driftwood stick, she ran down the beach, fluffy pink skirts flying around her, while the dogs chased her. Her hair had come loose from its pins and streamed behind her like a banner. To one side, on a path cut into the cliff, Nicca and Henwyn stood, the latter holding the baby. He clapped and his mouth was open in a huge grin. A gust of wind carried baby laughter to David's ears.

Baby and a woman's laughter.

Morwenna was laughing. At the end of the cove, she spun and threw the stick, and a shaft of sunlight breaking through the clouds shone on her face. It glowed as though the sun blazed from within her.

David's insides coiled and tightened. He gripped the edge of the windowsill as though he could hold on to his emotions, rein in his heart.

He failed.

"Dear Jesus, no, I cannot." He closed his eyes. "I cannot care for her. Please bring sense to my heart."

He opened his eyes, hoping to see her now and feel nothing but ordinary human kindness toward a lady who had been good to him regardless of her motivations.

She stood with the others, holding her son now while the dogs, their mouths lolling in canine grins, sat on either side of her as though guarding her.

Guarding her. Guarding . . . Guarding . . . As she said they had guarded him on the beach when she ran for help to carry him into the house, a lapse of time during which someone had stolen his medallion from the Trelawnys.

He pictured himself racing through the house and down the curving path cut into the cliff. In truth, he moved like a man three times his age, past two footmen who asked if they could be of service, through the parlor he had used the night before, and into the garden. It was stark and still nearly barren in early spring, its only advantage being shelter from the prevailing winds at the tops of the cliffs. The bar was off the door, probably removed by Morwenna. Fatigued from the hours of drawing, he leaned against the frame for a moment, listening to the distant-sounding surf, wanting to hear the laughter.

She was laughing.

Hoping he could hear it again, David pushed away from the sun-warmed stone of the wall and found the head of the path. Below him, Morwenna stood still holding her son, though he looked too heavy for her, and talking to Nicca and Henwyn. They were shaking their heads, but stopped and glanced up at David.

Morwenna turned. "Mr. Chastain, don't come down. The going up is too rough."

It looked it, steep and narrow.

"I'll wait for you then." He braced one hand against the face of the cliff from which the path had been blasted.

She had lost the light of laughter. Once again, her face had turned into that of a marble statue — smooth and perfect and expressionless. How he longed to change that back to something softer, happier.

When he carried no joy in his own heart?

He closed his eyes against the sting of wind and the sight of what he could not have. He hadn't even known he yearned for a family of his own until now, when he was in no position to go looking for a wife, especially not one who belonged to the gentry. Whatever she showed as her poverty, one day at Bastion Point told him it was of her own choosing.

"That's not an advisable place to sleep, Mr. Chastain." Her voice held a hint of amusement. "It's a long way down to the beach."

"It looks it." He opened his eyes in time to see Henwyn and Nicca disappearing around the headland with the dogs. "Is your play over?"

"My —"

"Dog!" Mihal shouted.

"The dogs will come back tomorrow." Morwenna shifted the boy to her other hip.

"May I carry him for you? He looks heavy."

"I'll set him down when we get inside the garden."

"Dog."

Morwenna grimaced. "I anxiously await the day when he says more to me than 'dog' and 'eat.' "

"Don't be so sure you want that." David turned back to the garden, and Morwenna fell into step beside him. "My brother's wife said something similar and now wishes my nephews would be quiet."

"I expect I'll be the same, especially when he says everything at such volume. Funny that. His father was gently spoken."

"And you?"

She snorted, but it wasn't as derisive as he had heard from her before, something closer to a genuine chuckle. "I am not quiet." She preceded David into the garden.

While she set down her son and ensured he stood on steady legs, David shut and barred the door.

"Did you want the fresh air," she asked him, "or did you wish to see me about something?"

"I wanted to see you about something." He looked at the child toddling along ahead of them. "Do you need to tend to him?"

She smoothed a strand of hair away from her face. "And my hair. Grandmother will flay me alive if she sees me with my hair falling down in the middle of the afternoon with callers expected."

"You're expecting callers? Not that I have any business asking. I merely don't wish to keep you if you are."

"We always expect callers." She glanced down to where sand fringed the hem of her skirt. "So I'd best change. Go into the drawing room. I will join you there. Feel free to order refreshments if no one offers them to you."

She picked up her son in one arm, started up the steps, her other hand lifting her hem just enough to keep herself from tripping on the gown, not enough to show her ankles. She might reject her grandparents' life in many ways, but her training ruled her life. She was a lady, the lady of the manor. She was the sort of female he glimpsed alighting from their carriages in Bristol or Bath, bestowing coins upon the urchins who offered to hold their horses or swept the walkways clear for them, and ignoring other people.

He didn't realize he was still gazing up the stairway though she had turned out of sight, until a footman cleared his throat. David started and glanced around.

The servant held open the drawing room door. "I will bring you tea and whatever else you wish. Perhaps some pasties?"

"Thank you." His face too warm, David

entered the drawing room, where a fire blazed on the hearth and, of all things, a cat lay curled up in sleep upon one of the velvet chairs. Tentatively, David paused to stroke the thick, gray fur. A low rumble rewarded his attention. Smiling, he took the adjacent chair. The cat lifted its head and regarded him with startlingly green eyes.

"Was I not supposed to stop, Mr. Feline? Or is it Miss Feline?"

"Miss, and she's not supposed to be in here." Lady Trelawny had entered without David's notice. "Come along, Tamsyn. You know better."

The cat leaped over the arms of two chairs and landed in David's lap. He laughed and curled a hand around her paws to keep her from clawing to hold her balance.

Lady Trelawny shook her head. "She thinks she's too good to be a mere kitchen cat."

"Shall I carry her back there for you?"

"Only if she annoys you. She's rather a matriarch around here and, now that Morwenna is back, wants to join the family." She glided across the room and settled on a chair across from David. "Morwenna has always loved the smaller animals, if anyone can call those deerhounds of Conan's small, and our other granddaughter, Elizabeth, loves horses. Do you like animals, Mr. Chastain?"

"Yes, my lady. We have several cats in the boatyard to keep the rats from eating the rope and canvas." He stroked the purring cat. "I usually have two or three keeping me company when I'm drawing."

"So you're the designer behind the boats?"

"I've been taking over from my father —" Suddenly, his throat closed and he turned his face to a fire that had grown blurry around the edges of the flames. "He hasn't done much design in the past few years. He said I was better. I think his eyesight was growing poor."

Suddenly, David wanted to be away, stop taking the hospitality of these people whose son and daughter-in-law probably had something to do with Papa's death or coincidence ran too deep for a man to manage on his own. The good manners drilled into him since childhood dictated that he couldn't walk out on her ladyship, and now a footman entered with a laden tray. David's stomach growled. Accepting food and kindness from these people should feel like treachery, betrayal to his family.

He rose, the cat still in his arms. He would excuse himself, go to his room, and think what he should do — stay or leave. He took a step toward the door, and in the great hall, the bell rang, heralding the arrival of guests. Then Morwenna appeared in the doorway.

"Tamsyn." Morwenna rushed forward and reached out her arms for the cat. Tamsyn leaped into her ladyship's hold, her purr louder than ever. "Oh, you dear thing." She rubbed her face against the soft fur.

David looked away, fully understanding that Morwenna's indifferent demeanor ran about as deep as skin or less. Her heart, on the other hand, was as warm as the flames leaping on the hearth.

She could not be responsible for harming anyone. She must be telling the truth about not knowing anything of her parents.

Don't trust anything by appearances, Papa had always said about business associates.

The advice probably applied to everyone. If Morwenna weren't so pretty, would he think the same of her, be so willing to set aside his distrust and now the new reasons for suspicions? He couldn't know because she was that pretty.

And apparently she attracted gentlemen callers. Jago Rodda and Tristan Pascoe headed straight for Morwenna.

David looked away and caught Lady Trelawny gazing upon him. "She is an extraordinary beauty, and we hope she will consider an alliance soon."

An alliance with one of these men of her own class.

David understood. "Perhaps I should excuse myself."

"Nonsense." Morwenna held the cat before her like a shield against the two other men. "You know Jago and Tristan."

Pascoe bowed to the ladies and gave David a friendly smile. "My father speaks highly of you, Mr. Chastain."

"Mine does not." Rodda tried to take Morwenna's hand.

Five needle-sharp claws shot out and slapped the reaching fingers.

"Tamsyn, you mind your manners," Morwenna crooned to the feline.

"Joseph," Lady Trelawny said, addressing one of the footmen, "take her back to the kitchen."

"I will." David did not want to remain amidst these people with one rudely hostile to him.

"But you haven't eaten your nuncheon," Morwenna protested.

"I expect the cook will have mercy on me?" David tried to smile.

Jago laughed.

"Sit down, Mr. Chastain." Lady Trelawny's tone demanded no disobedience. "Morwenna, give the cat to Joseph."

They both obeyed with reluctance. Morwenna played hostess, passing around plates of pasties and cakes and cups of tea, and talk began. It was talk about people David couldn't possibly know. Then talk about the storm and damage. Finally, talk turned to Penmara and the mines.

"I may have another investor for you, Lady P." Pascoe leaned forward, his face eager. "I didn't get the opportunity to tell you last night, but I was in Truro on some tin business for my father two days ago, and fell into conversation with two men from Falmouth up to buy tin. They said they can use a stake in the ore here, so I told them about Penmara."

"Two more investors. I shall soon have enough." Morwenna plucked a candied violet off the top of a cake and licked it with the tip of her tongue. "Perhaps they will join us when we meet other potential investors in Falmouth."

"When is that?" Rodda asked.

"As soon as Mr. Chastain is well enough to ride. He has business there as well."

"We'll all go," Pascoe said. "Make a party of it. Is that where you hail from, Chastain?"

"Bristol," David said.

"Can't you tell from his speech?" Rodda's

upper lip curled. "He builds rowboats or something."

"Occasionally." David couldn't keep his eyes off Morwenna licking that violet. "If you want to call a cutter a rowboat. It does, after all, have oars."

Pascoe guffawed. "He got you there, Jago."

"I guess he did." Rodda laughed without humor.

Morwenna finished with the violet, and David managed to return to his pasty, succulent meat and onions inside flaky pastry. He could have eaten the entire plateful, but restrained himself, sipping tea and nibbling at savory and sweet refreshments while the talk flowed, arrangements for the journey to Falmouth were set for the next week, and the gentlemen departed. David figured he should also excuse himself, retreat to the library or his room. Suddenly, however, he couldn't move. His legs felt as though they were overcooked carrots incapable of holding him up, and he was cold, so very cold.

"Was there something you wanted to ask me before we were interrupted, Mr. Chastain?" Morwenna seemed not to notice David's fogginess as she gathered up cups and plates. "We can go into the library or one of a dozen parlors —"

"You exaggerate, child. We do not have a

dozen parlors." Lady Trelawny's voice sounded a hundred feet away.

"Mr. Chastain?" Morwenna set the dishes on a table with a bang and rattle. "David?" She dropped to her knees before him and grasped his hands. "Are you all right?"

"I think," he said, managing to speak through lips that had grown numb, his voice slurring as though he had consumed spirits and not tea, "I've been drugged again."

CHAPTER 11

Morwenna flung her entire weight into stopping David from sliding to the floor. "He's unconscious," she shouted. "Run for the apothecary. Someone, help me."

Grandmother joined Morwenna holding David upright while issuing her own orders before turning her bright gaze on Morwenna. "What is wrong with him?"

"I don't know. I gave him laudanum at Penmara the first day or two because he was in such pain, but nothing since."

Except he had accused her of drugging him. She denied it. She had stopped. Laudanum wasn't safe to take for long. Everyone knew that. And he couldn't have drugged himself then or here. He didn't have access to opiates. Yet no one lost consciousness so quickly unless he was drugged, inebriated, or suffering from something far, far worse.

Had some lingering effect of one of his injuries caught up with the passage of time?

He seemed to be healing well. And yet . . .

She rested her hands on his shoulders, holding him upright in the chair, and looked into his face. His eyes were closed, his face slack. He wasn't intoxicated. She would smell that and, again, he had no way to procure spirits in this household where cordials were the strongest drink to be had. "Mr. Chastain." She spoke his name sharply. "David, open your eyes."

He didn't move. His lids didn't flutter. His lips didn't part. He seemed —

She released one shoulder and pressed two fingers to his throat to feel for a pulse. His cravat interfered. She yanked it off and unbuttoned his shirt. The placket opened.

"Morwenna." Grandmother looked shocked.

"His isn't the first male chest I've seen." Morwenna pressed her fingers against the base of his throat again.

He had a pulse — barely. She moved her hand to his lips and felt no breath. Just like on the beach. This time, no one had been assaulting him.

Not on the outside, but somehow on the inside, he had taken in a dangerous substance.

"Grandmama." The childhood name slipped from her lips on a wail of desperation. "He's not breathing."

And now she couldn't feel his pulse.

"I think he's-he's —" Her throat closed. Tears blurred her eyes. "David," she choked out.

Grandmother slapped his face. "Wake up, sirrah."

Nothing happened.

Morwenna worked hard to keep her own breath coming in regular exhalations. She reached for the tray and picked up the silver teapot. Its surface shone clear of spots. She held it to his face. In a moment, a moment that felt like an hour, a feather of fog marred the pristine surface of the silver.

She dropped to her knees and laid her head against his chest. Faint and quiet, his heart fluttered beneath the broad, muscular surface. The scent of vetiver rose from the warmth of his skin. "Thank you, God." She glanced up to see several shocked faces surrounding her — her grandparents' and two footmen's. "I didn't see anyone else here seeing if he's still alive." She heard the anger in her tone and felt it heating through her veins.

So quick to judge her and find her behavior wanting. She wanted to shout at them that she was living a different life now, a godly life, thanks to Elizabeth's loving-kindness before she departed. She was doing nothing wrong.

She glanced away before shock turned to disapproval or contempt. "We should carry him to his chamber."

"Coffee," Grandfather said. "I've seen this, especially on China runs when opium was too plentiful. He needs coffee poured down him and needs to be moving."

"How can he do that?" Needing to be moving herself to quell the words that might spill from her, Morwenna scrambled to her feet. "He's barely alive."

"Joseph, Carey?" Grandfather addressed the footmen. "The two of you are strong. Or we could get one or two of the gardeners."

"Aye, sir, we can manage him." Joseph spoke for them both.

They lifted David under his arms and began to perambulate him around the room. His legs didn't cooperate. He looked like nothing so much as a rag doll with half its stuffing missing.

Unable to bear the sight of it, Morwenna fled to the kitchen to ensure coffee was forthcoming. All activity ceased at her entrance — maids halted with knives poised, the bootblack stopped with a pair of shoes in hand, the housekeeper quieted her lecture or orders, her mouth still open. Only the cook remained in motion, stirring something savory in a pot.

"Coffee," Morwenna said.

"It's ready." The cook ceased her stirring to pour strong, black liquid into a silver pot and set it on a tray. "One of you girls stop your gawking and carry this."

"No need." Morwenna took the tray from the cook and rushed back to the drawing room. Grandmother was opening the doors to allow the chilly March wind into the room. "Cold air does wake a body." Her smile was forced.

Grandfather stood before the dying fire, his arms folded across his chest. "How did this happen?"

"I don't know." Morwenna looked him in the eye. "We all drank the same tea and are all right."

"Could he have put it in himself? Some men are addicted and take too much."

"And where would he have gotten it? I keep asking myself that. He hasn't been near any and didn't have it with him." Morwenna flicked a glance to David, where the footmen had set him in a chair and were trying to get coffee down his throat. They were surprisingly successful. "One of the servants or Jago or Tristan. I don't know how. I don't know why. I just know —"

She broke off, her heart squeezing with fear of being blamed and something worse — the depth of her panic that he might not be all right.

"Perhaps we should take him outside." Grandmother frowned at a trickle of coffee dribbling onto David's chest. "He could be ill . . ."

"It's too cold —" Morwenna's protest died on her lips as the footmen lifted David once more and half carried, half dragged him onto the terrace.

The footmen would listen to Grandmother. It was her house. They had taken over David's care. She stood helpless, useless in the middle of the parlor.

The doorbell rang. She spun, stopped herself in time from answering it. Servants did that here at Bastion Point. She was there to greet the apothecary and direct him out to the terrace. She followed in the event she could be useful. Unable to do anything, she leaned against the balustrade while medicines were poured down David's throat, encouraging his body to reject the drug, the poison. He had been so healthy earlier, looking stronger when he came to the cliff path to see her.

He wanted to tell her something. Then

the gentlemen arrived and David and she had no opportunity to talk.

The gentlemen. Talk. Drugs . . . It all whirled through Morwenna's mind. Investors. Mines. Attack on riding officers.

Life at Bastion Point had never been smooth. Drake was forever getting into scrapes of one sort or another. Morwenna's parents breezed in and out as though the house were an inn for overnight stays on their way to somewhere else. They brought her useless trinkets from around the world — a chunk of rock with leaf impressions, a hunk of quartz the size of her head, a nasty little doll she had tossed off the cliff at high tide. Then they vanished again and she sought for assurance elsewhere — a Carn, a Carter, a Polhenny. Because she was a Trelawny, people called her fast. The words would have been far less complimentary if she had been a village girl. She had done many things she regretted, but not once had she broken the law. Except no one believed her, and if David died, she would be suspected. Ah, she heard the gossip — he survived the wreck, and then he dies? What did he know?

David's death would hurt far more than her reputation. She would — well, she would miss him, not something she liked admitting to. Not something she would let herself think about because of its implications that she might care for him as a man and not simply a resource of information on who was leading wreckers to her beach.

Cold, she wrapped her arms around herself and began to pace along the terrace, keeping out of the way of the footmen and apothecary working over David. She didn't look. She couldn't. The idea of him slipping away there on the terrace in the cold spring sunshine brought tears to her eyes. Fear for herself and more, that something more she didn't want to think about.

"Morwenna," Grandmother called to her.

Morwenna turned, opened her mouth to respond, and looked straight into David's gray-green eyes.

Her knees weakened. She sank onto the flagstones, shaking. "You're awake."

He couldn't possibly hear her rasped words, but he managed to hold her gaze.

"Disappointed?" The single word was clear, not loud, but clear enough for everyone to hear the implied accusation.

She was going to be sick, cast up her accounts right there on the terrace in front of footmen, grandparents, and David. Her distress would look like guilt to David.

She pressed the back of her hand to her

lips. "How could you? Why — ?" She burst into tears and fled into the house. She fled where she always did — to her son, the one good, right thing she had done so far in her life.

He was playing with a pile of blocks. Each one bore a painting of an animal, paint that was bright and clear, not faded and chipped.

"Where did he get those?" Morwenna asked Miss Pross, who sat on a nearby chair, knitting with needles no thicker than toothpicks and thread as thin as a hair.

"Sir Petrok brought them up earlier." Miss Pross set the needles in her lap. "What's to do below?"

"Someone drugged or poisoned Mr. Chastain." Morwenna wiped her eyes on the edge of her shawl.

"Nonsense. Who would do such a thing?"

"Who indeed." Morwenna sank onto the floor beside Mihal and lifted a block. "This is a lion. What sound does a lion make?"

"Grrrr."

"You're brilliant." She handed him the block and picked up a cat. "Grrr?"

Mihal giggled in that way that never failed to make her heart melt. "Meow."

"Oh, silly me." She picked up a monkey, realized she had no idea what one sounded like, and replaced it with a cow.

"Did he do it himself?" Miss Pross asked.
"I don't see how."

Mihal mooed.

"Such a clever boy." Morwenna placed the cow with the other blocks. "He . . . no."

She couldn't bring herself to speak aloud David's accusation.

That was the last disaster for her, having a survivor of the latest wreck accuse her of trying to harm, trying to kill him. With the assault on the revenue officers who accused her of causing the wrecks, she was going to be doomed in the eyes of the villagers, in the eyes of the authorities, in the eyes of her grandparents.

She needed to return to Penmara, pack up her son, and leave before shiny new toys and Miss Pross's constant attentions lured Mihal from her, before she gave in to the lure of letting others control her life.

Grandfather had a right to dictate Mihal's care and upbringing until he reached his majority, being the boy's guardian under the law. The elder Pascoe and Rodda men were trustees of the estate and only allowed her to administer it, such as it was, and raise her son out of respect for Conan and his wishes. He might have been a smuggler, but he had been loved, and the Penvenans were one of the oldest families in the land. She was a Penvenan, mother to the heir, and she would make the estate pay again. As Conan's widow, she would then be able to take her widow's jointure and never need to rely on Trelawny largesse for survival.

From prison or New South Wales.

She couldn't take her son to New South Wales — or the gallows.

Capping the geyser of panic bubbling up inside her, Morwenna searched through the blocks until she found a dog. "Dog?"

Mihal yawned.

"Is it time for his nap?" She posed the question before realizing that no mother should be asking someone else such a thing.

Miss Pross set aside her knitting. "It is. Let me —"

"No, I will." Morwenna picked up Mihal and started for his crib, but once there, with his arms wrapped around her neck and his warm body snuggled against hers, she couldn't let him go. Instead of laying him down, she settled in the rocking chair. He nestled in her arms and was asleep in moments. So was Morwenna. She leaned her head into the curve of the back, closed her eyes, and knew nothing until Miss Pross laid a hand on her shoulder and shook her.

"You might wish to wake, my lady."

Mihal no longer cuddled on her lap. He

lay asleep in his crib, and Morwenna's neck was stiff. Sunlight slanting through the window spoke of late afternoon.

Morwenna sprang to her feet, swayed in a momentary dizziness, then glanced around the nursery as though it were a strange place.

"How did I sleep through you clearing up the blocks and putting Mihal down?"

Miss Pross smiled her gentle smile. "You looked worn to a thread. I hated to wake you, but you may wish to wash your face and change before dinner."

Morwenna knuckled her eyes, gritty from her earlier tears and nap. "I would rather sleep."

"Would you like me to have some coffee sent to your room? I have to go down and fetch his lordship's dinner."

"That would be kind of you, but I can —"

Miss Pross held up a staying hand. "No, you cannot, my lady. You can send a servant down to the kitchen, but going yourself is not done."

"I've done it all my life."

"You weren't Lady Penvenan all your life."

"I want to go home," she muttered as she exited the nursery.

At Penmara she didn't need to worry about such matters as offending the servants by appearing in their midst.

She needed to focus on dinner and what to wear, changing her dress yet again. How had Elizabeth borne life in London for six years? If nothing else, wearing stays from waking to sleeping was making Morwenna's ribs feel like David's had looked, though she barely had to lace them. She preferred her jumps, that more forgiving form of support. Another, if frivolous, reason to return to Penmara.

To run away?

All right, yes, to run away. Hide in her own walls. Order her own days.

"M'lady?" the footman at the head of the hall to her room called to her. "I have a message for you from Lady Trelawny."

Morwenna waited. He produced a sealed missive with her initials looping across it in Grandmother's elegant hand. "Thank you."

She read it on the way to her chamber. "Mr. Chastain is resting in his room. You will join us for dinner. The Kittos are joining us."

The vicar and his wife. Morwenna liked them. They were elderly and nosy, and Mrs. Kitto was a bit of a busybody, but neither had a malicious bone in their body. Even more so, they held hands in front of their parishioners. Once, Morwenna had seen them kissing in the garden of the vicarage. They hadn't even been embarrassed when they noticed her presence. Like them or not, she did not wish to entertain them, answer a dozen questions about the night before, or about David's mishap that afternoon.

Mishap indeed.

She tucked the note into her bodice, then reversed her steps and headed for the west wing.

A footman stepped into her path. "M'lady, Lady Trelawny said no one was to disturb Mr. Chastain."

Picturing how Elizabeth drew highborn lady airs around her when she wanted her way, Morwenna tipped back her head so she could look down her nose at the man who was at least a foot taller than she. "I am not no one." She then turned sideways and stepped around him.

He wouldn't dare lay hands on her to stop her. That would get him dismissed without specific orders to bodily prevent visitors to Mr. Chastain's room. As she had said, she was not no one. She was a baroness and daughter of the house. It held some privileges and perhaps she needed to use them if nothing more than to assure herself David was alive, breathing, past his notion that she had been the culprit who tried to harm him.

Heart thudding in her chest, she reached the end of the corridor and opened the door without knocking. Sunset filled the room, blinding her for a moment. She blinked several times, and when she regained her sight, she found David propped on one elbow and staring at her.

"To what do I owe this honor, my lady?" His voice was quiet, dry, but a spark flashed in his eyes like distant lightning over a storm-tossed sea.

A frisson of apprehension slid up Morwenna's spine and along her limbs. She touched her tongue to dry lips. "I wanted to see for myself that you are well."

"I'm not. I feel like I swallowed five clawing cats who left me as weak as a kitten. So please forgive me for not rising."

"Nothing to forgive." She clasped her upper arms, rubbing them through a shawl that had grown too thin. "I was concerned is all. I was asleep in the nursery. I wanted to see for myself. I don't want dinner —"

She stopped. Morwenna Trelawny Penvenan had never been so nervous around a male that she prattled. Men blathered around her.

David didn't babble. He was direct and quiet, speaking when he had something to say. At that moment, he apparently had nothing to say. He simply watched her, his gaze steady, if not entirely calm. Silence stretched between them, growing longer with each moment like the shadows made from the dropping sun. Their eyes locked in a dare to see who blinked first.

Morwenna moved first. Still looking into his eyes, she dropped her hands to her hips and stiffened her chin. "I did not poison you."

"Someone did."

"There were four people in that room besides you, plus several servants coming and going. Why do you think it was I who did it?"

"You're a Trelawny."

"So is Grandmother. What does that have to do with the price of tea in China?"

"Or opium?"

Morwenna ground her teeth.

The sun dropped below the windowsill, giving her an excuse to break eye contact and move around the room lighting a lamp, coaxing the embers on the hearth to lick flames around a fresh load of coal. Her back to him, she asked, "Would you like some dinner sent up?"

"Lady Trelawny is sending up a tray."

"Shall I bring you your book?"

"I doubt I have the energy to read."

Morwenna slid the poker into its stand with care. "I could read to you."

He didn't answer.

She faced him. "I did not drug you today or any day. I did not try to overdrug you so you would stop breathing."

"Who else would have reason to try to do me in?"

"Why would I?"

"A number of reasons if you're involved in the wrecking."

"I'm not —" She speared her fingers through her hair and realized what a mess it was from her nap in the nursery rocking chair. Only a few pins held it off her face. The rest tumbled down her back in an abandoned tangle of curls. She must look like a wanton. Miss Pross was right — she should flee to her room, set her appearance to right, and entertain the Kittos.

She stood her ground. "I saved your life after the wreck. I saved your life today. If I were afraid of you knowing something you shouldn't, why would I do that?"

"I don't know, but something is all wrong here." He held her with those stormy-sea eyes again — a contact powerful enough he may as well have gripped her with his hands. "You said someone must have taken my medallion while you fetched help."

"Yes, someone must have." Morwenna tensed, waiting for a blow of words.

"And the dogs were set to guard me, correct?"

"Yes, they —" She pressed the back of her hand to her lips, her eyes widening.

David smiled. "I see you caught on to what has taken me this long to work out. How did that person get past the dogs?"

CHAPTER 12

The dogs. Whoever had taken the medallion knew the dogs well enough to not only reach past them but make them remain afterward. Only three people Morwenna knew of could do this — Nicca, Henwyn, and her.

"It could have been others." Her voice held a note of desperation. "I don't know if one of my husband's cohorts was able to make the dogs behave fr-from their smuggling days. Conan and the others, that is, not the dogs of course." A nervous titter escaped her lips. "I knew Conan was deeply involved with the smugglers, but I never knew who they all were. No one does. It was too dangerous to know. But I think the dogs helped guard cargos. Conan might have entrusted someone else. He might have. Just because I don't know —"

She made herself stop talking. Babbling made her sound guilty. Her lack of knowledge about who could control her dogs sounded like a lame excuse and made her look guilty. David's lying there on the bed, his face pale and his pupils still too small from the drug, contributed to appearances of her guilt. She, after all, had served the tea.

"I have no defense except that I know of my innocence and —" A memory flashed through her mind — Jago bringing bones for the dogs to gnaw on and distract them from barking at his arrival. "Dogs — dogs listen to the man or woman with food in hand."

"They do." David looked thoughtful.

Shaking as though she stood in freezing rain, Morwenna turned toward the door just as someone knocked. She opened it to find a footman bearing a tray.

He started back. "M'lady, I didn't think to find you here."

"Well, I am." She took the tray from his hands. "You may inform my grandparents and tell them I won't be down to dinner."

She couldn't possibly be sociable.

She set the tray on a table inside the door and closed the portal in the footman's face. "Watch every move I make, Mr. Chastain, so you can see I am adding nothing to your food." She faced him, tray in hand.

He lay on his back, one hand flung across his eyes. He lay so still she thought he slept.

"Mr. Chastain?" She approached the bed. "Shouldn't you be watching me? I can send for more food and let the footman in this time."

"I don't think you're a stupid woman, Lady Penvenan." He lowered his arm and looked at her. "Even if you fed me something earlier, you wouldn't do so now when we're alone."

"If?" She seized on the word as though it were a lifeline, however gossamer a thread. "Are you saying you haven't tried and condemned me for certain?"

"Of course not. I'm a laborer with a Somerset accent, my lady, not a stupid man."

She set the tray on the bedside table. "Then may I help you with this?"

"I think I can manage." He levered himself to sit against the headboard. "Another meal of broth or gruel doesn't appeal much, but the apothecary said I need to eat to absorb any lingering effects of the drug . . . or poison."

"There's also bread and butter. And someone in the kitchen likes you." Though her tone was now too cheerful, she couldn't stop herself from the ebullient manner after he admitted he wasn't entirely convinced of her guilt. "You have some of those cakes with violet sugar. Those are my favorites."

"Then by all means help yourself to one." A half smile flitted across his lips. "And I'll manage the soup and bread and butter."

She leaned forward to set the tray on his lap. "It's white soup, very hearty, and blackberry cordial. That has strong healing properties, or so Grandmother always says. I never paid enough attention to her lessons in the stillroom. It's knowledge any mistress of an estate should know, but I never expected to be mistress of an estate."

"It's knowledge any lady of the house should have." He dipped his spoon into the soup. "Mama rarely calls in the apothecary when one of us is ill."

He called his mother "Mama."

Morwenna's insides went warm and soft. He said it with such depth of affection and respect, any female would be moved. She'd only known one man who spoke of his mother that way — Sam Carn. Mrs. Carn ruled her large brood with a strength and love that made everyone in the parish want her for their mother, including Morwenna.

"Have to think a moment before remembering what my mother looks like half the time." She spoke her thoughts aloud.

David's brows arched. "I should think she looks like you. You don't much resemble your grandparents except for the coloring."

"You mean because I'm so small? That much about Mother I know. She's little like I am. But her hair is red. Though she's past forty now, so it might be gray."

David sipped from the cordial glass and watched Morwenna from over the delicate crystal. "She might dye it or wear a wig."

"She might, but I don't think she cares much about her appearance. No woman who follows her husband to remote jungles and desert islands could be."

Morwenna never worried much about her appearance either. Yet all of a sudden, with David regarding her so intensely from less than a yard away, she grew conscious of her crumpled gown with baby drool on the shoulder, tearstained cheeks, and hair spilling down her back. She suddenly wanted to be wearing the pink satin ball gown hanging in her armoire, even if it was Elizabeth's gown and hadn't been cut down to fit Morwenna. She didn't even own any jewelry to draw a man's eyes with its sparkle.

All at once, her self-imposed poverty seemed like what it was — stupid pride doing nothing but making her guilt easy for others to believe. Yet now, if she accepted the wealth her grandparents wanted to offer her — a permanent home at Bastion Point even after David departed — she would compound people's belief in her guilt. They would suspect she wanted to give herself no reason to be part of the wreckers.

Too little too late.

She spun away from the side of the bed and paced the length of the chamber, her shawl wrapped around her, her fingers tangled in the fringe. This fine silk wrap wasn't even hers, but one of Grandmother's, the colors better suited to her pale coloring than Morwenna's darkness. She needed vibrant colors, pink and red and even yellow. She was out of mourning. No one would blame her.

And what was she thinking? Making herself more presentable to a man who thought her capable of attempted murder?

"I should go." She reached for the door handle.

"I thought you offered to read to me." His voice held a hint of amusement.

"I thought you didn't want me near you lest I harm you again."

"I'll risk it." Silver chimed against china. "I'm not used to being so much alone."

Oh, she understood that. The ache of loneliness, the tearing emptiness of abandonment crushed down upon her. She staggered against the weight of it and braced herself on the nearest piece of furniture. Her throat closed, her eyes burned. A single tear splashed onto the sheet of paper spread across the desk.

"My lady?" David's voice was soft, questioning. "Are you all right?"

"I am. Or rather, I will be." She shifted her shoulders to lift the burden, blinked away the rest of her tears, and turned toward David, her lips forced into a smile. "Shall I read *Joseph Andrews*?"

"Please." He was staring at her as though he had never seen her before.

She sped across the room. "Let me get that tray for you first. Are you certain you don't want more? You've scarcely touched your soup, and all the cakes are still there."

"I ate the bread and butter, ma'am."

"Yes, I suppose I couldn't have poisoned that." She leaned forward to retrieve the tray.

"Have a care for your shawl." He reached for the fringe of her shawl, but her hair slid forward and his fingers ended up tangled in her curls.

Her fingers loosened, and the tray remained across his thighs. She faced him, faced him from no more than a hand's breadth from his sea-storm eyes, his sculpture-perfect nose, his firm mouth. Warm breath from those lips fanned across hers, sending a shock wave through her entire body. If she moved just a little, more than his breath would touch her.

Blood roaring in her ears, she backed away. Her hair slid from his fingers and her shawl fringe dropped into the soup.

"I'm sorry." Her voice was a mere croak. "I'll call a footman to take the tray." She backed to the door as though she needed to keep an eye on a dangerous animal, though he had done nothing wrong. She was the wanton considering kissing him, not the other way around. "I-I should join my grandparents with their guests." The door handle caught her on the back. She closed her hand around it. "Sleep well."

"While you run away?" His voice was soft, his accent thick.

She gave him a direct look. "Yes, I am. For once in my life, I am running away from temptation."

And so she did, barely managing to walk down the hall to the nearest footman with dignity, give him her request to remove David's tray, then continue to her room where a maid waited to help her change for dinner. She allowed herself to be laced into a gown and have her hair pinned back atop her head, though she wanted to race all the way back to Penmara.

The Kittos were a distraction, a little dull, but kind and warm. Not once had they ever condemned her for her past behavior. They didn't condemn her now.

"We don't think you have done anything wrong today," Mrs. Kitto told Morwenna in the drawing room after dinner.

But then, Mrs. Kitto didn't know that Morwenna had nearly kissed their ailing houseguest. The vicar's wife didn't know that she might give in to weakness given another opportunity, not because she cared about him so much, but because he was there and lonely too. He was an attractive man who looked at her in those moments as though she were the violet sugar atop the cakes.

Conan, I am so sorry.

Burdened with guilt, she headed up to the nursery as soon as she was free to do so. Mihal slept. So did Miss Pross. Morwenna stood in the doorway and watched her baby's peaceful slumber and wished she could snatch him up and carry him to his home, wished his home were worth carrying him to.

I will save it for you, my precious baby. I will be a mother to make you proud, even if I wasn't a wife long enough to make your father proud.

She retreated to her room and picked up the volume of Shakespeare. She could improve her mind, read all those books she should have been reading instead of flirting with her dancing master or music master or the most inappropriate male nearby if he was good-looking enough.

David was just another — better than merely good-looking — man. That was the foundation of his appeal for her. She had no reason to like him otherwise. He thought her capable of trying to harm him. He thought her capable of helping wreckers. She needed to stay away from him.

She avoided him. For three days, she used the size of the house and a spate of beautiful weather to keep out of his presence. She insisted Miss Pross spend less time in the nursery so Morwenna could care for her son, taking her meals in the upper reaches of the house. She took him for walks in the parkland and helped him pick early wildflowers to present to his great-grandmother. She spent one day at Penmara overseeing plans for tilling at least one field as well as the kitchen garden. On the morning of the fourth day, she took the time to play with the dogs on the beach. While Henwyn entertained Mihal with some pretty shells, Morwenna questioned Nicca about whether anyone else could handle the dogs besides the people she knew of. "Did Lord Penvenan let anyone else handle them?"

"Mebbe." Nicca shrugged and stared out to sea, where a line of fishing boats headed toward shore. The hour was early for being out and about, but Grandmother had informed her a dressmaker from Truro was coming and under no circumstances could Morwenna wriggle out of being measured and fitted.

She glowered at Nicca in the few minutes she had left to question him. "Don't tell me you weren't ever out with the smugglers. They wouldn't let a strapping youth like you get away with not being involved."

He kept his gaze on the horizon, though the boats were closer in to be his focus. "I'm not saying I wasn't, not saying I was. I just don't know about them dogs."

Perhaps he didn't.

She let it go. The dogs lolled at her feet, calmly accepting how Mihal wound his arms around their necks. "Come this afternoon as well. I miss these overgrown beasts."

"Can't come later. Storm's brewing."

"Nonsense. The sky is cloudless."

"It won't stay that way. I'll stake a month's wages on it."

Morwenna laughed. "I take the warning seriously then. Come along, Mihal." She scooped up her son, much to his protests.

Another storm, of course, was no laughing matter. At any time, the wreckers could strike.

Her heart a heavier burden to carry than her son, Morwenna returned to the house. She reached the top of the cliff path as a quick breeze, not yet wind, blew off the sea and tugged at her hair and flirted with her skirt. A glance behind her showed a bank of clouds roiling out on the horizon, as black as smoke from burning oil, though still hours off before reaching landfall unless the breeze turned to wind gusts.

"Nicca was right." She hugged Mihal to her. "He knows his storms."

Did his uncanny ability to predict bad weather make him valuable to the wreckers?

For a moment, poised atop the cliffs, she wondered if she should keep watch again. But no, she needed to remain inside, remain where people could declare she never left their sight. Not that such word would hold much weight. She could direct the wreckers from afar.

She spun from the sight of sea and clouds and increased her pace away from the cliffs, Mihal squeezed hard to her side.

"Down." He squirmed in her arms.

"Another word." She let him slide down to the ground, then bent to take his hand and allow him to toddle beside her. It slowed her pace, but she would inhibit his bid for independence as little as she could while keeping him safe. "Can you say anything else new?"

She could have missed something.

Mihal paused to pluck a yellow flower from the hedge along the outside of the garden wall. "Good."

"Very good. May I have it?" She reached out her hand for the blossom.

He started to hand it to her, then pulled himself up straighter and broke into the shambling run of a baby not yet two years of age. "Daft."

"Daft?" Morwenna stared at her son. "Where did you learn that word?"

"I am thinking he means David," Mr. Chastain said.

Morwenna raised her gaze to adult level. "And when would he have learned your name?"

"When you were busy with tasks for your

grandmother." He stooped to Mihal's level. "We've had a fine time together, haven't we?"

Mihal handed him the flower and grinned.

Morwenna stared, torn between annoyance that this man had usurped her son's attention and grief that Mihal was growing up without a father. She wanted to think that she had grown up without a father and been all right, but that would be a lie. She hadn't done well just because she was now a baroness. Mihal needed a man to teach him things she could not. For that, she needed a husband, a worthy man — a man worthy of being her son's father. She wasn't certain she was worthy of being that sort of man's wife whatever her grandparents said.

"I thank you for taking the time with him." She spoke as stiffly as she felt.

"My pleasure. It helps." David rose, swinging Mihal onto his shoulders, much to the boy's delight. "He's a fine boy."

"I think so." She smiled at Mihal, who grinned down at her.

"Up, Ma."

"You are up." Her glance dropped to David's face.

He watched her with an intensity that heated her despite the chill of the rising wind. "There's a storm coming."

"So Nicca tells me." She glanced over her shoulder.

At the farthest horizon, the sea was turning the same color as David's eyes. "I plan to stay tucked up inside the house all night."

"Do we keep a vigil so we all can vouch for your presence?"

Eyes wide, she looked up at him to see if he was serious. He wasn't. At least his eyes sparkled, belying their sober coloring, and he was smiling. Oh, a man who looked like him should never smile. It was unfair to the females of the world, especially ones like her who found resisting an attractive man's charm difficult.

She took a step back. "I had best be going inside. It's time for Mihal's nap. And I'm certain you have much to do."

"Are you? I've done little more than sleep these past two weeks, these past three days especially."

"You are looking well for the rest."

There, she had admitted it. He looked better than well with the sun gleaming in his dark hair and his broad shoulders carrying her son.

"Do you think you're well enough to travel soon?"

"I'm well enough to go to Falmouth soon, yes." Holding Mihal steady with one hand, he opened the garden door with the other. "I will depart after Mama gets here."

Of course, with money for him, money she couldn't lend and her grandparents hadn't offered.

She offered him a better reason not to leave. "And the apothecary thinks you need to have a care for those ribs. Do they still pain you?"

"Only when I breathe."

"Then why are you carrying my — oh, it was a jest."

"A poor one."

"No, I'm simply not used to jesting. Conan loved his jokes, and so does my cousin Drake, but since then . . ." Her lower lip quivered and she drew it between her teeth.

He rested his hand on her shoulder, stopping her. "I've never lost a spouse, my lady, and losing my father hurts like a knife to the belly, especially if all was not well when the loved one passed."

"Of course all was well between us." She shook off his hand. "I adored my husband and him me."

"And I loved my father, but he left us —"

"Lady Penvenan." Jago's too-warm voice rang out from the terrace, interrupting what David had been about to confide.

David inclined his head. "I'll get this lad into the house. You have callers. I forgot to mention it."

"I'd rather take Mihal up myself."

But she could not. Jago, Caswyn, Tristan, Grandmother, and Mrs. Pascoe surrounded her the instant she stepped over the threshold, cutting David out as though he were nothing more than a servant.

"I need to get Mihal upstairs," Morwenna protested.

"I'll take him, my lady." David inclined his head to her in lieu of a bow.

"Good man." Jago took Morwenna's hand. "Have you forgotten we're going to see the mines today?"

"I had." She recalled no specific day being set. "But we can't go today. There's a storm coming."

"Not for hours." Tristan took her other hand, compelling Jago to let go. "It's the nicest day we've had in days, and if it does storm, who knows when we can go again."

Jago grinned. "Want to inspect my investment."

"Run along, child," Grandmother said. "You haven't been on an outing in weeks other than church. Wear a cloak and you'll be warm enough."

"But I can't go with three gentlemen

without a chaperone."

"You're a widow, not a green girl." Jago tugged her toward the door. "But we're collecting the Pascoes' sister on the way."

"She has come to allow my nieces and nephews to drive my parents into lunacy."

"Tristan, that isn't nice." Though Mrs. Pasco protested, she was there at Bastion Point instead of her own home with her grandchildren. "But Caroline can use the outing."

So Morwenna found herself herded upstairs, where Rowena waited with a riding habit Morwenna recognized as her own from before her banishment from Bastion Point more than two years ago, and her own boots. The latter fit just fine. The former was snug in the fitted bodice. For some reason, that made her smile.

Afraid if she breathed too deeply she would pop the frog closures on the jacket, she descended to the ground floor and the waiting gentlemen. Not until the butler opened the door did she wonder what she would ride.

"I haven't been on a horse in two years," she admitted.

And she wasn't the horsewoman her cousin was.

"Your grandfather kept your mare."

Grandmother followed the party onto the front steps. "Henry has been exercising her for you."

"And she's even gentler than she was two years ago, m'lady." Henry spoke from where he held Demelza's bridle. "You'll be having no trouble with her."

Morwenna ran her hand down the mare's glossy black mane. "I shouldn't have neglected you."

"You have those dogs," Tristan said. "They're nearly as big as horses."

"And nearly as difficult to keep in feed. Henry, will you help me mount?"

"I will." Jago appeared beside the mare, bent one knee, and cupped his hands atop it to make a step.

Morwenna grasped the reins and looped up her skirt so as not to catch it beneath her. She placed her left foot on Jago's hands and prepared to bounce off her right foot.

He curled his fingers around the arch of her foot and the other hand around her ankle. With him stooped, their eyes were on a level, and he held her captive, off balance, his dark eyes conveying a message she didn't want to read. "I'd rather go riding with only you." His voice was pitched for her ears alone.

"Jago, please don't." She tried to pull her

foot free. "I'm not interested in marriage."

An image of her lips mere inches from David's the other night flitted through her mind, and her cheeks warmed.

Jago laughed. "You're blushing. I think that means you're lying." His eyes holding triumph, he released his hold on her foot and ankle and gave her the leverage she needed to mount the dainty mare.

For the first mile, Morwenna felt insecure atop the horse, as though the slightest breeze could knock her from her perch. Then she settled into the rhythm of the mare's gait and began to enjoy the gentle pace. Added to the fact that away from the sea the wind bore less force, she truly enjoyed herself all the way to the Pascoes', where Caroline Pascoe Adair greeted them at the end of the drive.

"I had to come out here to keep the children from following me. Good afternoon, Lady Penvenan."

"Mrs. Adair." Morwenna nodded a greeting.

Caroline was ten years her senior, so they had never been friends, merely polite acquaintances when Caroline was home from school. She was a pretty woman with a slim, athletic figure despite her four children. Jago dismounted and assisted her onto her horse.

Though Morwenna watched, she couldn't see if he grasped Caroline's ankle. Morwenna wished he would so she could mark him as a frightful flirt and not truly interested in her.

Caroline's creamy coloring didn't change. She sat her mount with the ease of a born horsewoman, already chatting away with her brothers and Jago.

"Such a pity it's Lent and we can't have dancing," Caroline was saying. "I would dearly love a good village fete."

"Nothing would be wrong with a private house party with dancing." Jago glanced Morwenna's way. "My mother is willing to host one, if I can persuade Lady Penvenan to join us now that she's back into colors."

"Oh, do, my lady." Caroline's bright-blue eyes sparkled with anticipation. "I have boring sticklers for neighbors on that remote estate of my husband's."

"More remote than Cornwall?" Morwenna stared at her.

Caroline laughed. "It's in Ireland. That's why I'm here so rarely. So will you please say yes? We should be able to scrape together enough lively people to join in. Do you not have a houseguest who is, according to my naughty mama, better than passable looking?"

The idea of quiet Mrs. Pascoe being naughty made Morwenna laugh. "Your mother is correct," she found herself saying without thinking. "He —"

"Is hardly the sort we should be inviting to our home," Caswyn interjected.

"He probably can't dance." Jago took up the thread of condemning David in the eyes of Cornish society.

"He was seriously injured." Morwenna knew what Jago meant, but thought it unfair. If every miner and his lady in Cornwall could perform country dances, so could David, who surely attended parties there in Bristol.

"I think he's malingering," Jago said, "so he can stay in a fine home and not work. After all, he builds boats himself."

A defense rose to Morwenna's tongue, but she kept her mouth shut. They were rounding a curve in the rutted track called a road, heading back toward the sea, and a gust of wind caught at her hat. She needed all her concentration to keep her hat secure with one hand and hold the reins with the other.

"Why are we going to visit these mines?" Caroline asked.

"Because I am going to invest in them." Tristan raised a hand to his eyes and scanned the horizon. "Everyone says they are merely flooded, not paid out."

"With what will you invest, little brother?" Caroline poked Tristan with her riding crop. "Your good looks?"

"And charm." He glanced at Morwenna. "Of course, Jago thinks the same thing."

Everyone laughed except for Morwenna. She did not care for this feeling of being a bone over which two hungry hounds fought.

"I am not a good prospect as a bride." Perhaps she could discourage them. "I own nothing and cannot even be guardian of my son or his lands as merely his mother. If the trustees decide to sell Penmara, I can't stop them."

"But your husband could," Jago pointed out. "At the least, he would have a good say in it."

"And there is Bastion Point." Caroline slid a sidelong glance at Morwenna. "Are you not the grandchild in favor at the moment?"

The three men looked shocked that she would be so blunt.

Morwenna merely snorted. "I am the one here, but we will see how long I remain in favor if I refuse to marry."

"Rebellion runs in your veins." Caroline spurred ahead, then wheeled her mount with a grace that defied gravity and cantered back. "I always adored your parents. They were so adventurous. Did they ever find that sapphire mine they were after?"

Morwenna's chest felt as though a boulder lay upon it, and she looked away. "I don't know of any sapphire mine."

"I thought it was rubies," Jago said. "Somewhere in the east."

"It was emeralds." Caswyn reined in and gazed to the darkening sky in the west. "I remember Mr. Branek Trelawny talking about it at the pub in the village one night. He'd had a bit too much cider and started going on about emeralds in South America. Lost Spanish mines."

"How come I know nothing of this?" Tristan asked. "It sounds like something right out of a gothic novel."

"More like something the Minerva Press would publish." Jago gave Morwenna an approving glance. "I'm so glad you're practical, Morwenna, and didn't take after your parents."

"I won't abandon my son." Morwenna blinked, shocked at how much she wanted to weep.

She had forgotten why her parents left on that last expedition. Or perhaps she hadn't allowed herself to think about it until it slipped from her mind. Legends of lost emerald mines were more important to her parents than she was.

She didn't know how she would feel about them should they appear in her life again. She wished she loved them as David loved his mother and deceased father. She feared she didn't even like them much.

A light hand landed on Morwenna's arm. "And now we've made you sad with our talk of your parents." Caroline sounded contrite. "How long since you've heard from them?"

"Six years." Morwenna dashed her gloved hand across her eyes. "I presume they're dead."

"How perfectly beastly of me to bring them into the conversation." Caroline bit her lower lip and cast a look toward her younger brother.

Tristan halted his mount and held out an arm to stop the rest of them. "I think we should turn back. This storm is coming in faster than we thought."

Indeed, the dark clouds that had boiled on the distant horizon an hour ago now created a curtain of rain steaming across roiling waves with the speed of a frigate under full sale.

Caroline sighed loudly enough to be heard over the gusting wind. "Alas, I was so hoping for this outing to last. I've missed Cornwall's wildness."

Morwenna fixed her gaze on the storm, glad it was coming in the light of day.

No one would try to wreck a ship in the daylight.

Without waiting for the others, her taste for the excursion banished by talk of her parents and their fruitless seeking after riches, she wheeled her mount and headed back toward Bastion Point. The others followed, the horses' hooves thudding on the soft earth or occasionally ringing off an errant stone. From the sea, wind gusted like air through a giant's bellows, puffing, withdrawing, blowing harder. One gust caught beneath Morwenna's hat. She grabbed for it. Flipping off her head, it eluded her grasping fingers, soared over the mare's ears, and swooped past her nose.

Demelza shied and bolted.

CHAPTER 13

With only one hand on the reins and off-balance from snatching at her hat, Morwenna slipped from the mare's back. The ground flashed beneath the mare's hooves. In seconds, Morwenna was going to find herself beneath those hooves, trampled, dragged. Her foot wouldn't loosen from the stirrup. She opened her mouth to scream and inhaled a mouthful of her own hair tumbling around her face.

Hooves thundered. The storm rumbled, and a streak of lightning lanced across the heavens, sending Demelza bucking sideways. And Morwenna's foot slipped free. Seconds before her head struck the ground, strong arms caught her and lifted her away from impact, away from hooves, and onto her feet.

"My dear lady, are you all right?" The others swarmed around her, mounted and dismounted.

Morwenna shook her hair away from her face and gazed into Tristan's pretty dark-blue eyes. "I think you just saved my life."

"I'd say he did." Jago leaned down from the back of his mount and laid a hand on her cheek. "The lucky fellow."

"Lucky indeed." Tristan grinned. "I think I should perhaps make you an honest woman after . . . er . . . seeing you thus."

Head still spinning, legs wobbly, Morwenna blinked at him in confusion. Then the first drops of rain landed on her wetter and colder than they should have been.

"Don't be vulgar, little brother." Caswyn dropped his coat over Morwenna's shoulders. "I'll go after your mare."

Morwenna snatched at the coat to cover where the frog closures of her jacket had popped free of their moorings and her habit shirt gapped to expose a bit of embroidered stays and ruffled chemise. Her cheeks would have burned if not for the chill of the water tumbling from the heavens. "I was only funning." Tristan backed away. "You can't blame a man —"

"For not being a gentleman, of course you can." Caroline rapped him on the shoulder with her riding crop. "I should advise her not to give you another moment's notice."

Tristan glared at her and stalked to his

mount, who stood with its head down against the downpour.

"I'll take you up behind me." Jago dismounted. "My mount is the strongest."

"She's such a little thing, it doesn't matter," Caroline said.

"She's rather perfect." Jago grinned at Morwenna.

She used the need to slip her arms inside the sleeves of the too-large coat so her hands were free as an excuse not to respond.

Jago, apparently, needed no response. He grasped her around the waist and lifted her atop his gelding. Then he swung into the saddle in front of her. "Hold on."

He was lean around the middle, as he was lean all over, not particularly broad in the shoulders. She gripped the pockets of his short, wool coat. Shivering from cold and mortification and the lingering hurt of suspecting the reason why her parents had abandoned her, she wished Jago was someone she could wrap her arms around — Drake, Grandfather, . . . David.

The warmth of Jago's coat pockets sufficed for the moment. Despite the torrential rains, they took their time picking their way along the muddy, and thus slippery, track. In a few minutes, they came up with Tristan, then Caswyn, who had Demelza's reins in hand to lead her home.

None of them spoke on the return to Bastion Point. The crack of thunder and tumult of rain on the trees made conversation difficult. In what seemed twice as long as their ride out had taken, they reached the house. Stable lads rushed out to take the reins, while the riders mounted the steps to enter the entry hall, shivering and dripping.

"What happened?" Grandfather emerged from the nearest parlor, Grandmother and Mrs. Pascoe in his wake.

"We got caught in the rain is all," Caroline said. "Our apologies for soaking your floors."

"No matter." Grandmother began to issue orders for hot tea and blankets.

"Morwenna," Grandfather asked, one eyebrow arched, "why are you wearing Mr. Pascoe's coat?"

"Because I'm a hero." Tristan grinned at Morwenna.

"You're a nodcock, brother." Caswyn rubbed his shirt-clad arms. "Though you did save her."

"Save her?" Grandmother stopped in mid-order to fix Morwenna with her green eyes.

"Demelza bolted." Morwenna flung off Caswyn's coat and, holding her jacket together, ran up the steps. She kept her head down so her soaked hair didn't drip into her eyes.

And ran straight into David Chastain.

His arms closed around her. "My lady?"

"So terribly sorry." She lifted her head. "I wasn't watching where I was going. Did I hurt you?"

"I'm a'right. But you?" His gaze touched her face like gentle fingers. He released her and brushed her hair away from her cheek with a light hand.

The rasp of his calluses on her skin sent a shiver racing through her.

He jerked back. "I'm the one who's sorry. You're wet through."

"We got caught in the rain and — worse."

Her wet habit shirt was transparent enough to show the embroidery on her stays.

"I had a bit of an accident," she muttered, then fled the rest of the way down the corridor to her room. She stepped out again to call for the footman to send for a maid to assist her, though she didn't know why she needed to bother with dressing. She wanted to remain upstairs, return to Penmara, go anywhere but into the presence of David Chastain. If she saw him again, she feared she might throw herself into his arms, they had felt so good around her.

David descended the steps and joined the party below because he wanted to know why Lady Penvenan had barreled up the steps looking as though she had been assaulted. Looking beautifully disheveled and appealing and things he shouldn't think about but did.

He had thought about Lady Penvenan far too much in the days she went to absurd and obvious lengths to avoid him. He didn't blame her for doing so. He had accused her of trying to kill him. Few things ranked higher in ungentlemanly behavior than telling a lady she was capable of murder. Yet why would anyone else in the parlor the day he was poisoned want to harm him? The older ladies' involvement was surely out of the question. As for Rodda and Pascoe, David doubted they would wish to poison him to get rid of a rival. They knew he was no threat to their pursuit of Morwenna's hand in marriage. They were of her class. He was a boatbuilder.

On the other hand, one or both of them could be involved in the wrecking. After all, Conan, Lord Penvenan, had been the leader of a smuggling gang.

Apparently the local miners and farmers listened to young men because of their social rank, their role as leaders due them by birth.

David wanted Rodda or Pascoe to be guilty rather than Morwenna. Unfortunately, he wasn't so besotted with her he didn't recognize that being a woman was no defense to criminal behavior. She could be up to her pretty neck with the wreckers.

Dissatisfied with all these conclusions, David continued to the parlor and the assembled party. Not until he was seated in the drawing room with the Pascoes, two Trelawnys, and Jago Rodda did David think he should have a care regarding what he ate or drank. A tiny voice in the corner of his mind whispered that he need not worry because Morwenna wasn't there. He hushed it. Wanting to be near her and distrusting her at the same time seemed hypocritical or inconsistent at best.

He determined to watch whoever served him, but grew so engrossed in what had happened at the Penmara mines earlier he forgot until he had consumed a cup and a half of tea and one cake topped with a sugared violet.

He removed the violet and saved it with some romantic notion of presenting it to her ladyship. She wouldn't want it. She could have as many candied violets as she liked with a mere request. But she had looked to enjoy herself so much eating one the other day, he wanted to ensure she was able to again despite her absence.

He didn't think Lady Penvenan enjoyed herself much these days except when she played with the dogs on the beach, running and laughing with abandon like a girl with no cares.

Her cares were likely more than he knew, and those were enough. Today's embarrassing incident added one more burden to her slender shoulders. When Mrs. Adair concluded the story, everyone laughed except for Tristan, who glared at his siblings.

"Lady Penvenan was never such a prude," Tristan muttered.

"I think we overset her with talk of her parents going after an emerald mind," Mrs. Adair said.

David started, wondering how he could ask what she meant by that.

A strange quiet fell over the drawing room, broken by the lash of wind and rain against the windows. David didn't so much as want to lift his cup for fear it would make too much noise rattling against the saucer.

Then Morwenna walked into the room.

Once again, she wore a frothy pink dress that brought a rosy hue to her creamy skin. David remembered touching that skin, finding it as flawless as, but far warmer than, the porcelain cup beside him, and he barely found the stamina to stand at her arrival, so weak did his knees become.

"Money and lives wasted on imaginary emeralds." Contempt dripped from Morwenna's voice. "All while Penmara's mines lay silent and men here are out of work. Is that tea still hot?"

Immediately, the other men flanked her, walking her to a chair, fetching her tea and cakes, all but lifting her feet onto a footstool as though she were a queen. She accepted it with quiet grace, but once she was settled, she met David's gaze from across the room and winked one of her sparkling dark eyes.

Oh, how could he suspect her of anything?

She waved the gentlemen to sit, and talk commenced regarding some sort of party at the Roddas'. David realized he wasn't included in the plans, made his excuses, and left the room. He did gather up the sugared violets he saved from his cakes, wrapped them in a handkerchief with care, and removed himself to his chamber.

Already the storm was blowing itself out, leaving as swiftly as it had come. A bright line along the western horizon suggested sunlight before dusk. Not bright enough to help David draw, so he lit the lamps and set to work on the other peculiar part of his brother's letter.

Father had notes about a seagoing vessel, not something for Channel runs, but a true seagoing vessel. Do you know anything of this?

David didn't, but he would give the design a try. They couldn't possibly build such a thing now that the money was gone, but he could dream of multiple masts, a jib sail in front and a spanker behind, something graceful and fast, yet sturdy, something like the Americans were building.

As usual, the work absorbed him until a footman called him to dinner. "Unless you would care for a tray in your room."

"I'll go down."

Trays in his room were convenient but lonely.

Tonight the company consisted of the Trelawnys, Morwenna, and David seated at a gate-leg table before the fire in a cozy parlor. Though the storm had blown across Cornwall, a chill remained in the air and the parlor was a haven of warmth. So was the family gathering. They had received letters from across the ocean that Lady Trelawny said she would share after the meal.

They spoke of the storm, the oddness of a gentle horse like Demelza bolting over a mere hat, and a party Mrs. Adair wanted to give.

"No dancing," Lady Trelawny said. "It's Lent."

Morwenna shrugged, lifted a forkful of beef to her lips, then set it on her plate again. "Grandfather, Grandmother, did my parents truly go off seeking an emerald mine?"

"They did." Sir Petrok's face creased into sorrowful lines. "I told them it was a fool's errand, but they had a map and money from a previous excursion, so I couldn't stop them."

"Branek should have been born two hundred years ago." Lady Trelawny smiled, her eyes misty.

"Ridiculous." Morwenna snorted.

"Morwenna," Lady Trelawny admonished, "that is such a vulgar noise. What will Mr. Chastain think of your manners?"

He thought her amusing and charming with her forthrightness of feeling when she thought something absurd.

Lady Trelawny rang a little bell beside her plate. "Is everyone ready for coffee?"

Servants entered to clear the table and set out coffee and sweetmeats. Once they were gone, Lady Trelawny opened one of the letters.

"Elizabeth and Rowan are finally increasing their family." Lady Trelawny's exclamation broke into the moment of quiet. She fairly glowed with the news. "It should arrive — oh my, this letter took six months to reach us."

"I don't want to know how it reached us." Sir Petrok's grumble belied his grin.

"She said she couldn't get it to anyone sooner, so has added a note at the end. It's a boy. And they've given him a rather American-sounding name. Zachary. What sort of name is that?"

"I believe it is a more modern way of Zachariah, ma'am," David said.

"You clever lad, of course it is." Lady Trelawny resumed her perusal of the letter.

Across from David, Morwenna said nothing. He hoped he could have a moment with her perhaps after the coffee.

He found more than a moment. After dinner, the Trelawnys settled at one end of the parlor, and Morwenna led David to a game table at the other end. "Do you know how to play Spillikins?"

"I'm rarely beaten."

"Indeed?" Morwenna poked her nose in the air. "We shall see about that. I am considered the best around here now that my sister-in-law no longer lives in Cornwall."

"Prepare to lose that title, my lady."

"How ungentlemanly of you."

David laughed. "But I am no gentleman. I'm a poor boatbuilder."

Morwenna sobered. "Are you poor? Not that I have any right to ask."

"No, you do not, but I'll speak truth. A month ago I would say that I am not. Today . . . the Chastains are poor with only a hope of rebuilding what was stolen from us."

What her parents might have stolen from them. But why would they want to?

"I understand how one can work all day and still wonder where the next meal is coming from." Morwenna held out the can of colored sticks. "Pick one to see who goes first."

He dipped his hand into the canister and came out with a long, thin stick painted yellow. Morwenna chose a fat green stick.

"You go first." She poured the sticks onto

276

the table.

And the game was on, with his engineering training teaching him how one part was part of a whole. His sister, who never won, said he had an unfair advantage. He knew how to study the pile of sticks and choose the ones least likely to be holding up others, where removing them would cause a collapse of the mound.

Morwenna's advantage might have been her looks, able to distract the strongest of male hearts, except she didn't flirt or flutter. She studied each stick with care before choosing.

"I've been reading about mining," she admitted when she won the first game. "How they support deeper shafts. If I'm going to reopen Penmara's mines, I need to know what it's all about."

David opened his mouth to express his awe, but the Trelawnys rose at the far end of the room, and he stood out of deference for a lady standing. Disappointment ran through him at the notion the evening must end. Relief that the evening would end followed. Too much when alone with Morwenna, he wanted things he should not, like believing her innocent of wrongdoing, like wanting to spend more time with her, like simply wanting her.

"We're off to our chamber," Lady Trelawny said. "It's been an eventful day for two old people like us."

"Good night then." Morwenna stood with her hands folded in front of her like a miniature shield.

David bowed. "I expect I'm off to mine, too, if I may find another book."

"No need." Sir Petrok slipped a hand beneath his lady's elbow. "You're well enough chaperoned with the footmen outside the door."

"We'll leave it ajar," Lady Trelawny added. "No need to let Morwenna win for the evening." She flicked a glance at Morwenna. "Be kind to him, child."

Morwenna lifted her chin in the air. "I play to win."

"You are, after all, a Trelawny." Sir Petrok closed the distance between himself and his granddaughter and kissed her cheek. Then he shook David's hand without a single word of warning as to his behavior and returned to Lady Trelawny, taking her arm again and escorting her from the room.

Morwenna blinked hard a few times, then spun back to the table. "Another game?"

"I have to regain my pride somehow."

David took his seat. They drew sticks, then spilled the collection onto the table and began again. Neither spoke much. They concentrated on keeping the pile from collapsing, laughing when it did, cheering when it did not until the game ended with David the victor this time.

"Best of three?" Morwenna suggested.

David glanced at the clock. It was going onto midnight. "If you're not too weary after your disturbing day."

"Mortifying is more accurate." Morwenna scooped the sticks into the canister. "Would you like some tea, some cordial?"

They sent for tea. It arrived with cakes and David remembered the candied violets. Avoiding her eyes, he pulled them from his coat pocket. "You didn't eat anything this afternoon, and I thought you might be missing these."

"You saved them for me?" She looked as pleased as though he had given her a fine piece of jewelry. "How thoughtful." She pinched up one of the flowers and stuck it between her lips. "Mmm. I missed these after leaving here."

"I wish I had more for you."

"I shouldn't get used to having them around. There won't be luxuries like candied violets when I return to Penmara."

"When will that be?"

"As soon as you leave." She held up her

hand. "We aren't suggesting you leave. You may stay until you are comfortable leaving on the long journey home."

"I still need to find out more of what happened to my father."

"We'll go to Falmouth next week." She shook the can of sticks. "One more game?"

"One more." Or ten, anything to preserve this quiet time when the world and suspicions seemed foolish and far away.

Morwenna won again. "You shouldn't have pulled that red one. According to what I've been reading, an angled support can balance more weight." She went on to explain precisely why that was so, something he should have known but hadn't.

"You are a remarkable woman." David spoke with awe.

"Oh." She ducked her head as she scooped the sticks back into their canister for spilling out again. "I think that's the nicest compliment anyone's ever given me."

"I doubt that."

"Don't. Compliments of my looks are too easy." She peeked up at him from beneath her lashes in a flirtatious move. "But you wouldn't know anything of that."

"I know you are beautiful, aye."

"I'm referring to you, and you very well know it."

"I didn't. That is to say . . . I did not." David resisted the urge to press his cool hands to his hot cheeks.

"I didn't mean to embarrass you." She touched his hand on the table.

He turned his hand over and cupped her fingers in his. "I think you did, but I would rather you didn't flirt with me."

"You don't like me?"

"I like you too much." He ran his thumb across her knuckles. "But I don't know if I can trust you."

"That's honest, if not fair." She clung to his hand as though it anchored her. "It's not fair to me. And yet someone here isn't trustworthy."

"To say the least." The two-foot-wide table felt like too much of a barricade. He wanted to be holding both her hands, or better yet, have his hands on her waist, against her back, holding her to him.

Oh, he was lost. He should stand now and retreat. Her clinging to his hand spoke of flirtation now. Her gaze upon his was pleading, a little desperate.

"Why would anyone want to make me look guilty?" Her words emerged as a low cry.

"To draw attention from their own guilt?"

"But that means my grandparents, which

is beyond consideration, or else Jago or Tristan are involved. And that makes no sense either. They are of good families and wealthy."

"Some men never have enough wealth."

He would never have enough of cradling her hand in his or gazing at her lovely face, hearing her rich contralto voice, or inhaling the sweet tang of her lemon scent.

"Have you considered that the riding officers who searched Penmara are involved?" David asked.

Or her own parents.

He should ask her about them again, see if he could get her to admit she knew they were in England. He should tell her he knew.

"Don't you think it overly convenient they found evidence seeming to prove your guilt so easily?"

She grimaced. "As though I would be stupid enough to keep it that close to hand. But, no, I hadn't considered the officers themselves would be involved. It wouldn't be the first time those paid to protect are the ones from whom we need protecting."

"And we're both in the way of someone's plans." He cupped her hand between both of his, wanting to protect her, not sure if she needed it. "Perhaps you shouldn't leave here when I go."

"Perhaps you should go for your own sake, although" — she added her other hand to his hold of her — "you may be safer here with all of us than wandering Cornwall on your own." She stroked his hand, tracing her fingers over a serpentine scar across the back.

"If you want to stay."

He couldn't breathe enough to answer her. A band seemed to squeeze his chest, crushing his bruised ribs.

"This must have hurt." She traced the scar again. "How did it happen?"

"The adz slipped." His voice sounded like a mere croak. "I don't remember any pain."

"You're fortunate you didn't lose your hand." She ran her thumb from wrist to knuckles, then lifted his hand from hers and kissed the scar.

A distant warning told David to run, make his excuses and race for the safety of his room.

Instead, he rose, drawing Morwenna to her feet. "I'll stay."

"I'm sorry you got caught up in all of this." She cupped the palm of her hand to his cheek.

He pressed her hand between his face and his own fingers. "I'm not in some ways, like right now." He lifted her hand from his face, then kissed her fingertips one by one, watching her face for any sign of withdrawal, of protest. When she remained perfectly still, he released her. "I never thought I'd find myself welcome in a house like this."

"Welcome except for the little matter of someone poisoning you." She fluttered her fingers at her sides as though not certain what to do with them. "I would think that would give you a disgust of us, especially me."

"Perhaps it should."

"Sometimes it does?"

"Sometimes." He rested his hands on her shoulders. "But not right now."

"Right now?" She fluttered her lashes. Unlike her fingers, she knew exactly what she was doing with that luxurious fringe shadowing her eyes.

When she closed her eyes, he understood she didn't expect him to reply to her query with words.

CHAPTER 14

David was kissing her. She had encouraged him to do so. Still the contact stole her breath. Her head spun, and she clutched his shoulders, buried her fingers in the thick satin of his hair and allowed the contact to last as long as he liked, an interlude far too short and far more intense than she anticipated.

When he lifted his head, she was too shaken to release him. She dropped her head onto his broad chest and tried to catch her breath.

"My lady?" He curved one hand around the back of her neck, then slid his fingers into her knot of hair to cup the back of her head. "Morwenna?" He tilted her head up. Their gazes touched, then he kissed her again, longer this time and just as intensely.

If he hadn't held her so close, she might have dropped to the floor, her legs useless.

She had been kissed many times. Too

many times. She had been married for nearly a year. She didn't know this man well enough to be kissing him, and knew of his distrust of her even while he found her as appealing as she found him. He might even be kissing her to soften her into admitting something she couldn't admit because she was innocent of it. She wasn't convinced she wasn't kissing him to soften him into telling her whatever he was keeping from her. Yet this touch of lips, mingling of breaths, the taste of tea, and the solid strength of his arms around her with the gentleness of his hand in her hair, sliced her to her core, opening and unraveling pain and heartache and rage she kept under wraps.

She knew how to suppress the pain. She had done so too often in her life, letting passion and physical pleasure mask the fear and loneliness of being the one left behind when others sought a better life. She had encouraged David to kiss her for just that reason, she now realized. His swift response told her he was only a step away if she gave the word, a gesture. But she couldn't go through with it. The unhealed rawness of her heart stung too much for bad behavior to rescue her this time, especially at the expense of a good and godly man.

Slowly, reluctantly, she released him. Cold washed over her where they had touched. Inside she burned — longing for what she would not take, anger over what she had lost, the boiling up of tears for her grief. She could deny the wanting. She could clamp down the anger. Usually, she could stifle the grief. But the sweetness, the gentle hunger of David's kiss had torn her heart open too wide for that.

The first sob rose unbidden. She clamped her teeth together to hold it back. Yet others followed in rapid succession, threatening to choke her if she didn't let them out.

No, no, no, she could not, she would not burst into tears in front of him. She couldn't weep in front of him after enticing him into that embrace. She. Could. Not.

She pressed her hands to her mouth to stifle the sobs and spun on her heel to flee. Blinded by tears, she ran in the opposite direction of the door and bumbled into the French windows. Her fingers fumbled at the latch. Once, twice, she tried to lift it and failed.

"It's locked, my lady." David's warm voice with its broad vowels and throaty *r*'s purred behind her.

The lock clicked. The door popped open on a blast of cold March night.

And her tears fell faster. She couldn't even attempt to stop her weeping now. She had lost control.

Blinded, she stumbled onto the terrace and across the flagstones to grip the balustrade. She leaned over it as though the cold stone could stop the pain rising inside her like waves on an incoming tide, and with each sob, words emerged, three words again and again. "I am sorry. I am sorry. I am sorry."

He said nothing. He was there beside her, his large hand with its scars of a laboring man resting on her back, warm through her shawl and gown. He remained silent and still beside her, a rock to cling to in the storm of her grief, until her weeping ceased from sheer exhaustion if not an end to the artesian well of her pain. When she fell silent and was able to straighten, he gave her his handkerchief and still said nothing.

She applied the soft linen to her eyes and nose, managed to breathe normally for several moments, then lowered the handkerchief to look up at him.

Light from the parlor silhouetted his profile, and part of her still quivered. It was such a beautiful profile, his features chiseled strength, a steady stability she so lacked in herself.

"Thank you." She swallowed. "That was a wholly humiliating display."

"But a long time coming, I'm thinking." He brushed his scarred knuckles across her cheekbone. "And it's sorry I am if I caused it."

"You? How could you cause it?" She twisted the handkerchief between her hands.

He bowed his head. "I had no business kissing you. You're a lady, and I —"

"I am a lady by birth and marriage." She pressed her palm against his cheek. "That is where my ladyship ends. My behavior —" She choked on the next word she should say.

"You have been graciousness itself."

"Because I want to know what you know about the wreck." As she made that confession, she knew exactly how she could keep him from feeling that the kiss was his fault and suffering guilt over it. She knew how she could keep him away from her where she might succumb to temptation again and bring him down to her level of reprehensible behavior. "I am well aware of how my looks affect men, and I tempted you into kissing me."

"I am capable of resisting temptation and did not."

"And I would have kissed you if you

hadn't kissed me." She hugged her arms beneath her bust and stepped back far enough to break the contact between them. The physical contact. "I cannot help but suspect you are keeping something from me, and I learned a long time ago that men have a difficult time keeping secrets from a lady they are enamored of in a physical way."

In silence, he gazed down at her, his expression inscrutable with the light behind him. Then he sighed and she expected him to condemn her, accuse her of being the immoral woman she thought she had left behind with her marriage and faith.

"My lady, who's to say I did not kiss you for the same reason, or would not have embraced you whether or not you encouraged it?" Of all things, his voice held a lightness, as though he smiled.

Speechless, she stared at him.

"Why," he continued, "would you think I am such a weak man that I cannot make these decisions on my own? The truth is, I've been wanting to kiss you since I woke to the sight of your beautiful face leaning over me. The wanting has only grown the stronger with more time in your company. That said, I do not believe for a minute that you kissed me to get secrets from me. I have lived my life in a way I hope is pleasing to the Lord, and I am no saint, as none of us are, whether 'tis telling a white lie to remain out of trouble, or kissing a beautiful lady."

"I have done a great deal more than kiss handsome men." If one strategy didn't work, then she would try another — giving him a disgust of her.

"Ah, my lady." The kindness of his voice and ghosting touch of his fingertips on her face nearly brought her to tears again. "There is no degree of sin. We all need forgiveness, is what I'm saying to you. It's how we go forward once we've received the forgiveness that matters. And I've seen enough to believe you have not gone forward as you went on in the past."

"I might have with you."

"But you did not." He stepped closer so he could cup her chin in his hand and raise her face so, no doubt, he could see her expression in the light spilling from the parlor. "What I'm wanting to know is why you wish to convince me now that you are a lady of loose moral character and not a lady who honors God's Word in her life that I believe you to be."

"Because —" She took a long, shuddering breath. "Because I don't want you to care for me."

"I'm afraid 'tis too late for that already, or do you think I go about kissing ladies for whom I care naught?" He bent his head and brushed his lips across hers in a gesture holding more affection than passion. Then he took her elbow and urged her to the house. "I'm thinking it's time for you to go to your bed and me mine before the footmen send for your grandparents and Sir Petrok has me tossed out on my ear."

"More like they'd have me tossed out on mine. It wouldn't be the first time." She managed a half smile and stepped over the windowsill to see a footman peeking around the edge of the door. "We're all right, Joseph. I needed air, and Mr. Chastain was kind enough not to let me go into the night alone."

The footman raised one eyebrow but said nothing as he opened the door wider to let them pass before him. "Shall I be putting out the lights, my lady?"

"Yes, and bank the fire." She reached the steps and grasped the rail with one hand and her skirts with the other, removing her arm from David's hold. "Good night, Mr. Chastain. Sleep well."

"And you, my lady." He didn't follow her up the steps.

All the way to the landing where the steps

split between wings, Morwenna felt his gaze upon her as though his hand rested on the center of her back in such a lovingly gentle gesture of kindness.

"I'm afraid 'tis too late for that already," he had said, *"or do you think I go about kissing ladies for whom I care naught?"*

He had admitted that he cared for her. He had made a declaration of feelings far deeper than she suspected he felt for her. Lust in a man she could manage. Love was something different. She needed to have a care of the heart of a man who loved her. The last time she hadn't taken care, she had ended up married to him. She honored him with everything she could, and she adored him for accepting her with all the black marks against her.

But had she loved him?

She shoved open her bedchamber door and sought solitude behind the heavy panel. She would take refuge in sleep, in helping Grandmother with the garden on the morrow, in playing with her son, in entertaining whoever came to call. She would not think about whether or not she had loved her husband. She feared that answer, for it made her a worse woman than she thought she already was. The answer didn't matter now anyway. He was gone, as her parents were gone, as her cousins were gone, as her grandparents would go one day, likely sooner than any of them were ready to go.

As David would go, the best reason in the world to not let herself love anyone. They all left in one way or another.

Besides, her practical self remembered that David was poor, a mere boatbuilder. She needed money from a husband. If she married, her grandparents must approve of the man or they would not release her dowry. They would not approve of David, the boatbuilder, for all their kindness to him. Besides, David's life lay in Bristol, not Cornwall. Her future rested in Penmara, in making up to Conan for not loving him the way he wanted her to.

And there, the answer slipped out despite her efforts to keep it hidden even from herself. She did not love Conan with the devoted passion he felt for her. She loved him as a friend. She adored him for giving her something better than what she had as the Trelawny grandchild who didn't know how to behave — the respectability of being a baroness. But the growing devotion to him she experienced died in anger over his death. He should have done what she was doing — seeking investors for the mines — instead of smuggling and dying like a common criminal.

"So I will do it for you and prove to everyone I am not useless." She flung herself onto the bed, already turned down by a thoughtful maid, and buried her face in the pillows.

Somehow, somehow, somehow, she would prove she wasn't involved with the wreckers. She would find enough investors for the mines. She would secure her son's future as the baron of an estate prosperous enough he could take his rightful place in the House of Lords. She would do it without Trelawny money so everyone knew she had done it, not her grandparents. The only way to survive, to keep her heart from breaking, was to succeed on her own.

David took his brother's letter out of its hiding place and reread the part where they would see him home as soon as they could manage the money to come to Cornwall. Someone should arrive at any time, he hoped. "Be honest with yourself." He spoke the admonition aloud. "Before you succumb." He didn't need to be more enmeshed with Lady Penvenan. He had no business kissing her, let alone kissing her as he had. He was in no position to marry her or anyone else. Even if she would have a poor boatbuilder, far beneath her in social rank, the poor part was a stumbling block. She needed money. Why she needed it when her grandparents were so obviously possessed of overflowing coffers, David didn't know. Nor was it any of his concern. What did concern him was his own behavior toward a lady he had no intention of wedding.

Her bringing up the notion that she had lured him into her arms with the purpose of drawing secrets from him made him wonder if his motivations were indeed the same. He hadn't thought so at the time. Candlelight playing over her porcelain skin, her eyes alight with laughter during their game, her nearness were all enough of a lure on their own, yet now, in the quiet of his chamber with the sea crashing on the rocky cliffs below his window, he remembered something his brother-in-law had said after David's sister had gone shopping in Bath without anyone in the family knowing of her excursion.

"She can say she only went with friends, but I'll get her to tell the truth tonight. She can't keep secrets from me when her head is next to mine on the pillow in the dark."

Jack had been right, and Rebecca had confessed nothing so terrible the two of them weren't cooing over one another in the morning. David had been amused at the time. Now he felt a little sick that part of his mind might have been considering something similar only without the benefit of marriage.

If only he could leave that moment and not face Morwenna in the morning, all the same. Of his behavior resting upon his shoulders for everyone to see, he was quite certain. Yet not even the shirt on his back was his own. Though his brother Martin had slipped a guinea beneath the wax seal, it wasn't enough to get David very far toward Bristol, and he could scarcely walk as far as Penmara village in the thin shoes that were his only footwear, let alone farther. And what if he missed Will or Mama or whoever was coming to see him? Most importantly, could he truly leave Cornwall without discovering what his father was doing in Falmouth when he died, what had happened to the money, and how to explain away the shipwreck that dropped David nearly on the doorstep of the family who bore the crest of the pendant his father had been clutching when he died?

Quite simply, he could not leave. He was here to find answers, and answers he would find without saying anything himself. If

Morwenna had been determined to get answers from him, he must stay to find out what she wanted.

No, my lady, you are not the innocent I wish you were, but not for the reasons you think. That thought, along with his pricking conscience over his behavior that night, did not give him a restful night. He woke as soon as enough light allowed him to do so, washed in cold water left over from the night before, and began to work on his drawings. A maid brought in hot water and tea and rebuilt the fire, all without a word, and he kept working until hunger reminded him of the time and he gathered his nerve enough to descend to breakfast.

"How dare he do something so stupid?" Sir Petrok's bellow stopped David in his tracks. For a missed heartbeat, he thought perhaps Morwenna or even one of the servants had said what happened the night before, then the voice that must have reached from quarterdeck to fo'c'sle in his seafaring days rang out again. "Will my grandson never learn his lesson?" A crash of rattling china followed this rhetorical question.

David met the amused gaze of the footman outside the breakfast room door and arched a brow in query.

298

In response, the stone-faced servant opened the door for David to enter the cheerful room.

"I should have sent him into the military as soon as he was old enough to carry a musket." Sir Petrok was still raging, albeit more quietly. "Or perhaps the navy. A few rounds kissing the gunner's daughter with the bosun's cane might have taught him obedience."

Above a napkin held to her lips, Morwenna's dark eyes danced with amusement. Across from her, Lady Trelawny's lips twitched.

David tried hard not to laugh himself, partly at the absurd expression of "kissing the gunner's daughter," which usually referred to one of the "young gentlemen" or midshipmen bent over a gun while the bosun applied his rattan cane where it would do the most good, according to naval discipline. Ordinary seamen got that cane across their backs and counted themselves fortunate not to get the cat-o'-nine-tails. David's brother had felt that cane many times himself before leaving the navy for a merchantman.

"My grandson will not be a privateer." Sir Petrok shoved back his chair and rose. "Decent Englishmen are not —" He saw

David standing in the doorway and stopped. "I beg your pardon, Mr. Chastain. Do come in and seat yourself. Samuel, why aren't you fetching our guest a cup of coffee?"

The footman at the sideboard sprang into action, collecting cup and saucer and pouring coffee, nodding to another servant to fill a plate.

David drew out the fourth chair at the small gate-leg table and seated himself beside Morwenna. He wanted to reach out to her, take her hand in both of his, brush his fingertips across her incredibly silky skin until those circles beneath her eyes were smoothed away.

He wanted to kiss her again, not because he wanted to gain any information from her. That, he now knew, as he slid a sidelong glance at her from the corner of his eye, was not why he had kissed her the night before. He had embraced her then for the same reason he wished to close the distance between them now.

He had found the lady with whom he wished to spend his life, and they had no future together with her parents somehow tangled up in his father's death.

CHAPTER 15

"Are you not hungry, Mr. Chastain?" Lady Trelawny's solicitous tones drew David from his discomfiting thoughts.

He startled, then smiled and turned his attention to his plate. "I was woolgathering, I'm afraid. Perhaps I should take my breakfast to my room and not interrupt your family discussion."

"No family discussion here." Morwenna lifted her coffee cup and eyed David over the rim. "Grandfather was railing against my eldest cousin. Drake has become a privateer. It's a family tradition, apparently, but Grandfather does not approve."

"Things are different now." Sir Petrok stuffed a letter into the pocket of his coat. "We have a respectable navy now. In my day, we did not have enough ships and privateering was necessary to fight back the French from our colonies."

"We also have fewer colonies now that

America is independent," Morwenna pointed out.

"Hmph." Sir Petrok carried his own cup to the sideboard for coffee, dismissing the servants as he did so. "We shall see how long that lasts with their eighteen ships to our five hundred and more."

"And their privateers."

"Morwenna," Lady Trelawny murmured, "do not provoke him."

"They build fine vessels, those Americans," David said. "I was able to examine one we captured last autumn. I'd love to sail one and see if they are as fast and maneuverable as I've heard. They look it from the design with their —" He stopped, his cheeks growing warm at how he had been about to launch into a discussion of angles and planes.

But Sir Petrok had returned to the table and was smiling at him. "Do tell me more. My brig was the fastest on the seas fifty years ago."

Lady Trelawny and Morwenna exchanged glances and stood simultaneously.

"We shall leave you gentlemen to business talk." Lady Trelawny nodded to David, brushed her hand across her husband's shoulder as she passed him, and left, Morwenna following without acknowledging either man.

"They don't like sailing on the sea." Sir Petrok sighed. "It brings them poor memories. It took Morwenna's parents from her too many times and now, quite likely, forever, and her husband in a way, and now the wrecking . . . We could make things easy for her, if only she would ask, but she's always made life harder than it needs to be."

"She seems to hold a surfeit of pride." David focused his gaze on a point past his host's shoulder rather than look him in the eye and give away his feelings.

Sir Petrok chuckled. "Morwenna has a surfeit of many things — pride, beauty, rebellion. With the pride and rebellion, she is too much like me in my youth. It works well for a young man wanting to restore his family's lost fortunes, but it doesn't work for a lady. It only brings them loneliness."

"I should think she could have her pick of gentlemen should she wish to marry and end any loneliness." David lifted a forkful of ham he didn't wish to eat.

"Jago and Tristan are both more than eligible. They have both adored her for years, especially Tristan when he's been here and not up at university or off visiting friends. Caswyn Pascoe would be a better match, being the elder son, but he shows no more than a passing interest in Morwenna. But she'll have none of them for more than investors in her mines." Sir Petrok emitted a sound rather like a growl. "Sometimes I would like to set charges in those mines and blow them up rather than see her sink good money into restoring them."

David arched a brow. "They're not worth it?"

"I expect they are. It's only flooding why they closed down, not because they're paid out. The previous baron of Penmara, not Morwenna's husband, but his father, gambled away any money that might have been used to restore or purchase new engines. Conan barely managed to hold body and soul together, but Morwenna is determined to get the money if it kills her."

David switched his gaze to his host. "Surely you don't think she is — that she has anything to do with the — the wrecking."

"You were there." Sir Petrok held David's gaze. "You tell me."

"I don't remember anything, sir, not after I went into the water."

"And before?"

"We saw lights. I wasn't privy to where the captain thought we were or that he should steer toward them. I was a mere passenger going by sea because I thought it a faster and more comfortable way to Falmouth than overland."

"And what's in Falmouth that takes you back?"

David shrugged this time. "I don't know."

"And what's in your heart?"

"Sir?" David sloshed coffee onto his saucer.

"If I allow one granddaughter to wed an American, I won't shrink at an Englishman, with an honest trade, courting her, but I warn you to guard your heart where she is concerned. She won't take money from us, but she may be forced to marry for it if she can't get her investors on her own. Do you have money, when you haven't been robbed of the ready, that is?"

It might have been a rude question had Sir Petrok not guessed that David's feelings ran more deeply for Morwenna than appreciation for all she had done for him. The question deserved an honest answer, but the truth was so painful, David's throat closed.

"Your silence says no," Sir Petrok said.

David bowed his head. "Not now." Lest Sir Petrok think him a profligate spender or worse, a gambler, he admitted the truth. "My father emptied the family and the boatyard coffers before his last journey to Falmouth. We don't know why or where the money has gone, but we do know that the yard will go bankrupt if we don't find out within the month."

"Do you need investors?"

Hope flared in David's soul. "We're too small to attract attention, sir."

"But you don't need to remain small." Sir Petrok looked thoughtful. "I own shares in many merchantmen, but I've never taken up the actual construction of vessels. If you're a good enough designer . . ." He gave David an encouraging glance.

David swallowed against dryness in his mouth. "I may not be. I only have preliminary sketches for a seagoing brig. We do, however, wish to expand in that direction. My brother is fully qualified to captain his own vessel and —" Truth drowned the spark of hope — this man's son and daughter-in-law were involved with Father's death somehow. "I need answers before I can move forward with even thinking about investors."

"Thus you need to go to Falmouth." Sir Petrok's voice held understanding, not condemnation.

David nodded.

"But you haven't the money to get there."

David nodded again.

"Do you feel physically fit enough for the ride?"

"I believe so, sir."

"Then we'll leave in three days' time. I can't get away before then."

"But, sir —"

Sir Petrok rose, ending the discussion.

David stood and reached the door before his host. His hand on the latch, he faced the older man. "How did you know — about my feelings for Lady Penvenan, that is?"

"The way you looked at her when you walked into this room this morning."

"I thought you were . . . er . . ."

"Ranting about my grandson?" Sir Petrok let out a roar of mirth. "I didn't make a fortune on the high seas during the old war with France by not noticing more than one thing at a time." He clapped David on the shoulder and gestured for him to open the door. "We want to join our ladies and get the Falmouth journey planned. After that journey, we will discuss building ships further."

Jago Rodda and Tristan Pascoe arrived in the middle of planning for the Falmouth journey. After greeting them and seeing they had refreshments before them, Morwenna said she believed David couldn't possibly be healed enough to ride that far. She excused herself and left her grandparents to entertain their granddaughter's suitors.

"I apologize for my granddaughter's rudeness," Lady Trelawny said. "But she won't neglect her son for anyone."

"Admirable." Pascoe nodded in approval.

Rodda merely lifted his cup to his lips.

David neither ate nor drank. He sat gazing out the window. A few moments later, he saw her walking across the garden with her son toddling along beside her. A quick calculation told him the tide would be out, which meant the dogs were with Nicca.

"Why don't you all join them?" Lady Trelawny pulled an embroidery frame out of her basket. "You young men can't want to sit in here with an old lady while the sun is shining."

"The sun might be shining," Rodda said, "but that wind off the sea feels like January, not March."

"She's off to meet those dogs." Rodda grimaced. "I don't understand why a beautiful lady like her wishes to romp on the sand with those overgrown beasts of hers."

"I'm thinking," David said, "they make her feel carefree and young." He rose and bowed to the Trelawnys, both of whom looked upon him with approval, then he exited the drawing room for the ground-floor parlor that gave easy access to the garden and then the cliffs. He wasn't half-way down the terrace steps, having hesitated just a moment to savor a memory of the night before when he had held Morwenna in that parlor, when the other men joined him. They flanked him at the top of the cliff.

"You'll catch cold at casting your eye in her direction, you know," Pascoe said.

"She won't marry for anything but money," Rodda said.

"And we doubt you have any," Pascoe added.

David let them continue their attempts at discouragement. They said nothing he didn't already know, and he knew more reasons why he could never court Morwenna. That made his heart heavy at the same time he laughed inside over the other men's persistence in listing reasons why he had no chance of gaining Morwenna's attention — they weren't as sure of their own suits as they wished they were. David had seen her shrink from Jago Rodda's attentions and treat Pascoe like a youth. Whatever her reasons, she had let David kiss her.

And at that moment, below them on the

beach, she was letting one of the dogs kiss her with a slavering tongue. She fended off the beast without much sincerity in the protests. Rodda shuddered with an expression of disgust.

Pascoe scrubbed a hand down his face as though he were the one being licked by a canine tongue. "How can she bear it?"

"Who cares if they make her happy?" David started down the path.

Rodda followed close behind. "She shouldn't have dogs to make her happy." He half turned back. "Coming, Pascoe?"

Pascoe shook his head. "I don't like those dogs."

"You ride a horse like a centaur and are afraid of these dogs?" Rodda laughed at his friend and rival.

David increased his pace and reached the foot of the cliff, where Nicca stood with his hands shoved into his pockets.

"Fine morning, sir."

"It is. All well at Penmara?"

Nicca shrugged. "Will be if we don't have no more storms, I'm thinking."

"Is that likely?"

"It's spring. Allus storms in the spring. But the riding officers been patrolling the beach if the tide's out."

"And the cliffs when it is in?"

"Haven't seen them. They got a new —" Nicca broke off to stop Mihal from running too close to the surf.

Dogs at her heels, Morwenna joined him and scooped the boy into her arms. "You do that again, Mihal, and I won't bring you with me."

The dogs' barks drowned her next words to her son. Both deerhounds charged the cliff and the other two men descending.

They had raced right past David.

"Enough," Pascoe shouted.

The dogs quieted.

"Sit." As the dogs obeyed Rodda, he turned to Pascoe. "Thought you didn't like them."

"The best way to control something you don't like is to speak with authority. Dogs will recognize a firm tone."

"So whoever took the medallion didn't necessarily need to be friends with the dogs," David said loudly enough for only Morwenna to hear.

She looked up at him, startled. "I didn't realize that. I've rarely seen them with anyone but Nicca and Henwyn, besides myself, and you there at Penmara. That leaves far too many people to choose from."

"They would like as not respond well to someone carrying a juicy bone." David shoved his own hands into his pockets to stop himself from brushing an errant strand of hair from her cheek. Too well he remembered the silkiness of that hair, the smoothness of her skin. "Dogs seem to forever be hunting food."

"Indeed they do." She set Mihal on the sand and called the dogs to her. They bounded over to her, and she sent a stick skimming down the beach for them to chase. Then she raised her gaze to the men still on the path. "To what do I owe this honor?"

"Sunshine that scarce matches your beauty," Pascoe said.

Morwenna laughed. "You, sir, should purchase spectacles in Falmouth to call me beautiful when I am all over sand and my hair is tumbling down."

"False modesty does not suit you, my lady." David took the stick from the returning Pastie and threw it farther than she had. "It diminishes what you know we see."

"You are unkind to my lady." Rodda cast David a disapproving glance.

Pascoe looked hurt. "You toss my compliment away like that stick."

"It's coin so plentiful I fear it is merely gold plating." Her tone was light, but her cheeks flushed. She ducked her head and brushed off her skirt. "I should take Mihal in for his nap."

"Allow me." David picked up the boy, who immediately began to cry in protest. "Stay with the dogs."

"That would be kind of you. But he'll need changing and Miss Pross is occupied in the stillroom."

"I have done my fair share of changing babies."

The other men, including Nicca, stared at David.

"What freakish behavior," Pascoe muttered.

"Heaven forfend the lower classes gain any influence in this world," Rodda said, "or we'll all be doing women's work."

"Giving birth is the only work I know that only women can do." David lifted Mihal to his shoulders and grinned. "That isn't to say I'd rather leave many tasks to the ladies, but there've been times in our household when the women are all occupied and have asked us for assistance with a task or two. I cannot say nay to my mother when she tells me to do something while I live under her roof."

Her roof, not Father's now.

Saddened after the flash of remembered happiness over memories of the whole family together for a Christmas Day feast not so long ago, David headed up the path with the not yet two-year-old baron. He heard no words spoken behind him, and he suspected everyone stared after him.

Good. Now he had disarmed them where he was concerned. They already believed he had no chance to win Morwenna — sadly true — and they thought him a weakling living under the cat's paw, cheerfully willing to do women's work.

He would cheerfully do women's work for those he loved, and now Morwenna counted amongst them.

More fool you, David Chastain.

Morwenna scooped up the stick and tossed it for the dogs, then chased after them to avoid watching David walk away with her son. In himself he was pleasing to observe. Seeing him carry a cranky child who needed changing made her wish her life was a great deal different. But now, after last night, she couldn't even look him in the eye. If she did, she feared she would throw herself at him and —

She tripped over a chunk of driftwood and sprawled on the sand. The dogs raced up to her and began to lick her face and nuzzle at her.

"Off with you." She pushed them away.

"Let her up." Tristan held his hands out to her. "How can you bear to have them do that to you?"

"We all need some affection in our lives."

"If that is what you wish, my lady" — Tristan hauled her to her feet — "and you weren't all over dog slobber, I would be more than willing to provide affection and more."

"You are kind, Tris, but you're too young for me." She patted his cheek.

He brushed the sand away with an impatient gesture. "I'm your age."

"And not half so worldly."

"I've lived outside of Cornwall most of my life, unlike you."

"But you haven't buried a spouse and been accused of a crime." She scratched Oggy behind one pert ear. He leaned his head against her leg.

Facing her, Pastie leaned against Tristan's leg. He started to scratch her head, then snatched his hand away. "You dogs smell terrible."

"And now you will too." Jago was staring at Tristan. "I thought you didn't like them."

"So did I." Morwenna stared at Pastie's adoring gaze pointed at Tristan.

He rolled his shoulders as though shaking

315

off a wet cloak. "The beasts always like me. They will like anyone who feeds them, though."

As she had thought before, the dogs might have let him — or anyone else with a juicy bone in hand — take something from around David's neck in those minutes he lay alone on the sand.

But what was she thinking? Tristan was from a family nearly as wealthy as the Trelawnys. He had actually taken a degree at Cambridge instead of simply attending classes as did most men of finer families. He had no reason in the world to participate with wrecking unless he wished for the thrill of it like her cousin Drake, who had smuggled for the excitement of it. Because of Conan and Drake's social rank, the village men listened to them. Class rank ruled even in the underworld of lawlessness, so she could not discount any local man — or woman — from being the guilty party leading the smugglers.

Bewildered at her own thoughts, Morwenna called the dogs to heel and returned to where Nicca waited at the foot of the path. "Go on without me." She gestured to her suitors. "I need a word with my manservant here."

Jago and Tristan climbed to the top of the

cliff, then waited, looking back.

Morwenna turned her attention to Nicca. "I want to ask you without Henwyn present . . . Did you ever give Mr. Chastain laudanum in his food when we were still at Penmara?"

"I wouldn't do that, m'lady. Not unless you told me to." Nicca reached for Pastie and rubbed her head, not meeting Morwenna's eyes. "Henwyn, well, she didn't much like him there."

"And might have drugged him because of that?"

Nicca said nothing.

Morwenna sighed. "Your loyalty to her is commendable, but I pay your wages, poor as they are."

Nicca's head shot up. "I never saw her do nothin', m'lady."

"Of course not."

And now he would warn Henwyn of Morwenna's suspicions. But she knew all she needed to — Henwyn had drugged David without permission. *Why* was a matter of speculation and not something Morwenna could dwell upon at the moment.

Wondering how she could ever control a household full of servants if her two acted beyond her wishes, she climbed the cliff path to face the men waiting for her attention. "I am going inside to wash and see to my son. I shouldn't have left Mr. Chastain to it."

"You should hire a nursery maid," Jago said. "No need for a lady to spend her days cooped up with a child."

"I like my son. Being with him isn't cooped up to me."

Tristan sighed. "Which makes you even more beautiful."

"And you absurd." Morwenna shook sand off her skirt as best she could and started up the path, calling over her shoulder, "See you bright and early in three days." She hastened so she could enter the garden well enough ahead of them that she could bar the door and prevent them from following her. They would take her hint that they needn't stay. She did need to get herself up to the nursery.

She rested in the garden for a few minutes, leaning against the trunk of a peach tree where a haze of green along the branches suggested budding leaves might be forthcoming in the next week or two. The walls would protect those buds, then the flowers and fruit that followed, from storm winds.

Nothing but exposure would protect her from storm winds, and she didn't know how to go about that in any way beyond catching the men in the act. She wished she didn't have to, that the men would stop on their own. She didn't like the idea of the brothers and husbands of poor villagers going to prison or even hanging. Yet she couldn't go there either, and now a new notion rang in her head — the idea that the sons of local gentry families were the perpetrators. If she was going to suspect Tristan, if only for a moment, she needed to take Jago under consideration. Or why not the Kittos' grandson who came to visit them upon occasion? And others returned home to the county as well. The Chinoweths, the Blameys, the Bolithos . . .

She feared Sam Carn was the ringleader now that he was no longer constable sworn to uphold the law. Men and women alike followed Sam since he was a youth. Hadn't she lowered herself to dallying with the son of a miner?

She burned with shame at the memory and entered the house through the garden room, where she left her sandy half boots, before she made her way up to the nursery.

David sat there with Mihal. The latter slept soundly in his crib. David sat on a chair nearby, his burly frame dwarfing the rocking chair, his hair loose from its queue and slipping over his face as he leaned his head on his hand and slept.

Morwenna crossed the room and brushed his hair back, letting her fingers linger in the thick, dark mass. His eyes opened. He smiled.

And Morwenna admitted she had fallen in love for the first time in her life.

CHAPTER 16

Morwenna peeled Mihal away from her skirt and handed him over to Miss Pross. "I hate leaving him, but taking him on horseback isn't practical."

"He'll be all right once you're out of sight." Miss Pross raised her voice to be heard above Mihal's wails. "He's a good boy."

"He is."

That he would stop crying and likely not start up again until perhaps bedtime, if then, disturbed Morwenna. She was too much separated from him there at Bastion Point, as she had feared she would be, and now she was leaving him overnight for the first time in his twenty-one months of life. She lingered in the nursery doorway, reluctant to leave.

"Morwenna," Grandfather called up the stairway, "we need to be on our way."

"I have to go to Falmouth." She spoke her

excuse aloud more for her own sake than anyone else's. "This is for Mihal's future."

Everyone knew that. She headed for Falmouth to meet with men who were potential investors in the mines. No one blamed her for going. Only she blamed herself.

She was not much older than Mihal when her parents left her for the first time. She didn't remember their departure. She only remembered not having parents like the other children. Even Elizabeth and Drake's parents arrived from London upon occasion in those days. Morwenna remembered her parents coming home when she was five years of age. They brought gifts of ivory and gold, crystals and rare woods. They spoke strange languages. Mammik and Tasik they taught her to call them, from the old Cornish tongue few people knew anymore. Mammik's skin was bronzed as dark as any sailor's. With her red hair and blue eyes, she didn't resemble Morwenna with her porcelain skin. Before Morwenna grew used to her parents as relatives and not exotic visitors from afar, they were off again, jesting about dragon hunting. That time, they were gone for five years, and then five more, and then —

"Morwenna, we're leaving in five minutes," Grandfather's powerful voice rang out.

She snatched Mihal from Miss Pross again, hugging him close. "I will return, I promise, sweetling. I won't leave forever."

Before she changed her mind and left the investors solely to the men, she set Mihal on the floor, picked up the trailing skirt of her new riding habit, and fled down the corridor to the steps. She ran so fast she slipped on the last set of treads and would have landed in a heap in the front hall if David hadn't caught her and set her on her feet.

"Are you all right?" He gazed at her with such concern she wanted to rest her head on his shoulder and let him hold her.

She backed away from him as she had backed away from him the day after she woke him in the nursery and, in doing so, awakened her own heart. She would not love him. She would not love anyone. That was too risky to her heart.

She fluffed out her skirt. "Riding boots and steps don't go well together."

"And speaking of going." Grandfather tapped his riding crop against his thigh.

They followed him out the front door and onto the drive where the riding and pack-horses with their grooms awaited. Were they headed for Truro, they would have taken the carriage, slow going as it needed to be on the rough road. But Falmouth lay on the southern coast, and between Bastion Point and the port city rose the spine of Cornwall, rugged rocky hills and the merest suggestion of a road impassable by a wheeled vehicle, barely passable by horse.

Watching David mount, seeing he still held himself stiffly, Morwenna wondered why they hadn't thought to take the Fal River instead of riding. He could ride in a carriage as far as Truro and then take the smoother passage of the boat. Smoother and a slower way to go by the time they made the drive into town and the sail downriver. This way, they were likely to reach Falmouth before dark.

Morwenna allowed Henry to assist her into the saddle, where she perched, admiring how her grandmother, three times her own age, mounted with such grace. She hoped she looked half so well when she was old. With a sleepless night behind her, she felt at least twice her age.

She was bound to feel older by the end of the day. Riding for long distances took practice and stamina. Riding with her grandparents and three gentlemen took a different kind of practice and stamina. Jago and Tristan rode on either side of her and vied for her attention with flirtatious quips and conversational gambits. She parried each remark tossed her way, while watching David to ensure he was faring all right considering his injuries and his lack of experience riding.

He appeared well and in no need of her care. Her grandparents had stationed themselves on either side of him. From the snatches of dialogue blown back to her on the brisk morning breeze, they were discussing boat design and business. Once, David's words, "I'd like to build a sloop," rang out clearly.

Jago and Tristan guffawed.

"The rowboat maker wants to build a fishing smack perhaps?" Tristan laughed at his own jest.

Morwenna wanted to slap him. One did not mock the ambitions of the lower classes. One did not mock the lower classes. In Morwenna's life, one was nothing but kind to those born into fewer privileges than those like the Pascoes, Roddas, and Trelawnys enjoyed. Half of her friends growing up had been the sons of miners and fishermen.

She would have edged her mare away from Tristan to state her disapproval, but that would take her closer to Jago. He needed no encouragement. So she maintained her position equidistant between the two gentlemen and focused her gaze straight ahead.

"I think you've displeased her ladyship." Jago snickered. "You know she won't let anyone speak ill of anyone else."

"One of her few flaws." Tristan grinned at her. "You are too much like those Americans who think all men are created equal or some such nonsense. I mean, just look ahead of us. He isn't my equal. You just have to listen to him talk to know it."

"I completely agree." Morwenna slid Tristan a sidelong glance. "Listening to him talk proves a great deal about his character."

"So you are wise, my lady." Tristan's blue eyes brightened. "You recognize that the way a man speaks says a great deal about his breeding."

"Indeed it does." Morwenna inclined her head.

"Every time that boatbuilder opens his mouth —"

"Tris," Jago interjected, "I'd give over, were I you."

"He reveals his background," Tristan finished.

"Indeed he does." Morwenna flashed Tristan a glare that should have knocked him from his mount. "He reveals that he is courteous, thoughtful, and raised with a strong faith in God. Yes, Mr. Pascoe, you would do well to listen to a man like David Chastain and learn a great deal about how he was raised."

Tristan's mouth dropped open, but no words emerged.

From Morwenna's other side, Jago laughed so hard he nearly toppled from his horse.

The three ahead glanced back with questioning looks.

"Mr. Rodda appreciates my witty repartee on breeding and the raising of children," Morwenna said. "Mr. Pascoe does not."

"Morwenna." Grandmother's mouth flattened. "Be nice."

"I am, Grandmother."

"To the wrong party," Tristan muttered.

That made Jago laugh again. "I warned you, Tris. You need to learn that our Lady Penvenan can spring a trap faster than any poacher."

"She's not the poacher." Tristan sent a vicious glare at David's back. "He needs to learn that his territory for hunting the fairer sex is not amongst the upper classes."

"Nor am I game." Morwenna tightened her gloved hands on her reins. "I am mistress of my own life."

But not her heart, foolish woman that she

was. She had lost that to the most unsuit-able man she could have come up with — one who was poor by his own admission. And a man who spoke truth to her about herself, if not himself.

And she wanted to be near him, touching his hand, his face, his shoulders that looked as though they could bear any number of burdens without bowing under the weight. That was new for her — a man who drew her to him because of who he was and not because she wanted to use him in some way. She still needed information from him, why he had that medallion for one thing, but she went for whole days forgetting he held secrets she needed.

She longed for a lifetime of forgetting he held secrets she needed to know. At that moment, she wished she were riding with him, discussing his plans for building bigger boats than cutters and gigs for naval cap-tains and merchantmen. If she were to do that, she might give her feelings away to the others or, worse, David himself. He must not know how she felt.

"We are doomed to ever win your heart," Jago was saying.

Morwenna snorted. "You don't want my heart."

She would have mentioned how he wanted

the dowry her grandparents would likely give a spouse, not her heart. They both knew it, that talk of her heart was a jest.

"I don't have a heart for you to win," she said instead.

"I believe that." Tristan still looked sulky. He might be her age, but he was a mere boy.

Unbidden, her gaze strayed to David. He was a man, calm and confident of his own worth. Appealing. He would never resort to smuggling or other unlawful activity to fill empty coffers.

She winced at this disloyalty to her late husband. Conan had an estate dependent on his prosperity. Yet what had he done with the money he made? He hadn't invested in the mines. The house was falling down around his ears, and he hadn't spent a great deal on the farmlands.

More disloyalty, yet questions she had found no answers for. She had looked in the house for secret compartments. The closest she came was that he felt obligated to pay his father's gaming debts, some misguided male honor notion. The gaming houses couldn't demand payment for those debts, couldn't send Conan to a sponging house or debtor's prison for not paying them. Yet Conan had wasted money paying those debts. Letters to that effect were abundant among Conan's papers.

Had Conan been a gamester himself? Of course he had. He smuggled. That was a form of gambling — with his life. He had promised to stop smuggling as soon as all debts were paid off. He just needed one more run to clear all financial obligations. That was no different than the gamester who said he only needed one more game to win back his losses. And Conan had lost the toss of the dice. He had paid the debt with his life.

Why she should wonder this now, she didn't know. She felt as though her feelings for David had brushed aside a layer of gauze she had hung between her thinking brain and the truth regarding Conan, Lord Penvenan. She wanted him to be good since he had saved her from her poor choices in life. But he wasn't, not in truth. He worked with violent men and died accordingly. Perhaps he had even engaged in violence.

Of course he had. His closest friend, her cousin Drake, thought fights with the excise officers were entertainment, and Conan had joined him by his own will. Conan had continued to engage in smuggling, though he had come too close to being caught several times. He must have loved the excitement of the danger well after he had a wife and child. If he had gone to her grandfather for assistance, he could have stopped sooner, ceased breaking the law before he was killed by his fellow smugglers. But he'd been determined to take Penmara out of debt on his own.

Just like you are.

She started so abruptly she reined in her mare. Her grandparents and David, still engaged in conversation, and Jago and Tristan likewise discussing something past her, didn't notice at first that she had stopped. They all rode on for a quarter mile before Jago shouted for them all to stop.

He wheeled his mount and cantered back to her. "My lady, what's amiss?"

"Nothing." Morwenna curled her hands around her reins to disguise their shaking.

Surely her situation was different and she wasn't rejecting her inheritance out of pride.

"I-I had a thought that startled me is all."

"I hope you realized that marrying me is the best thing possible for the two of us." Jago grinned as though he wanted to add, "Just making a jest."

She made herself laugh at the poor joke. "If we want to end up in early graves it is the best for both of us. Now turn your mount around and let us not hold up the party. I believe we are expected for a nuncheon at the Bolithos'."

She took her place in the cavalcade again and managed to indulge in the two young men's banter. Doing so kept her mind from returning to Conan and money, Conan and smuggling, Conan and prideful refusal of help.

Around noon, they reached the Bolithos' snug cottage orné tucked into a sheltered pocket of budding greenery. A mere ten miles from the coast, the season seemed far more advanced than along the north coast with tulips blooming in profusion along the front of the fifteen-room house, small by manor standards. The Bolithos were an elderly couple who liked a quiet life in the country except on the occasions when their children and grandchildren came to visit. This was not one of those occasions.

The Bolithos greeted the Bastion Point party in a sunny parlor, offered refreshment in the form of hot tea, then led them into an equally cozy dining room, where the table seated no more than ten people, for a cold collation of sliced roasted meats, bread rolls, and salad.

After an initial showing of surprise at David's Somerset accent, the older couple welcomed him with the same courtesy they afforded all their guests, and the hour the Falmouth-bound party took for repose and to allow their horses rest, passed pleasantly.

Stiffening up already, Morwenna wished she could stay in the cottage. It seemed so much more like a home than Penmara with its near empty rooms and water-spotted ceilings, and certainly more than Bastion Point with its dozens of chambers filled with treasures few people ever saw. The Bolithos had hung charcoal drawings of their children and grandchildren around the walls of the dining room.

Almost too weary to eat, Morwenna scanned the pictures. Odd that she had grown up ten miles from these people and didn't remember meeting their family more than half a dozen times in her life. They seemed to have a grandson near her age. Vaguely she recalled dancing with him at some village fete.

"Margh," Mr. Bolitho, to Morwenna's left, said. "He goes by the English Mark now. Got teased too much about his foreign name at school."

"So did I with Morwenna."

"It's a beautiful name, just like you."

Morwenna smiled at the old man's flirtation. "You flatter me."

"You should be used to it by now." Mr. Bolitho patted her hand. "Margh still talks about dancing with you at that fete. Perhaps he shall call on you next time he comes to visit."

Morwenna suppressed a groan and inclined her head. "We are nothing if not hospitable, sir."

The Bolithos certainly were hospitable. Besides the meal, they packed pasties and bottles of cider for sustenance along the rest of the journey. Then the travelers mounted up and were on their way again.

Not one word had Morwenna exchanged with David. Seating at the table and courtesy to her host and hostess had kept him on the opposite side of the room from her. She wanted to ask him how he was faring. He looked fatigued, not as upright and steady in the saddle as he had been before lunch. She wanted to inquire if his healing wounds hurt, if he was distressed about returning to the same place his father had died, if he wished to talk to her . . .

Though he rode a mere dozen feet ahead of her, she missed him. Jago and Tristan tried to engage her in conversation, but she wasn't interested in the banal banter. She tried to get Tristan to talk about his time at Cambridge, but he waved his hand as though erasing her words from the air. "You don't need to fill your head with philosophy and history."

"Why not?" She wasn't certain she would understand, and yet she needed to if she was to ensure her son was educated enough to hold his own in society after he reached his majority and took his seat in the House of Lords. Perhaps he would attend one of the universities.

But the men were laughing at her for asking such silly questions.

"You don't need to act the bluestocking to get attention, my dear." Tristan reached across the space between their mounts and squeezed her hand.

Annoyed, Morwenna spurred Demelza forward. Forget pride. She would stop waiting for David to acknowledge her presence and simply ride up beside him and engage him in conversation.

In order to insinuate herself and her mare between Grandmother and David, Morwenna needed to ride close; thus, she was mere inches from David when he slumped sideways and began to fall.

CHAPTER 17

This time, David was horribly, embarrassingly sick from whatever drug had been slipped into his food. Not one Trelawny or the other two men had been near enough to his food to slip some foreign substance into his drink, but he had been around the Trelawnys long enough now to know they could afford to pay for any number of servants to poison him.

This felt like poison rather than the sleep-inducing effects of opium. Before, he merely slipped into unconsciousness. This time, his insides burned and roiled, and he grew terribly weak before he slipped to the ground, gently, thanks to her ladyship's maneuvering with her horse, but not gently enough to prevent him from landing with a thud that broke his fragile control on his illness before he lost awareness.

He left consciousness on the rugged road to Falmouth, cries and shouts ringing in his

ears. He regained his senses to quiet dim-
ness, the softness of a bed beneath him, and
a feeling like someone had used emery grit
to cleanse his insides.

"Water." The word sounded more like a
frog's "ribbit" than a human request for
something wet to soothe his raw throat.

The request must have been comprehen-
sible enough, for in a moment, a rustle of
fabric and the splash of liquid came to his
ears. A soft hand slid along the back of his
neck, lifting him just enough for the rim of
a glass to slide against his lower lip.

Not just any soft hand — Morwenna's.
He smelled her sweet lemon fragrance. He
opened his eyes to see her beautiful face,
her eyes too big and too dark, as though she
wore spectacles.

No, those were tears magnifying her eyes.
They swam and pooled on her lower lids.
One or two trickled down her cheek.

With great effort, he raised his hand and
brushed one tear away with the pad of his
thumb. "Why this? I'm alive." He tried to
smile, but feared he merely grimaced. "Or
is that the cause."

"Don't be a widgeon." She tilted the glass
so the cool water slipped down his throat.

Not until he swallowed did he wonder if
perhaps he should not take refreshment

from her.

Then she removed the glass and pressed her lips to his brow. "The physician says only a little at a time." She eased him back onto the pillows.

He pressed his hand to his brow to hold the kiss close. "What?" He couldn't find the strength to ask for more details.

"You were poisoned." The mattress shifted as she perched on the side of the bed and took his hand in hers. "Not opium this time, but something almost worse. The physician is analyzing what it might be, but he thinks it was dealt with an inexpert hand, perhaps too much so you rejected it, or perhaps too little so it simply made you ill. Whatever the dosage, you-you —" Her voice broke on a sob, and she slid to her knees beside the bed. She clasped his hand in both of hers, and a few tears seeped through her lashes.

He rolled onto his side and rested his other hand on her neatly coiled hair. "Why are you weeping?"

"Why do you think?" She sounded angry. "I want you dead? I want you alive so no one can accuse me of trying to kill you? Poison is known as a woman's tool of murder, you know."

"I did not know." He found one of her pins and tugged it free. Her hair held in

338

place, but he curled his fingers around the bone clip as a keepsake. "I seem to know too little for my own good."

"Or you know too much for your own good." She raised her head. Her lips trembled.

He wanted to be well so he could kiss her again, see that those lips only quivered because his own covered them and not because she still fought emotion.

But he wasn't well. He was so unwell he wished for her to leave him.

"Why are you here alone with me?" he asked instead of requesting she leave, a request he knew she would ignore.

"We are in an inn in Falmouth, and Grandmother left a maid to look over you during the night, but I looked in on you and the poor child was sound asleep. I sent her to her bed and stayed myself."

"Reputation." It was the only word he could manage now.

"It's of no consequence."

"Your investors?"

"They won't invest if you succumb to poison, now, will they?"

"Ah." Another dose of poison couldn't hurt so much as her proclamation.

He let himself fall back on the pillows and willed himself into wellness. Weakness before a lady was too humiliating, and she had already seen him at his worst.

Fabric rustled, and she released his hand. "I'll fetch the innkeeper's lad. He's a bit of a mooncalf, but capable and kind."

So she understood.

She spoke truth about the innkeeper's lad, and when she returned, morning had come without him realizing he lost consciousness again. She brought the physician and her grandfather with her.

"Are you improved from the night, Mr. Chastain?" The physician was a stoop-shouldered gentleman with thinning gray hair, spectacles, and an easy smile. "Lady Penvenan says you had a difficult night."

"To my humiliation." David tried to return the smile.

He caught Sir Petrok's scowl and glanced to Morwenna.

"Grandfather disapproves of me being here last night." She approached the bed and rested her hand over his. "But the maid was doing you no good."

"And you're doing yourself no good." Sir Petrok sighed. "Headstrong as ever."

"Kindhearted," David said.

"I think you should both leave me alone with Mr. Chastain," the physician said. "I wish to examine him more fully now that he is awake and sensible."

The Trelawnys left, still arguing with one another over Morwenna slipping into David's room during the night. Alone with him, the physician gave him a thorough examination, listening to his heart and lungs with the aid of a long metal tube, and poking and prodding.

At last, he grunted, gave David more water, then drew a chair up to the bed and sat. "I suspect you ingested too much tansy. It's plentiful this time of year."

"Would I not have tasted that?"

"I understand you all had salad for lunch. Was it dressed?"

"Some sort of sauce. Vinegar. Lemons, maybe. I don't honestly know. I didn't care much for it, but I could scarcely refuse it."

"No, and it would mask the flavor, and you might not notice more herbs among spring greens from a hothouse, as the Bolithos have."

"But those kind old people would never —"

The physician chuckled. "Not in a thousand years. But servants can be bribed. I wouldn't be at all surprised to learn that one of them has left their employment without notice."

David's head began to ache. "But why?

I'm a stranger in these parts."

"Or are you?" The physician leaned forward and looked into David's face. "Are you of any relation to the late William Chastain?"

David shot upright. "Why do you ask?"

"Are you?"

"My father."

"Oh, I am sorry." The physician rubbed his knuckles on his chin. "I was afraid of that. You have much the look of him, and then there's the Somerset accent." He heaved a sigh and brought his gaze back to David's face. "I attended him when he grew ill here at the inn. My surgery is only a step from here, so I am often called for ailing guests."

Heart racing, David waited for more.

"He didn't have much to say, being far gone when I got here," the physician obliged him. "I helped him write a letter for his family. Did you receive it with that medallion?"

"I did." David's throat closed and his eyes burned.

"I'm sorry I couldn't deliver it myself, but I had to go to a difficult lying-in for a friend's wife in Plymouth and was not here when a family member arrived. Was that you?"

David nodded, not trusting his voice.

"A bad business. And now you as well."
He rubbed his chin again. "A bad business
indeed."

"What . . . do you know of his death?"
David asked, his words a mere whisper.

"I'm afraid," the physician said, "that he,
too, was poisoned, only not being of as
hearty a constitution as you, he suc-
cumbed."

Not some illness he gathered on the road
to Falmouth, but poison just like David.

David wanted to shout, throw something
against the whitewashed wall of the inn bedchamber, drag whoever was responsible into
court, and see justice done to the maximum
extent of criminal punishment.

He lay perfectly still, his head spinning
from weakness and the news, mostly the
news. Poisoned. Murdered. Father murdered with poison because he was in Falmouth and not Scotland.

And where was the money? No doubt
stolen by whoever had killed him.

"I think," David said, "I would like to be
alone."

"And I shall leave you alone, but not
before I see you take some broth. It should
be arriving soon."

"Can I trust anything I eat?"

"I suggest you only eat from the same vessels as others eat from and only be served by someone you trust. And perhaps you wish to send for the constable?"

"I doubt a constable can do anything to help." David gathered his wits around him. "What else can you tell me of my father's last hours?"

"Too little, I'm afraid. He said he had only eaten at public inns on his way here. But you know how most inns are. A common table where anyone could slip something into a stew or tankard."

A knock sounded on the door, and the innkeeper's son entered with soup and tea. The physician brought them in, made a show of drinking some of both, then set the tray across David's knees. "Take each mouthful slowly. I will stay to see if you manage to keep it down."

David did as the physician ordered, talking in between sips. "Whom can I trust then?"

"I'm thinking you will have to work that out for yourself, young man. Lady Penvenan seems quite concerned."

She did. He wanted her to be. But he had wound up on her beach after his father had died, and now he had nearly died for the same reason.

"I don't know. I cannot —" He closed his

eyes, too weary to eat, too weary to think. Most of all, he was too weary to let his heart be vulnerable. It felt scraped raw by the pain of what felt like losing his father all over again and too many coincidences to be coincidences.

The physician rose and removed the cup from David's hand. "I shall return in the forenoon. You rest until then. Have someone send for me if . . ." He named a number of unpleasant symptoms, then departed.

Poisoned. He had been poisoned. He had come closer to death than before. Someone was growing more serious about seeing him done in. Surely the suspects were finite. Too finite. Pascoe and Rodda didn't like him around Morwenna, yet he was no competition to them. They were the sort of men ladies like her married. Those two gentlemen should view David as no competition and certainly not so much one of them would need to resort to murder to be rid of him. He would be gone as soon as he was well.

He would be gone because all his calculations returned to Morwenna.

"Why?" He posed the question to the next person who walked into his chamber.

He knew it was her from the lightness of her tread, the sharp sweetness of lemon blossoms, the way his entire being ached to reach out to her.

He opened his eyes and gazed at her portrait-perfect face, glowing even in the pearly gray of a rainy morning. "Why?"

"Why what?" Her skirt rustled as though she wore taffeta beneath her blue muslin gown, an alluring whisper his eldest brother had explained to him when telling him how females used their wiles to catch husbands. Martin had gotten caught in a whispering web and seemed most happy with the entanglement. David wanted to be happy with such an arrangement for his heart.

"Why would someone want to kill me?" He gazed at her, pleading for an answer that didn't involve her.

She most improperly perched on the edge of the bed instead of taking the chair the physician had vacated, and took his hand in hers. "To stop you from talking."

"About what?"

She laid one hand along his cheek and turned his face toward her, gazing into his eyes. "You tell me."

"Tell you what?" He drank in the sight of her features, committing each detail to memory so he would remember in days to come that he had been this close to her, that he had been closer. "Shall I tell you that I think you're the most likely person to be drugging my food? Shall I tell you that I think you know perfectly well where the medallion is? Shall I tell you that right now I don't care about any of that because I love you? Shall —"

"No, you cannot." She pressed her fingers to his lips.

He drew them gently away and spoke above her protests. "Shall I tell you I want to forget about wrecks and —"

"David, stop. You don't understand —"

"Forget about murders and attempted murder and . . . everything but you?" He leaned forward, cupping her face in his hands. "For this?"

He kissed her. His fingers splayed across her cheeks and his thumbs caressing the smooth skin beneath her jaw, he parted her lips with his as though he could draw truth from her with the intensity of the contact.

She made a wordless sound somewhere between a whimper and a sigh of contentment and buried her fingers in his hair, drawing it down to curtain their faces. She kissed him back as though she were starving, as though nothing but propriety kept them apart.

Then, when the contact strained propriety and proper behavior to the breaking point, he released her and leaned back against the headboard, shaken to the core, filled with wanting her, hollow with guilt, especially when Morwenna slid to her knees on the floor and buried her face in the bedclothes. And she wept hard enough to shake the bed ropes.

He rested his hand on the neat coil of her hair. "I must be doing well. Twice now I have kissed you and twice now I have made you cry."

"You haven't." She raised her face with its drowned pansy eyes melting every hard thought he'd ever had about her. "You haven't made me cry, that is. It is I, my past . . ." She wiped her face on her shawl. "Do you ever wonder why I am so easily believed to be guilty of the wrecking despite being a Trelawny?"

David's eyes widened at this abrupt change in topic. "It's your beach, and your husband was in the smuggling trade."

"Those are your reasons, and I can distract you from them. I've done it again today. You start to accuse me and you end up kissing me like — well . . ." Her cheeks turned the color of peonies.

"Like I have no business kissing a lady to whom I am not even betrothed." He cringed inwardly. "I am sorry. I don't regret it as perhaps I should, but I regret hurting you."

"You haven't hurt me, David. You are such a good man."

His conscience pricked him, urging him to speak, even to tell her what the physician had said about his father. But the less he told her, the more he could learn what she knew of the information — limited as it was — he had been able to gather.

He held up a staying hand, his conscience smiting him. "Not so much forthright as you think.

"A good man wouldn't have kissed you today or the other night."

"Not if you knew —" She shot to her feet and paced across the room to shovel a load of coal onto the smoldering fire, then stalked across the room in the other direction and pushed open the casement to a billow of cold air smelling of rain and the sea. "I left my sinful life behind three years ago when I married Conan, Lord Penvenan. I wouldn't say I lived a Christian life then, but I didn't live as I had before. The Christian life came later, after Mihal's birth, after I saw what God had done in the lives of my cousin Elizabeth and her husband. But before then, before my marriage, I was . . . wicked."

David wanted to protest, wanted to tell

her he doubted she could have ever been wicked. Yet he could not when he held his own condemning suspicions against her. Yet her smooth, contralto voice grated with pain, as though each word she spoke scraped her throat raw, so all he could do was listen and pray, take in each word and hope she gave him even a gossamer thread of hope to believe she was innocent of harming anyone with unlawful acts.

Gripping the windowsill with white-knuckled hands, as though the painted wood were stopping her from being swept downstream, she continued to face the courtyard beyond the window. "After my parents left for the last time, I, um, went looking for love and affection where I could find it. My grandparents tried to rein me in. They locked me in my room. They tried sending me into Devonshire for schooling, and they prayed for me. I climbed out my bedroom window and nearly broke my neck, but I escaped. I ran away from school with the music master. I broke as many rules of proper behavior as I could."

And he had just helped her break one more.

He wanted to play the craven and duck beneath the bedclothes to hide his shame. He made himself listen to her in silence, watching her, praying for wisdom for once in his life.

"Conan wanted a wife and heir," she pressed on. "He knew all about me and didn't care. In fact, it made getting me to wed him easy, I expect. We had to keep our marriage secret so no one would kill our son, or me for that matter, especially after he was murdered. We had planned to tell my grandparents so we could collect the dowry and rescue Penmara, but Conan died and my grandparents were not so kind about me bearing a child, as they thought, without the benefit of marriage, so I determined to save Penmara without their help. But that's beside the point here. What matters is that I didn't love my husband as I should have, as he deserved. He was my friend and I loved him for that, but Penmara came first in his life, and he died for it. He married me to save it and he died because of it, and I'm glad I didn't love him. I'm glad my parents left before I was old enough to love them. I'm glad Conan died before I could love him. And now I'm glad you think ill of me, even while you think you love me, so I remember not to love you. I will not let myself love anyone." She pounded one fist on the sill to emphasize each word. Then she slammed the window and charged toward the door.

"My lady, Morwenna." David spoke her name quietly.

She checked her flight but didn't look at him.

"I want to believe you innocent of all wrongdoing more than I want to stop loving you."

She gave her head a hard shake. "As I said, you're a good man. You want me, and your goodness tells you that has to mean you love me. Don't let that hurt you in the end. You're far safer with the part of you that is thinking in your head and telling you I'm guilty. Either go to the authorities with that information, or go home to Bristol where you're safe."

"Morwenna —"

She slipped out the door before he could even think to look for his clothes, let alone don them. By the time he located them folded into a chest, she was nowhere to be found in the inn. None of the Trelawny party were to be found in the inn according to the young man with a pistol stationed outside his chamber door.

"Sir Petrok hired me to guard you and taste your food," explained the youth, who looked as solid as the truncheon hanging from his belt along with the pistol. "If you

352

want to go somewhere, I'll be going with you."

"No, thank you. I'm staying right here."

He was staying in Cornwall until he had his answers and until he won Morwenna's heart. Neither task was going to be easy, but one thing he now knew for certain.

Morwenna Trelawny Penvenan was not among the guilty.

CHAPTER 18

Morwenna was not only slumping, she supported her sagging head and shoulders with her elbows on a table in the inn's coffee room and held her chin in her cupped hands. Grandmother had already admonished her about her elbows on the table and her poor posture. She ignored it. She ignored the talk between Tristan, Jago, and Grandfather. Her gaze rested on the rain-streaked window and the blurry image of the inn yard beyond, without seeing any of the carriages or horses coming and going. She wasn't thinking of David — much. All but that corner of her mind into which she relegated David for the moment, she held fixed on the meeting that had ended no more than a quarter hour earlier.

A wholly disastrous meeting.

"We cannot invest in mines on an estate riddled with scandal," one of the potential investors declared, speaking for all his cohorts. "If Lady Penvenan is innocent of helping wreckers, then we will reconsider. The land there should still be rich in ore, so you should perhaps consider selling now that the entail on the land is broken."

Repeating those words in her head again and again, Morwenna slouched farther, going so far as to cover her face with her hands. She kept hearing "sell Penmara" from all sides. Grandfather could do it too. The disposal of Mihal's inheritance lay in the hands of the trustees, and with this failure, they might decide selling was in Mihal's best interest. What monies it brought could be placed in trust for his majority. Morwenna would be forced to raise him in the rigid rules of Bastion Point. With herself and Drake as examples of what that produced, she didn't want her son growing up there, however much her grandparents claimed the Lord had changed their hearts. She still saw them as autocratic.

An alternative was to wed.

She peeked through her fingers at Jago and Tristan. They were such good catches, intelligent, attractive, enamored of her. Neither had his own home, and Grandfather could still sell Penmara, but her dowry from Bastion Point's vast wealth would more than provide for purchasing lands and a house, if not Penmara itself.

But she could still feel David's lips on hers. Even the memory hours later set her pulse racing and warm softness spreading through her. He was a terrible choice. Better looking than either Tristan or Jago. He was kinder, certainly, with his heart more in tune with what the Lord wanted of a man than either of the others. But there the pros ended. David was poor. David lived in Bristol. He claimed to love her.

She shouldn't have let that happen. She should have done a better job of discouraging him from caring for her. She shouldn't have let him kiss her once, let alone more. She knew quite well that physical wanting got mistaken for love. He'd looked upon her with longing and hunger from the beginning. She should have taken more care of his heart — or attraction. But she flirted and touched, cared for him and showed interest in him because she wanted information. He had given her all too little of that which she wanted and all too much of what she did not.

No, not that. She wanted — his companionship, his touch, his heart. But she would conquer that wanting as she would conquer everything else. That was how she survived. She would not let herself love a most unsuit-able man who would come to his senses and head back for Bristol the instant he could. His nice family wouldn't want her, so he would think better of suggesting she join it. He hadn't even mentioned marriage except in his apology for kissing her. That mention hadn't preceded an offer. Too easily he accepted her pronouncement that she would not love him. Then, after her revelations about herself, he had likely changed his mind about her already. She couldn't bear to look in on him and see the truth of that — abandonment — before he left her vicinity.

"Morwenna, you are in public." Grandmother never raised her voice. Nor did she speak sharply. The enunciation of each word conveyed her disapproval. "If you are weary, go to your room."

This time, Morwenna made herself straighten and lower her hands to her lap. "I should look in on Mr. Chastain."

She should stay away from him, sever the ties.

She waited for Grandmother or Grandfather to tell her that was improper. They did not. Tristan and Jago stopped talking and gave her expressions of disapproval so much like elders frowning down on a lesser being she let out a snort of amusement.

"You need to be above reproach, my lady," Tristan said.

"I am already far below reproach, Tristan Pascoe." Morwenna rose. "Nothing short of my exoneration will make matters better."

"Exoneration and marriage to someone respectable." Jago rose and started toward her. "You've been a widow too long."

"And everyone knows ladies should not be left widows for too long or they get up to mischief." Morwenna turned her back on the company and stalked to the door. "I shall go to my room. I need rest if we are to leave for Bastion Point in the morning."

"Unless the rain remains this heavy," Grandfather said. "Our old bones can't take that much exposure to the wet, and I doubt Mr. Chastain is up to the discomforts."

"Will he be returning with us?" Jago asked. "I mean, he has had singularly unpleasant experiences here in Cornwall."

"He's waiting for his family to either send or bring money," Morwenna said.

"Why doesn't someone just give him the money to move along?" Tristan asked. "I am happy to do so."

"I tried." Grandfather stared hard at Morwenna. "He has nearly as much pride as my granddaughter and perhaps a bit more stubbornness."

"Perhaps all the laborers have is their pride." Morwenna lifted the door latch.

"My dear," Grandfather said, "Mr. Chastain is far more than a laborer. He is an artisan. Where seafaring vessels are concerned, he is an artist."

"A silk purse from a sow's ear." Tristan spoke *sotto voce,* clearly for everyone to hear, even Morwenna at the door.

She opened the door. "I will accept your judgment on that, Grandfather. I know nothing of boats."

For all she had lived in sight of the sea all her life, she had only sailed once — when Conan took her to Guernsey where they could be married in secret without banns or licenses. She had been so ill she wasn't all that eager to repeat the experience.

Another reason why she and David didn't suit. Too many reasons from the gulf between their social statuses, to their mutual poverty, to her unwillingness to risk her heart. Despite all that, she found herself outside his door instead of her own.

"Is he sleeping?" she asked the guard Grandfather had hired.

"I hear him moving about some, m'lady. He asked for paper and ink."

"Of course he did." A reluctant smile tugged at Morwenna's lips. "I'll just look in on him and see if he needs anything he won't ask for."

The guard wasn't about to stop a Trelawny. He moved aside so she could tap on the door. Beyond the heavy panel she heard David's quiet, "Enter," and her heart began to race.

He sat at the simple table that served as a desk in the room. A branch of candles shone on the papers spread before him and drew reddish lights from hair he had combed but not tied back.

"If you brought tea," he said without looking up, "please set it beside the bed so I don't have to move any of these papers."

"I didn't bring tea, but I can send for it if you like."

"My lady." He scrambled to his feet. "I thought it was the guard or a maid, or I would have risen sooner."

"No need to stand on ceremony with me." She studied his pallor, obvious even in contrast with his white shirt, especially noticeable against his dark hair. "Should you be up and about at all?"

"I feel well enough now." He glanced around, then drew his chair farther from the desk. "This seems to be the only chair, so do, please, take it."

"I shouldn't stay." She formed a barrier

between them with her folded arms. "I shouldn't have come."

"I'm glad you did. I want to talk to you —"

"No." She flung up her hands, palms out. "I only came to see about your welfare."

"Did you?" He closed the distance between them.

Morwenna folded her arms again. Only a hand's breadth of space and her folded arms lay between them.

"Are you certain you came simply to see if I'm faring well?" David hooked his thumbs into his waistband. "Or do you dislike being away from me as much as I dislike being away from you?"

She would have backed away, except the door rose behind her and she feared if she opened it, David would follow her into the corridor and expose his feelings for her to everyone.

She closed her eyes so she couldn't see his enticing face and form. If she took shallow breaths, she couldn't inhale his clean-as-nature freshness of vetiver. "You should know how my reputation precedes me to Falmouth. The potential investors withdrew because of the wrecking, because of the riding officers who were set upon, because my grandfather won't put up any kind of surety for the venture." She leaned her head back against the door. "Grandfather could buy engines for a dozen mines, but will not because he wants us at Bastion Point. He wants me to fail."

"And so does someone else."

"What?" Her eyes popped open.

"Your beach has been picked as a place for the wrecking, though, from what I observed in my travels, Cornwall offers scores of miles of suitable cliffs to accomplish their end, but they pick yours." He hooked his thumbs into the slits of his breeches' pockets. "Riding officers are set upon on their way from trying to arrest you, again making you look guilty. So I believe the question we should be asking is not who is doing this, but why do they want people to believe it's you. If we work that out, we will come at the an— why are you staring at me like that?" He grinned down at her as though he already knew the answer.

She licked her lips. She swallowed. Her mouth remained dry, and she could only manage a whispered, "You don't think I'm guilty?"

"I don't. I think you're understanding why I did, but no lady as kind and giving as you is capable of perpetrating such a heinous crime."

"But, David — Mr. Chastain, how came you to change your mind? Not so long ago, you were accusing me of trying to poison you."

"Because that's the easy way to think of answers. You are the obvious culprit. Too easy a culprit." He leaned against the wall beside her, his arm brushing hers. "As I was lying there trying to work out how I could think ill of you and be so certain of loving you, I realized that I had to be wrong in one way or the other. You tried to talk me out of loving you more than you tried to talk me out of thinking ill of you."

"I cannot protest enough to prove my innocence."

"But you could tell me of your past, thinking it would give me a disgust of you. Am I not correct in this?"

She shrugged.

David chuckled. "It had the opposite effect, you know." He rubbed his thumb along the sensitive skin behind her earlobe. "You told me of a lady who deeply regrets her past and showed me one willing to sacrifice her own happiness for the sake of her son and a husband who isn't even around now to know. You were more interested in preserving my heart than hurting me. You —"

He hesitated as several voices rang in the

corridor, then returned his attention to her, sliding his thumb from her ear to her chin. "Your behavior and your words support the lady I see; they do not support the sort of lady who would resort to murder to protect a —" The footfalls and voices grew louder, pausing outside the chamber door, and David broke off again. His hand fell away, and he strode around her to fling open the door just as a lady in widow's weeds, the veil of her hat flung back over the brim, raised her hand to knock.

Stunned by David's words, Morwenna stared into a pair of gray-green eyes set into the face of a middle-aged beauty, and her insides twisted.

She was alone in David's bedchamber with him in naught save shirt and breeches, and she facing his mother.

"Mama." David's heart eased to see his pretty, petite mother standing before him, even if her coffee-colored brows were drawn together in a frown of disapproval. "It's good to have you here at last."

"But you were not expecting me, I can see." Her precise, cool voice rang clearly, if not loudly, through the room and beyond to a corridor full of the Trelawny party and physician. "Otherwise, you would not have a female in here with you only half dressed."

"This is Lady Penvenan." Lips twitching, David grasped Morwenna's hand and drew her forward.

"Then she outranks me and I should have been presented to her, not the other way around." She dropped Morwenna a curtsy. "I thank you for writing to me as soon as you had my direction. We were worried about David sailing right before that storm hit."

"With reason, ma'am." Morwenna sounded subdued. Her hand shook in his.

He squeezed it. "She was looking in on my well-being, nothing more, Mama. I expect you heard?"

"That Cornwall is not a safe place for you? Indeed I have." Mama glanced at the Trelawny party. "You are kind to take care of my son. He looks better than I expected to find him to."

"We were happy to do so." Morwenna still spoke with the restraint of the highest born of ladies, her voice the low thrum of a half-asleep kitten — barely audible. "And now we happily leave you two alone." With a gracious inclination of her head, Morwenna slipped past Mama with a rustle of skirts and drew the door shut behind her.

Mama wrapped her arms around David

and rested her head against his chest. "I so feared we had lost you."

"There've been a few times I was afraid you were going to lose me as well." David patted her shoulder. "But I'm alive and thinking there's little better than seeing at least one member of my family again."

"I want my chicks gathered around me again. Andrew wrote from Southampton. He'll be back in Bristol any day now. And if you come home with me, we will be together again and be able to plan what we do now — now that my William is gone."

"I want to do that." David shoved his hands into his pockets and toyed with Morwenna's hairpin as he gazed at the blank door through which Morwenna had walked with nothing settled between them. "But I won't be leaving with you anytime soon."

"Why not?" Mama backed away far enough to look into his face.

David wouldn't meet her eyes. "I need to stay here in Cornwall."

Mama took several steps into the room, the flowing black fabric of her skirt hissing across the floor, the veil drifting behind her like smoke. When she reached the chair, she faced him, her hands on her hips. "Tell me everything, David."

Oddly, David was reluctant to start. "Shall we wait until tea arrives?"

"I didn't order tea. Did you?"

"No, but I have gotten to understand how these people live. We will receive refreshment in —"

A knock sounded on the door. David opened it to find a maidservant on the threshold bearing a tray with teapot, cups, and plates of pasties and cakes.

"Thank you." David took the tray from her and carried it to the desk.

Mama stood looking down at his drawings. "That is a fine vessel you're planning there, but nothing we're likely to build."

"Martin asked me to design it anyway. He found notes in Father's desk . . ." David brushed the papers aside with one hand and set the tray in their place. "Will you do the honors?"

Mama sat and poured tea and milk into a cup, then eyed the food. "Meat pies?"

"Pasties. Everyone eats them here from miners to noblemen. I think only the ingredients change. The miners get potatoes and the gentries get beef."

"We're eating a great many potatoes these days." Mama picked up a pasty. "Will this be beef?"

"It was ordered by the Trelawnys. It will

have beef."

"I saw Bastion Point. I went there first, then came this way by boat." Mama bit into the pastry and sighed with contentment.

David smiled and carried his own refreshment to the table beside the bed so he could sit. He didn't much feel like eating, but nibbled to make Mama happy.

"Are they as wealthy as they look?" Mama asked.

"I believe they are. One of those young men with them said something once about fifty thousand pounds a year."

Mama choked on her tea. "And we consider ourselves blessed with one thousand a year."

"We are." David sipped his tea, though he wanted to gulp it. "We love one another."

"And the Trelawnys do not?"

"They are too prideful and determined to have their own way to truly love."

Mama eyed him above the rim of her cup. "Including Lady Penvenan?"

David met Mama's gaze. "Including Lady Penvenan."

"Yet you're sweet on her anyway."

"I'd say it's more than sweet on her. I'd marry her if she'd have me."

"But she won't." It was a statement, not a question, and Mama finished with a sigh.

"Peeresses do not marry boatbuilders. Heir-esses do not marry boatbuilders."

"You married Father."

"I was the youngest of too many daughters of a mere baronet. An impoverished bar-onet. A man with a large house and good income was the best I could expect." Ma-ma's eyes filled with tears. "And he loved me and I him. I doubt I would have traded your father for any number of well-set-up gentlemen even if I had enjoyed the op-portunity."

"Lady Penvenan has opportunities. Good opportunities. She doesn't need a penniless boatbuilder." David stared into his teacup, as empty as his heart's future. "She's afraid to love anyone, I'm thinking. For all the Trelawny wealth, she has had an unhappy life. Her grandparents are autocratic, her husband was murdered, and her parents —"

"Yes, let us discuss her parents. Did you know they are at Bastion Point?"

CHAPTER 19

The Trelawnys, Morwenna's parents thought dead for years, were in Cornwall. Should he or should he not tell Morwenna before she met her parents face-to-face for the first time in six years? And if he told her, would he not have to admit he knew, that he had known all along, that they were alive? Then he would have to admit that he had kept the information from Morwenna just as soon as he had told her he believed her, he trusted her because he loved her.

Having given up his chamber for his mother's comfort in the crowded inn, David pondered these questions as he paced the taproom, now empty at four of the clock in the morning. A truckle bed had been set up for him in the chamber Rodda and Pascoe shared, but David had been unable to rest with them so close. Servants slept on truckle beds, and he wasn't about to play the role of a servant with those two. Without rest, he would fare poorly on his way back to Bastion Point in the morning, and working out what to say to Morwenna — if anything — was far more important.

What to say to the Trelawnys when he encountered them was perhaps more important.

"You murdered my father," scarcely seemed appropriate.

He didn't know if they had directly. He only had coincidence and circumstance to conclude any wrongdoing on their part. They paid Father a late-night visit.

Two days later, he disappeared with nearly every penny the business and family possessed. Then he died. A month later, David nearly died — three times.

When the Trelawnys were nowhere about.

Not that they had been about Father died either.

David slumped on the snug beside the banked fire and rubbed his aching eyes. "Heavenly Father, I can't tell her anything. I can't *not* tell her anything. Now, if I had any chance with her, it's likely gone unless you make this right." With a sigh, he added, "If you want to make it right."

Of course the Lord might not want them together. David had to accept that as much as he didn't want to. An unblessed union was worthless.

And they were so disparate in their lives, perhaps he was a fool for thinking for a moment they could share more than what they already had.

She thought him a good man. Once she learned what he'd kept from her, she would know he was not. If he did not give in to the Lord's will for his life, he was not a good man, as much as any man was good on his own merit.

He must simply face what the Lord set forth before him instead of trying to manage things on his own. He had certainly failed at that, nearly paid for his efforts with his life.

Weary to the bone, David fell asleep on the high-backed seat. He woke to the sound of carriage wheels rumbling over the cobblestones in the yard and the shout of the hostlers. Any moment, the maid was likely to rush through with refreshment for the travelers unless the travelers themselves entered the premises. Either way, David needed to get himself up to his shared chamber to wash and shave, if he could get hot water so early.

A peek through the window at the stable clock told him the hour was not so early after all. Daylight was breaking enough to dim the lights on the carriage and above the stable door.

He hastened up to the top floor and along the gallery to his room. Cans of water indeed already sat outside the door. David carried one inside and poured steaming liquid into the basin as quietly as he could manage. By the time he shaved, brushed and tied back his hair, and donned fresh linens, the other men were rousing themselves and grumbling about having to carry in their own water.

David considered leaving the others with their grumbling, but remembered how Morwenna had called him a good man, and retrieved the other can of water for Pascoe and Rodda. Neither man thanked him. He merely smiled at them and departed.

As he passed her door, Morwenna stepped onto the gallery. She jumped at the sight of him, then offered him a tentative smile. "Is your mother well?"

"She is, though was weary, so I left her to sleep."

"She's very pretty." Morwenna's eyes danced. "But then, you favor her."

"Are you saying I'm pretty?" David paused beside her, hands shoved into his coat pockets to stop himself from drawing her to him.

She shook her head, sending the silly little feather on her hat bobbing. "You're too big to be called pretty. You're simply a pleasure to the eyes."

He drank in her beauty with the first rays of the sun kissing her cheeks. "Are you flirting with me, my lady?"

"I'm afraid it's second nature to me. Or perhaps first nature. I say things without thinking about how one might take them."

"I'd like to take them to heart." He gave in and traced a fingertip along the path of a sunbeam on her skin.

Her lashes dropped over her eyes. "Do not. I . . . cannot until I solve the disarray in which I find my son's inheritance."

"On your own, of course."

"Of course."

"And being on your own has done so well for you thus far?"

"And how will you help when you are a self-proclaimed poor man?" She turned away and started for the steps. "Now that your mother is here, I expect you'll be heading back to Bristol."

"We will be heading back to Bastion Point."

She halted and stared back at him over her shoulder. "Why?"

"I have unfinished business there. You see,

Morwenna —"

Footfalls rang on the wooden planks of the gallery. "You dare call her by her Christian name?" Tristan Pascoe strode between them and offered Morwenna his arm. "I should have been here sooner, my lady, to prevent this insult to your dignity."

David waited to see if she would renounce him for the low-class clod he knew most people thought him. If she did, she wasn't the lady he thought her.

"I am not insulted, Mr. Pascoe." Eschewing Pascoe's proffered arm, she started down the steps ahead of all of them.

"She is such a kindhearted lady, even to your sort." Tristan shot David a glare that should have shriveled him, and followed Morwenna.

David started to follow, his heart lightened by her championship of him, but someone called his name and he turned back to see Sir Petrok holding open the door to his chamber. "Will you join us, Mr. Chastain?"

Did the man expect him to say no?

David nodded and retraced his steps as far as the Trelawnys' room. They seem to have had coffee carried up to them — service for three, as their room was large enough to sport a table and chairs. Lady Trelawny already resided there.

Sir Petrok motioned David to take one of the other chairs. "We may not gain another opportunity to speak."

"About what, sir?" David drew out the chair but waited for the older man to sit first.

"You have nice manners," Lady Trelawny said. "Though I can see why after meeting your mother. Her family is from near Bath, is it not?"

"Yes, my lady." David accepted the cup of coffee she poured for him. "She married far beneath her."

"So did our elder granddaughter. She married an American." Sir Petrok's eyes twinkled. "Some would say that's worse than her marrying a poor Englishman."

David stirred sugar he didn't want into his coffee to have something to do with his hands. "I have never met an American, so hold no opinion on the merits or demerits of their character."

Sir Petrok laughed. "You are diplomatic, I see. Well, we aren't from the highest stock. Let me be more accurate and say that, once upon a time, the Trelawnys of our branch and Phoebe's family, especially Phoebe's family, were fine stock. But they fled during the Civil War in the 1640s and lived by their wits and not always lawfully for many decades until they found their way back here. Many consider our bloodline polluted or diluted with common stock. We prefer to think that we look at the character of a man before the history of his family."

"Except for our elder son." Lady Trelawny sighed. "He and his wife are inclined to prefer blood over character."

David concentrated on removing the spoon from his cup and setting it on his saucer without spilling a drop of coffee. He wanted to drink some of the rich brew, but his heart pounded so quickly his hands shook, and he feared pouring the contents down his front if he lifted the cup.

"We have said we are not opposed to you courting our granddaughter," Sir Petrok continued. "And, with the events of two days ago so recent, I think we need to know why someone is trying to kill you."

David curled his fingers around the edge of the table and chose his words with care. "I believe someone fears my father left me some kind of message before he died. Or I saw something during the wreck, or . . ." Weariness overwhelmed him, and he bowed his head. "I wish I knew for certain. It might be as simple as the fact that —"

The words choked in his throat. He could not tell these people, these kind people who overlooked his lowly station in life in giving him permission to court their granddaughter, that his life could be endangered because of their own son and his wife. The Trelawnys, the younger ones, were the key to all of this for certain, and he couldn't breathe a word of it, could not make accusations against the son and daughter-in-law of his host without more information.

"I'm going to ask some questions at the Bolithos', with your permission," he concluded. "The physician here said something must have been put into my food there."

"Servants, alas," Lady Trelawny said, "are all too easily bribed."

"You have our permission and any aid we can provide." Sir Petrok rose, signaling an end to the interview. "Tell us if you learn or remember anything."

"Of course."

"Let us go down to our breakfast. It'll be a long day's ride."

They left the chamber and headed for the ground-floor parlor. On the way, David detoured to fetch Mama. She appeared more rested, but a tremor around her mouth suggested she was troubled in her mind.

"You must tell her of her parents' return, David," Mama said as she greeted him. "I have reached this conclusion this morning upon waking."

"I think I cannot win either way." He offered Mama his arm. "And opportunity is going to be scarce."

He tried. He offered to help her mount, hoping he could then ride beside her, but she accepted the aid of a hostler from the inn and drew up beside her grandfather. Though the conformation of the party changed, seven riders this time, David never managed to find himself beside her when he could talk to her.

He might have done so at the Bolithos' cottage, but he had other matters he wished to tend to there. With the excuse — a true one — that he needed a walk after the long ride, David made his way around the house and into the kitchens. The staff stared at him, their silence crying out their discomfort to have a guest invade their domain, but then he spoke and his accent, perhaps a little exaggerated for the purpose, gave him entrée. A giggling maid offered him tea, the elderly cook gave him thick slices of dark bread and thicker slices of ham — "Instead of that dainty fare the quality demands" — and soon David found himself seated at the scrubbed kitchen table with a repast he far preferred to more cold meats and salad.

For a moment, his conscience pricked him about leaving Mama on her own, but only momentarily. Mama was better equipped to hold her own amongst the gentry than was he. She had lived with people like the Bolithos and Trelawnys, if not with as wealthy a people, until she was two and twenty when she met Father quite by accident while visiting friends in Bristol and wed him two months later. They had been happy together for over thirty years. She deserved to know why he had betrayed her and the family in the end and died so horribly.

"Do you all get weary of working in such a remote location?" he asked the assembled servants. "At least I think it remote after living in the city all my life."

"It's not so bad." The giggly maid fluttered her gold-tipped lashes. "We get plenty of visitors, though none so handsome as you."

"Chesten." The cook rapped the girl's knuckles with a wooden spoon.

David laughed. "I expect your visitors don't come here to the kitchen either."

"Too good for the likes of us." One of the footmen sneered into his tankard of ale. " 'Cept when they're wanting one of our girls."

While the others hushed the youth, David sat up straighter, every fiber alert. "They bother the maids?"

"Never you mind, young sir." The cook tramped back to the fire and began to stir a pot of something savory. "He was sweet on one of the maids, but after one of the gentlemen came calling here, she left us showing a lot of coin."

"And there's only one thing a girl does to get that much of the ready that quickly." The footman's mouth quivered. "And she been going to chapel with me every week."

Perhaps not just one thing.

David made himself take a large bite of his sandwich and chew slowly before speaking so as not to let anyone think he was too interested. "That seems ungrateful, just leaving without notice." David took another bite and waited.

"Without notice or where we can find her." The cook slammed the lid onto the pot. "Ungrateful chit."

So he couldn't follow up with the maid. But how did he ask who had sent for her without sounding salacious?

A ringing of a bell from the dining room made the point moot. The servants went scurrying to their duties, scooping up plates of cheese, nuts, and hothouse strawberries or empty trays. David's own repast was finished, and he had no more excuse to remain. So he thanked the cook and departed, making his way to a bench outside the stable as though he had merely been soaking in sunshine instead of going back inside after his walk. He considered questioning the grooms, but they were too busy taking care of the horses to give David opportunity to engage them in conversation.

He had learned something, though. One of the maids had disappeared just as the physician in Falmouth said was likely to have happened. She could have placed something noxious into his food and ensured the right plate set down before him. But she certainly hadn't acted on her own. Someone had paid her. She probably didn't even know why or what was the intended result.

David rose and returned to the house in time to greet everyone as they exited the dining room and entered the parlor. He sought out Mama to ensure she was all right. She was deep in discussion about the benefits of orgeat over cordial with Mrs. Bolitho and merely nodded at him. But Morwenna walked right up to him, her eyes full of concern.

"You never rejoined us."

"The lure of a fine day and country fare in the kitchen was too much for this simple man." He held out his arm. "Shall I escort you into the parlor?"

She tucked her hand into the crook of his elbow. "I'd rather a walk outside myself, but am afraid that won't do. Tristan and Jago will join us, and I cannot go walking with three gentlemen."

"Will you ride beside me? I need to talk to you."

"I don't know. You see —"

What she saw he wasn't to know then. Pascoe and Rodda commandeered her attention, and David crossed the room to make his apologies to his hostess for abandoning her table.

"I understand you did not fare well after your last visit here." Mrs. Bolitho's wrinkled face crumpled further. "I hope you are improved now?"

"Yes, ma'am. A momentary disposition is all." He bowed, accepted her offer of a cup of tea, though he had already had more than he wanted, and moved to Mama's side.

"I think," she said for his ears alone, "these people have empty lives."

"Not at all. At least the Trelawnys spend a great deal of time and money helping those less fortunate around them. Lady Trelawny is always planning some function to entertain or raise money for the good or making warm clothes for the children. And Sir Petrok is a magistrate and — you're laughing at me."

"You champion them well despite how things have gone for you here."

David allowed his gaze to stray toward Morwenna. She had extricated herself from Rodda and Pascoe to talk to Mr. Bolitho — or rather listen to him with seeming interest in whatever he was saying. She was pretty and kind, and she also enjoyed entertainment, simple entertainment, like romping on the beach with two dogs nearly the size of ponies.

"She thinks I'll abandon her like everyone else she has loved."

He wouldn't abandon her if he could manage it, but he had betrayed her belief in him.

If only he could talk to her before they reached Bastion Point . . .

He didn't have an opportunity to talk to Morwenna before they departed from the Bolitho home; however, he did grasp the chance to talk to one of the grooms. He dropped his purse containing its single guinea, to give himself an excuse to ride back to the Bolithos'. "I'll come up with you all shortly." He wheeled his mount around.

Sir Petrok looked dubious. "Should you be traveling alone after . . . knowing someone doesn't want your existence to continue?"

"I'm likely safer alone, sir." David spurred his mount ahead before anyone could think of a way to keep him with them or decide to accompany him.

He reached the stable yard in moments and asked a lounging groom if he'd found the purse. "It's light enough as it is."

"Here you go, sir." A boy with a pitchfork hurried up to hand David the pitiful excuse for a purse. "I put it aside thinking it were sommit you'd be back for, seeing as Sir Petrok left handsome vailes for us."

"Vailes?" David didn't know the word.

The outdoor servants, all appearing now, stared at him as though he were daft.

"You know, vailes. Money for our service," the youth tried to explain.

"Kinda like a tip in a chophouse," one of the older men explained.

Chophouses, David knew — establishments where a man could get a hearty meal for little money. They weren't fancy like many inns; they simply provided meat and bread for working men. One laid down a few pence to ensure good service.

"So do you give good service to those who give better vailes?" he asked.

The grooms exchanged glances and didn't reply.

David laughed. "Don't dare admit it, eh? Does anyone come calling who doesn't give good vailes?"

They shrugged.

David decided to take a chance. "Anyone been here who might have given that maid good enough vailes she could leave her post?"

"Lots of folk could have persuaded our Nell away," the stable boy said.

The others made gestures for him to be quiet.

"What's it to you?" the eldest groom asked.

"I'm looking for whoever that is. I owe him something." Empty though it was, David tossed his purse in the air and caught it. A guinea was nothing to turn one's nose up at, and if one of them talked enough, he would give it up.

But silence prevailed for so long he knew he would have to ride along soon or be benighted.

"I respect your loyalty to the guests of your employers." He tucked his purse into his pocket and gathered his reins. "I needs be on my way then."

"It's not that we won't talk," one of the younger grooms said. "It's just that we've had a lot of callers of late. All of you today and t'other day, and that pretty lady, and one of the gents and any number of folk."

Not helpful, but he tossed them the guinea anyway. "Divide it among yourselves for what you did tell me — and for my vailes to those in the kitchen for their care." Without looking back, he rode off in search of his party.

He knew only a little more than he had. The pretty lady would have been Mama. Lots of gentlemen could be anyone in the county or beyond. No one mentioned a couple, folk who had known them. That would have commanded comment if the Trelawnys had been there.

Thought of the Trelawnys now at Bastion Point urged David to ride faster than his usual trot, the only speed at which he was comfortable. He was already sore from the long ride two days ago. Tomorrow he might not be able to walk from the sort of exercise he was unused to and his weakened constitution of late. He needed to reach the Trelawnys and — what? Confront them? Outright accuse them? Just because the Bolitho servants hadn't seen them didn't mean they hadn't been there.

Yet if they were responsible for the attempts on his life and his father's death, why had they been surprised to learn of Father's death and been distressed about it?

He didn't know those answers, but he could answer that they were involved in all of this. As much as he might wish to deny it, he could not. And he needed to tell Morwenna.

But clouds began to roll in from the sea, bringing on darkness early. His mount began to weary, and he had to slow long before he caught up with the party. By the time he spotted his traveling companions, they had nearly reached Bastion Point and the sun hung from the cliffs, ready to plunge into the sea. They had reached the gates with their lion guards by the time David drew within hailing distance, and then warning Morwenna was too late, for as the porter swung the gates open, a man and woman appeared on the drive holding hands and all but running.

"Morwenna." David edged his mount beside hers. "I wanted —"

But she was reining in and sliding to the ground, her face white. "Mammik? Tasik?" Her voice breathy and strained, she stumbled forward on her overly long habit skirt.

David dismounted as well and grabbed her mare's reins along with his own. The others had halted, their faces registering shock. Morwenna looked about to faint, and David released the horses to stand behind her.

The couple gathered before her, holding out their hands as though waiting for her to make the first move of welcome.

"It is you." Morwenna did not hold out her hands or take theirs. "You're not dead."

"We're very much alive." The man David had glimpsed in Father's office, looking younger than what must be well past forty years, stepped closer and took one of her hands in both of his. "It's been a long time coming."

"We've missed you, child." The lady took Morwenna's other hand. "Except you're not a child now, are you?"

"I haven't been for years." Morwenna freed her hands and crossed them to grip her upper arms. Her voice was as cold as the Irish Sea.

Tears filled Mrs. Trelawny's eyes. "We can explain . . ." She blinked and looked past her daughter — to David. Her face brightened.

He realized his error in being with Morwenna at that moment, but the time for making himself scarce had passed.

Mrs. Trelawny looked to her husband. "Branek, look, this must be the other Mr. Chastain."

"You know them?" Morwenna turned on David, her eyes flashing, her fists clenched. "You know my parents?"

"I haven't met them officially —"

"But you knew they were alive? All this time, you knew —" She choked and pressed her hand to her lips.

"I think," Sir Petrok said from behind David, "this is not the place for this reunion. Branek, Arabella, we are happy you are home at last. Let us continue to the house —"

"How could you not tell me?" Morwenna seized David's lapels. "How could you?"

"It's a complicated story —" David's explanations all jumbled in his head until nothing would emerge with any coherence.

"I think," Branek Trelawny said, "he didn't want to tell you we're responsible for the death of his father."

CHAPTER 20

Morwenna felt as though someone had punched her in the belly. "You lied to me." She yanked so hard on David's lapels a button flew off. "How could you? How —"

"M'lady." David's fingers curled around her wrists and gently removed her hands from his coat. "I did not lie. I didn't tell you . . . I couldn't . . ." He closed his eyes and his face twisted.

"I think," Tristan said, "I shall ride on for home. Care to join me, Jago?"

"I do." Jago bowed from his saddle. "I shall call in the morning, Lady Penvenan."

"Do what you like." Morwenna still glared at David as she dismissed Jago and Tristan. "You let me talk about my parents. You listened to me talking about them vanishing and probably being dead. And you never . . . You never . . ." Her throat closed and tears burned her eyes.

"Leave the poor lad alone, child." Her

father grasped her shoulders and drew her from David. "We shall talk in the house."

"I'm thinking Pascoe has the better notion." David managed a half smile.

Morwenna wrenched herself free and headed up the drive. Her father, her grandfather, perhaps Mammik called after her. She ignored them. Footfalls and hoof beats followed her. She walked faster, wanting, needing to be alone even for the few minutes' trek along the drive. Her heart raced ahead of her, her thoughts close behind.

She loved David. She had begun to trust him, and he had betrayed her.

"Why, why, why?"

What was wrong with her that everyone left her in spirit, if not body? David washed ashore in her life and created havoc. Her parents returned and created havoc. She was better off alone.

She reached the front steps. The entry doors stood open with footmen ready to take up bags and see to everyone's needs waiting on either side. Morwenna rushed between them and headed up the two flights of steps to the nursery, to her son, whom she would not abandon. The hour was late and Mihal slept while Miss Pross worked embroidery onto the hem of a petticoat.

She glanced up at Morwenna, set her

needlework aside, and rose, motioning Morwenna back into the corridor. Morwenna shook her head and stood beside the crib, gazing at her son. She might have only chipped blocks and dented tin soldiers for him to play with, but he would grow up knowing he was loved. Surely that was more important than all the advantages of wealth.

"I will try to give you both."

She would manage on her own somehow. No more letting others lie to her, if only by omission. No chaos of heart and mind.

She ghosted her fingers along his thick, dark hair, then left the nursery to speak with Miss Pross. "Thank you for taking such good care of him."

"It's been a joy to me." The glow in Miss Pross's eyes said she spoke truth.

Truth, yes, she spoke truth and, to Morwenna's knowledge, always had. And if she could do so, surely others did as well.

She believed David spoke truth to her, but he had kept secrets from her, important information.

Yes, she was better off on her own, away from love, away from lies. Yet if she returned to Penmara, she would rob dear Miss Pross of the joy of caring for a child when life had denied her her own offspring. What if she didn't clear her name and find investors for the mines? She might lose Mihal to his guardian, Penmara to the trustees. She hadn't done so well on her own so far, not since she refused to live at Bastion Point and let her grandparents help her. Conan might have lived had she insisted she bring her grandfather to help. Conan had been just as determined to manage on his own . . . and he was dead. Though she didn't fear for her life, Morwenna found herself struggling with her thoughts as she descended to the first floor. Everyone was gathered in the parlor with cups of coffee or tea, plates of sandwiches, pasties, and cakes. A fire blazed against the chill of an early spring evening. In the candlelight, everyone appeared weary.

She scanned the room in search of David. He perched on the edge of a settee beside his mother to one side of the room. Mrs. Chastain was drawn but composed. David met Morwenna's gaze and his eyes, more gray than green, held pain, before he looked away from her.

Of course he did. The Trelawnys had wronged him. How could he bear to remain there with people who admitted they had caused his father's death?

She approached her parents, who sat in adjacent chairs beside the fire. Mammik wore a woolen gown and shawl as though the temperature were one of deep winter. Or perhaps she was ill? She didn't look ill. Her face, though lined at the corners of her eyes and creased at her lips as though she spent much time smiling, was still beautiful. Her hair was now threaded with gray, startling against sun-darkened skin, making her look anything but English.

She smiled at Morwenna and rose to embrace her. "You have every reason to be angry with us, but please try not to be. We never forgot you."

"You have odd ways of showing it." Grandfather spoke the words Morwenna couldn't bring herself to say aloud to her parents. "A single letter would have sufficed some."

"We haven't been where letters can get delivered," Tasik said.

"Or written," Mammik added.

"But you have been in England for some time, have you not?" David rose and crossed the room to stand with his hands in his pockets and one shoulder propped against the mantel. He fixed his gaze on the younger Trelawny couple, and his face was hard.

Mammik sank onto her chair as though all her woolen trappings were too heavy for her to hold them upright. "We landed in Bristol over two months ago."

"And after we concluded our business there —"

"After you hired my father to — what? Build a boat in secret even from his family?" David interjected.

"We didn't tell him to keep secrets from his family. We said only to be discreet in whom he confided. We were discreet in choosing Chastain's, and then further as we traveled down to Plymouth." Tasik reached for a pasty and bit into the flaky crust. "That's where the trouble started." He spoke with his mouth full.

Grandmother shuddered. "Branek, you have forgotten your manners."

"I have forgotten good English fare." He took another healthy bite.

"From my perspective," David said in his gentle Somerset accent, "the trouble started in Bristol."

"Yes, well . . ." Tasik inhaled another bite of pasty, then chewed with agonizing slowness.

"You came to Chastain's in Bristol straightaway, came to ruin us with your dealings, whatever they are." If ever David's eyes resembled the color of a stormy sea, it was then, complete with the flash of lightning.

Morwenna looked away from him, jolted

as though lightning had struck her. He had so many reasons to detest her family. He would not continue to love her. Somehow, her parents had been the cause of his father's death, and now the death of his love for her — surely.

I should have known better than to care too much. She closed her eyes until tears ceased burning the backs of her lids.

"We needed a vessel built as quickly as possible, by autumn so we can sail south after hurricane season," Mammik said. "But we wanted a lesser known boatyard. We asked around and learned that Chastain's has a reputation for good design and construction and honest dealings."

"A pity," Mrs. Chastain said in her clear, crisp voice, "that your dealings were not so honest."

"Not dishonest at all. We were going to bring the money as soon as we had it. And we did have it to pay him back as soon as we met up with him in Falmouth. We went to Plymouth to sell something where all the naval men coming and going with their prizes from foreign lands and ship captures make things like this less conspicuous." Tasik reached inside his coat, drew something from an inner pocket, and tossed it onto the table amid the refreshments.

Green fire blazed from a stone the size of a man's thumb, the brilliance seeming to dull flames on the hearth, the myriad candles, the reflecting glow of silver dishes. Outside, lightning flashed, and around the room, a collective gasp rose from the assembly.

"An emerald?" Morwenna's knees weakened.

"A Columbian emerald." Mammik drew a necklace from inside her gown. Smaller chunks of uncut but still bright stones dangled from her fingers. "We found a lost Spanish mine in the jungle."

"And have been running for fear of thieves stealing them and taking our lives ever since." Tasik picked up another pasty and grinned. "Not that that will stop us from going back."

David strode forward and picked up the gemstone. "You may be running for your life, but my father died for this."

"He did." Mammik and Tasik bowed their heads, and the pasty crumbled in Tasik's hand. "We thought —" He cleared his throat.

"Mr. Chastain was to go to Falmouth and hire workers," Mammik said. "We gave him the Trelawny medallion so Cornishmen would trust him that his word was good in the event that we were delayed in meeting him with the money."

"And we were delayed. Selling the emerald even in Plymouth was more difficult than we thought it would be. Most jewelers do not have that kind of money . . ." Tasik's voice trailed off and he looked to Grandfather. "I know. We should have come here, but we wanted to arrive home in triumph."

Across the room, Morwenna met David's eyes, and her heart twisted. Her parents' determination to succeed on their own had caused the death of David's father. She felt guilty by way of being their daughter — and more. No wonder he had said nothing to her.

She knew doing so was wrong, but in that moment, she wished her parents had remained lost to her. They had caused nothing but grief since they landed on England's shores.

David returned the emerald to the table and paced to the window, where he stared into the night.

Tasik cleared his throat in the ensuing silence. "All we have been able to work out is that someone got suspicious when they saw the Trelawny crest on that medallion with Mr. Chastain. Or perhaps someone saw us trying to sell the emerald in Plymouth and followed us. We knew nothing of Mr. Chastain's death until a few weeks ago because we were set upon outside Falmouth and knocked over our heads."

No one asked if they were all right. They both looked well and strong and alive.

"They stole the money we were bringing to Mr. Chastain, as well as two emeralds that were in my reticule," Mammik said. "The only reason they didn't get the rest is because I had them sewn into my stays as though they are the boning."

Grandmother looked pained at the mention of a lady's undergarments in mixed company.

"My husband," Mrs. Chastain said, "was poisoned."

"To make him talk?" Tasik suggested.

"To keep him from talking." David spoke without turning around. "Just as I was, even if I knew nothing."

"Your father knew nothing either," Tasik told David. "We only said we needed a vessel."

"And then went off to Plymouth to sell an emerald. And my father took most of the money we had and left for Falmouth to hire builders." David swung to face the room. "A clever man could work out that the Trelawnys might need a vessel by autumn because they were going to the southern hemisphere for something worth the expense. So all they had to do was wait for you on the road. Once they found the emeralds, it was all over."

"Who in Cornwall would do such a thing?" Grandmother asked.

Morwenna gave her an exasperated and sadly affectionate glance. "Who in Cornwall would murder a peer of the realm? Someone greedy."

"The medallion was a mistake." With a sigh, Mammik rose, retrieved the emerald from the table and the rope of them from around her neck. She crossed the room and pressed the gems into Mrs. Chastain's hand. "This is far from enough to pay for a life, but perhaps it will help restore the money your family has lost."

Morwenna held her breath, half expecting Mrs. Chastain to throw the beads into Mammik's face. But she was too much a lady to do more than incline her head, murmur something like "Thank you," and tuck the stones into her bodice. "I will take these because my family needs the money."

"We would still like you to build us that brig," Tasik said.

David shook his head. "Not until this monster is caught. I'm thinking not ever.

My father lost his life. You two could have lost yours, and I have come too close to losing mine over these jewels."

"I think," Grandfather said, "that profound wealth, as much good as it can do, isn't worth risking more lives to obtain."

"But once we find who is behind these misdeeds," Tasik protested, "I see no reason —"

"How is this tied to the wrecking?" Morwenna spoke over her father. "Or does no one else think D— Mr. David Chastain landing on my beach is too much of a coincidence?"

"My thought precisely." David glanced around the room. "I suppose whoever killed my father followed me back to Bristol. Or perhaps he tracked me down in Bristol in the event I knew something he didn't want me to."

"You had that letter your father wrote before he died." Morwenna gazed at David, trying to get him to look her way.

He looked past her. "The letter was little more than the ramblings of a dying man."

"But his killer wouldn't know that," Morwenna persisted.

"No, he would not." David glanced at his mother, taut and quiet alone on her settee. "I expect this person was on the brig I was on. I was never supposed to get back to Falmouth, and easier to do me in at sea than in either Bristol or Falmouth. If there hadn't been a storm for the wreckers, then I would have ended some other way."

"But David," Mrs. Chastain spoke up, "how could this person survive the wreck and you be attacked?"

Grandfather stiffened his already straight spine and suddenly looked old and tired. "Then this must be someone local, someone who could blend in with the wreckers, if that's the way this happened."

"Someone who wasn't surprised by the wreck and got to safety himself." A lump of ice in Morwenna's middle began to spread frost throughout her veins. She gripped the back of her father's chair so hard her nails cut into the brocade. "Someone clever enough to connect emeralds with shipbuilding and the Trelawnys. Someone who knew of their quest for the mines."

Everyone stared at her as though she spoke a foreign language. But of course, they weren't on that ride to the Penmara mines when Caroline Adair mentioned the emerald mine quest. But the others knew. Jago, Caswyn, Tristan . . . Caroline was not in England until recently. Caswyn was simply not bright enough. Jago or Tristan?

"I know —" Morwenna began, but at that moment, a scream ripped through the house and Mihal began to cry far too close at hand for him to still be in his bed in the nursery.

CHAPTER 21

"Morwenna, don't —" David shouted the warning knowing Morwenna wouldn't listen to him, not with her son crying somewhere close at hand. "Wait." He charged for the door, skirting tables and chairs and pushing Branek Trelawny out of his way. "It's a lure."

Vaguely, he understood the shouts and protests behind him, though perhaps others followed. He focused on the patter of Morwenna's boot heels on the floor, the direction from which the baby's wails emanated.

Not far. The entry hall. More shadow than light with only a handful of candles burning, the cloaked figure holding Mihal looked like an actor's depiction of death — all darkness and hollow eyes. And Morwenna sped toward him, her feet skimming the risers.

"Let him go. Let him go, Tristan."

David gripped the banister, reeling as though the name she called were a blow to his chest. Flirtatious, sometimes sulky, sometimes charming Tristan Pascoe?

David started down the steps, slowly. Too slowly. Too painfully.

"Halt, Chastain." Pascoe held up one hand from which the blade of a knife flashed. "Morwenna, will you exchange yourself for your baby?"

"You know I will." Breathless, she reached for Mihal.

The word *don't* burned on David's tongue, but he saved his breath. No mother would save herself over her child, especially not Morwenna. From the stillness of the others behind him, David understood they had reached the same conclusion.

"Come here then." Pascoe wrapped the arm with the knife-holding hand around her neck, the tip of the blade at the side of her throat. "If any of you follow, they die." With that pronouncement, he thrust Mihal into Morwenna's arms. "Walk."

They vanished into one of the parlors that led into the garden and thus onto the cliff.

"He's going to kill them anyway." Miss Pross crouched on the upper staircase, a hand fisted against her lips and tears streaking her face.

"I'll gather the servants and send for the riding officers." Sir Petrok glanced around.

"Where are the footmen?"

David began his painstaking way down the steps.

"David, you're not fit enough to go after heroics," Mama called after him.

"He's going to kill them," Miss Pross wailed.

"Where. Are. The servants?" Sir Petrok bellowed.

"I'll go." Branek Trelawny started to bolt past David.

He held out an arm and stopped him. "If we send out a brigade, I don't give any hope for their chances of survival."

"He might let them go once he's ready to escape." David began to descend again. "Besides that, how many of the servants are truly trustworthy? If Pascoe is running the wreckers, the servants might be involved and more inclined to listen to him."

"They wouldn't dare." Sir Petrok's tone lacked the conviction of his words.

"We don't know where he's taken them." Trelawny pounded his fist on the balustrade. "Oh, why did we go about this all wrong?"

"I'm thinking pride and stubbornness run in your family, sir." David reached the bottom of the steps.

"Where are you going, Mr. Chastain?" Sir Petrok called down to him.

"Penmara. I'll be starting at Penmara where he's been causing havoc for my lady."

"Then take a pistol." Sir Petrok charged down the steps at a speed belying his age and entered his study.

David followed to stop the older man. "I don't know how to use a pistol."

"Take one anyway." Sir Petrok removed a gun from a case and tossed it to David.

"Like a club." Trelawny sped into the room. "Where else should we look?"

David hesitated, thinking. "Any direction that will get him out of Cornwall."

The Trelawnys exchanged looks from landing to entryway.

Branek groaned. "Cornwall has miles of coastline and it's dark."

"Then we cannot delay." David headed across the parlor, where the door to the terrace stood open, swinging in gusts of rain-soaked wind. David hesitated on the threshold. Pascoe could have them in the garden waiting to see if anyone followed. He could have his compatriots with the wreckers waiting for him. Knocked down or even dead, he would be of no use to Morwenna and Mihal. Standing still he was of no use to them.

He headed across the terrace, down the steps, and along the path to the cliff top entrance. The door stood open, the source of the gusting wind. Below, the white caps of the waves glistened against the blackness of the incoming tide. Incoming tide meant a blocked beach access to Penmara. Going around was inconceivable. Either they were there or they were not. The sooner he discovered which, the sooner he would be able to seek in another direction.

Mouth set against the lingering weakness of illness trembling through his limbs, David commenced the treacherous descent down the cliff path. Too slowly, he reached the water. The cold shot through him, numbing his feet in an instant. Waves buffeted his legs, pushing him against the cliff, threatening to drag him out to sea as they retreated. He resisted the urge to hasten so he didn't slip. Hand on the cliff face, he plodded on, digging in his heels, pressing against the rock for balance. Ten yards felt like a hundred. Water splashed him as high as his waist. As high as the pistol.

It would now be truly useless except as a club, presuming he could get that close. Presuming he headed in the right direction to reach Morwenna.

At last, soaked and shivering, he reached the Penmara beach. He found it empty of people. But above him on the top of the cliff, a light flashed off the silvery shafts of rain.

That could be wreckers happy to simply throw David off the cliff. Pascoe might have taken Morwenna in a wholly other direction. Nonetheless, David scrambled up the path to the top. This one was wider, not as steep.

He should have gone faster. His body, so abused over the past month, refused to let him. Lead had replaced his feet. The light was moving away. He would never catch up.

Then the light returned his way, a bright, swinging lantern in the blackness. And in one flash from the lantern, hooded beneath a glass bell to protect the light from the wet, he caught a glimpse of Morwenna's face and heard the faint wail of a child.

He saw her face in the light because she held the lantern — not her son.

The light swung away from her before he could detect whether or not she was alone. Of course she wasn't. David simply didn't know where Pascoe might be.

Knowing he could be assaulted and stabbed, or even shot from any number of directions should Pascoe have accomplices or a gun himself, David shouted her name. "Morwenna, I'm here."

She halted. The lantern stilled. "David, be

careful." She accompanied the warning with a thrust of her arm that sent the lantern sailing out over the cliff to crash and die somewhere below.

A shot rang out. Morwenna screamed.

And David's insides turned to water. "Morwenna, my lady?"

"Here." Her voice was strangled, gasping.

A surge of energy roared through David, urging him to leap for Morwenna, find her wound, save her — if it wasn't too late.

"If you killed her," he called to the other man, "you had better disappear like smoke." With each word, he took a step toward where Morwenna had been, from where the shot rang out. "You won't live long enough to get off Penmara land, let alone Cornwall." He had caught a glimpse of a patch of brush, rhododendron struggling for survival on the cliff top. Eyes narrowed against the rain, he peered through the near total darkness for the shrubs, for a man . . .

For a baby . . . for a woman's body on the ground.

He saw two figures standing. Poised on the edge of the cliff, the phosphorescent crests of the waves below silhouetted their stance on the brink.

No child. No Mihal on the edge. Yet his wails rang over the roar of surf and rain.

"She's still breathing," Pascoe shouted above the roar of the surf. "But if you don't leave, I will throw her off the cliff."

Perhaps the cold had deadened all feeling inside David. He certainly experienced no fear or regret or even anger. As though striding up to a sunny garden, he paced toward Pascoe and Morwenna, stopped just beyond arm's length. "It's over, man. Let her go." His voice was as calm and cold as his numb insides.

"I still have my life," Pascoe said. "I can flee the country."

"Do you think the Trelawnys won't hunt you down if you kill one of their own?" David risked a fraction of a step closer.

Pascoe laughed. "They could never find me."

"He has nothing to lose now." Morwenna's words were weak, but she was still alive, conscious.

"Don't come closer." Pascoe's tone, for the first time, held a note of panic. "I have nothing to lose now, but you do. If you go back to Bastion Point, I'll let her go."

"Where's the baby?" David tried to remain calm, as though he carried on a normal conversation.

"Henwyn has him, the treacherous —" Morwenna's words ended in a groan.

"Then I can't risk leaving them here, Tristan." David used the man's Christian name on purpose. "If you don't kill her and the baby, you'll get transportation. You can build a new life in New South Wales."

David didn't know that, but it sounded promising, hopeful, a reason to not commit another murder.

He took a deep breath to say his next words with emotion. "There's no proof you killed my father or tried to kill me."

"I could have had everything here." Pascoe's voice broke. "Morwenna, and with her, this land. No more being the baby brother to poke and prod and dismiss as unimportant. I took a degree from Cambridge, and they treat me like I'm an idiot. But not with my own land or money from my wife's dowry for restoring these mines myself. I could have lived like a king."

"And now you'll live like a rat scuttling from the light and the trap." David moved a fraction of a step closer. "You were bound to get caught with the wrecking."

"The wrecking?" Tristan's tone was dismissive. "I wouldn't risk everything for the paltry income from wrecking."

David staggered under the impact of the buffeting wind.

Morwenna gasped loudly enough to be

heard over the roar of sea and storm. "Not a wrecker? But what about David?"

"My dear." Tristan's tone had grown affectionate. "You were the only prize I wanted — until I saw people trying to sell emeralds in Plymouth and realized they were your parents."

David took advantage of the moment to move another step closer. "Let her go."

"You go or she dies. And if she dies, the boy dies."

Mihal might already be dead. His wails had ceased.

Checkmate, unless David did something daring or foolish — or both. "All right, Tristan." He made himself smile in the hope of disarming the other man. "I'll let you go so we can get her help. See, I'm even throwing away my weapon." He made a show of tossing aside the useless and heavy pistol. He took a casual stance, hands in his pockets, and curled his fingers around Morwenna's hairpin kept out of sentimentality.

Now a weapon — maybe.

He took a step back, then dove. With one hand, he grabbed Morwenna, spinning her away from the cliff. With the other, he drove the hairpin straight for Tristan's eye.

With a scream, Tristan flung himself away

from the threat to his face. He flung himself to the side. Rain made the rocks slick. With his head thrown back, he was already off-balance. When his foot slipped, he couldn't save himself from plunging down and down to the white-edged blackness of the incoming tide.

CHAPTER 22

For some reason, all the images of angels Morwenna had ever seen were of gentle females or fierce males. The one gazing down at her from beside the bed was certainly male, but anything other than fierce — now.

She smiled at him. "Good morning, David."

"Morwenna, my lady." He emphasized the "my" as he reached for her hand atop the coverlet and laced his fingers with hers. "It's afternoon."

"Then I'm not in my room?" She glanced toward the window, where sun slanted through the leaded panes of glass.

"You're in the one beside mine."

"Scandalous." She drew his hand to her cheek.

"You're not alone." Mammik's voice came from the far side of the chamber. "I've been a terrible mother, but not so much of one I will let you be alone in a bedchamber with a man to whom you are not married."

Morwenna tried to sit upright. Her head swam, and pain shot through her side from hip to shoulder. "And speaking of terrible mothers, where is Mihal?"

"In his nursery." David rested a hand on her shoulder, holding her still. "Your father has learned a few things about sneaking up on people from his travels and surprised Henwyn before she could do any harm."

"And I thought her loyal to me." Morwenna flung her arm across her eyes. "I suppose he paid her."

"To help with the wrecking, to drug me too much to keep me senseless so I wouldn't talk, to plant evidence of you being involved in the wrecking."

"By whose orders if not Tristan's?" Morwenna tried to make sense of it all, but her head felt as though someone had used it for a tennis ball.

"Nicca," David said. "Henwyn was happy to talk for a promise of transportation rather than hanging."

"But —" Morwenna couldn't make sense of anything through her aching head and body. "Nicca is so quiet and . . . slow."

"And big enough to make others obey him." David caressed her cheek. "And Pascoe was persuasive enough to convince Henwyn and Nicca and other servants to help him get you to marry him."

"By killing you." Mrs. Chastain spoke up for the first time.

Morwenna twisted her head around to find the lady seated in the opposite corner of the room from Mammik. Apparently forgiving the Trelawnys did not come quickly or easily. Morwenna understood. They were her parents and in a corner of her mind, she admired them for chasing after their dreams. On the other hand, they had caused terrible trouble with their selfishness.

"I don't die easily," David addressed his mother. "Not when I have something to live for." He didn't look at Morwenna, but his fingers laced through hers, and she hoped.

"What's happened to Nicca?" Morwenna asked.

"I'm afraid he disappeared before we knew to catch him," David said.

"With the dogs," Mammik added. "Of all things, he used them to hold the servants in their hall for Tristan, then escaped with the disloyal beasts the minute Tristan ran off with you."

"Dogs are loyal to those who feed them." Morwenna grimaced. "Greed for food like man is greedy for wealth without hard work. A good thing all younger brothers don't behave like Tristan, considering you are a younger brother." She tried to laugh at her own lame jest, but pain shot through her and she gasped instead.

David leaned closer. "Are you in pain?"

"Only when I laugh." Morwenna moved her hand to her side. "He shot me, didn't he?"

"Only a graze along your ribs. It wouldn't have been much of a wound if I hadn't thrown you halfway back to Bastion Point."

Mammik approached the bed. "Would you like some lavender water? I was shot in India ten years ago and found it helped with the inflammation that causes pain."

"Thank you." Morwenna let David ease her to an upright position and sipped at the glass Mammik put to her lips. The water was cool, aromatic, a little bitter. She drank more deeply, then looked into her mother's face. "You were shot?"

"I was. We thought to save a widow from being burned on her husband's funeral pyre, but the villagers didn't like it. Or maybe it was the guards."

"The poor woman."

"Nothing of it. We still got her away."

"Bravery must run in your blood, my

lady." David drew her closer to him.

She rested her head on his shoulder. "And yours. I was so afraid he had killed you, and then you would go over the cliff with him." She shuddered.

David held her more tightly. "It was worth it, if it spared you."

"He must have been mad," Mrs. Chastain said.

Morwenna fixed her own mother with a piercing stare. "He was greedy."

"I think we were the greedy ones, and in that we are to blame." Mammik lowered her head. "Perhaps one day you and your family can forgive us, Mrs. Chastain, Mr. Chastain."

Mrs. Chastain crossed the room to stand before Mammik. "My husband and I have brought our children up to have faith in the Lord. We would be a poor example if I did not forgive you." She smiled. "Besides, I think our families are going to see more of each other." With a nod to David and a curtsy to Morwenna, she swept from the chamber.

"So is she a good example, David?" Morwenna ventured to ask.

"I must forgive even without her example." His voice was a low rumble beneath Morwenna's ear, the purr of a large cat.

Did he want to forgive her because his mother was right and he wanted to be a part of her family, or had her insistence in turning him away worked? Surely not. Surely not after the night before and what he had done for her.

"The Bible tells us to forgive if we want to be forgiven. And more . . ." He trailed off and released Morwenna to recline on her pillows. "With God's strength, the hurt will fade."

"I hope so." Mammik wiped her eyes on a lace handkerchief. "We are devastated at what we brought about. But if you're happy . . ."

Morwenna waited for David to speak up, but he remained silent. Too much silence remained.

"I don't know what will be my future," Morwenna spoke aloud to push aside the oppressive cloud of quiet. "I don't know what the trustees will do with Penmara now."

"I think," David said, "they should sell the land and restore the mines to bring work to the miners."

"Sell my son's inheritance?" Morwenna couldn't disguise her shock.

David's features stiffened and he rose. "Of course not. I am forgetting you want to save every precious stone."

"If I can." She raised herself on her elbow.

"I believe your grandfather is advising the sale of Penmara after all the grief it has caused."

That news hurt worse than the gunshot wound. Penmara and the dogs gone. Now Mihal was her only tie to Conan.

"Is Tristan —" Morwenna couldn't ask the question she should have posed immediately.

"They found him at the bottom of the cliff." David's face was bleak. "There's an inquest tomorrow."

Morwenna reached out to him. "No one will blame you, will they?"

"Not for a moment." Grandfather, Grandmother, and Tasik entered the room.

"We were just with the coroner. He found this on Pascoe's body." Tasik drew something from his pocket and tossed it to David.

It flashed in the stream of sunlight, and David caught it, then held it up to the light. "Isn't this yours, sir?" He held out the blue and silver medallion.

"You earned it," Tasik said. "You saved my daughter's life."

"And she saved mine." David tucked the medallion into his pocket.

Silence settled over the chamber. Then Grandfather cleared his throat. "We have not done well by our children and grand-children. In our efforts to not have you all follow in the miscreant steps I, and, yes, even Phoebe took in our youth, we tried to manipulate you all to our will using our wealth and the power it has brought. It's come too close to costing too many of you your lives." He sighed and looked like a tired old man.

Tasik gripped his father's shoulder. "But it's made us all independent."

"Too independent." Morwenna dashed a hand across her eyes. "If I weren't always so determined to succeed without anyone's help, this could all have been avoided. Even last night. I worked out that Tristan was who we were looking for, but I ran off without telling any of you." She avoided looking at David in the event he had not yet made up his mind about her — or had and it was the opposite of what she wanted. "I have made amok of being alone and going my own way. Perhaps if we all work together instead of trying to bend one another to our will, we can build a better future for all of us, for this county, for our children."

Mammik began to weep with silent tears and darted across the room to embrace

Morwenna. "I never knew I loved you for more than because you're my daughter until last night."

Tasik joined her, surrounding her with bergamot and a hint of Grandfather's pipe tobacco scents. "We've been beastly parents. But you've grown into a wonderful young lady without us."

"Perhaps because you were without us." Mammik laughed through her tears.

Morwenna wrapped her arms around both of them as best she could. "I think I rather like you, though. You and your adventurous spirits. I'd like to know more of your adventures . . . But you'll be off to your emerald mine? No doubt you can get investors."

"We think we will let someone else find that mine," Mammik said. "It's brought too much sorrow and grief."

"We'll sell the emeralds we have and invest in the Penmara mines," Tasik added.

Grandfather cleared his throat. "If you weren't full of so much stiff-necked pride, Morwenna, you could simply accept my assistance."

Morwenna extricated herself from her parents and looked to her grandparents. "I was still angry about two years ago." She held up her hand. "I know — because I was going to suffer on my own then too. But

God blessed me with this family for a reason. It's time I forgave the past and let myself be a part of it."

"At last." Grandmother wiped her eyes on a lace-edged handkerchief.

Grandfather rubbed one hand across his face. "Well then, much good has come from this. At least some of my sheep are back in the fold. Perhaps we can get Drake to come home before he gets himself killed."

"I saw how important family was to David —" Morwenna broke off and glanced around. "Where is he?"

"He left a moment ago," Mammik said.

"Why?" Morwenna started to get out of bed, realized a lack of dress, and beat her fists on the mattress.

"He's a polite young man," Tasik said. "He thought to leave us all alone."

"Not necessary." Unless he didn't want to be a part of the family. "Do I have anything decent to wear here?"

Grandmother and Mammik shooed the men from the room and bundled Morwenna into a simple round gown over her shift without stays. Her hair was such a tangle, Mammik took a silver ribbon from her own hair and tied back Morwenna's curls.

"You are so pretty, child, he won't care if your gown is a bit rumpled and your hair is unkempt." Mammik kissed Morwenna's cheek. "I am blessed."

Grandmother nodded. "I admit we weren't always certain of that, but Morwenna has become a fine lady." She opened the door to find Tasik and Grandfather waiting right outside.

"You may go in to see him," Tasik said, "but we expect you to behave yourself."

Morwenna hesitated on the threshold. "If-if this works out . . ." She fiddled with the bow beneath her bust. "He's not of our society. I think he's probably of a lower order even than Elizabeth wed."

"Considering we thought Tristan good enough for you," Grandfather said, "we have nothing to say about whom your heart chooses."

"None of us does," Mammik said, giving Tasik such a loving glance Morwenna's heart melted toward them.

They might not stay in England as they claimed they would now. Tasik might wish to discover some other part of the world, and Mammik would go with him. But Morwenna took comfort in knowing how much they adored one another. If they didn't have quite as much room in their lives for her as she might like, they still possessed the sort of love for one another she could use as an example. That was enough for her to feel they had given her a great gift as her parents.

If she hadn't sent David away once too often with her planned or careless words, she, too, would have the sort of love her parents shared.

"And there is your dowry," Grandfather pointed out. "Perhaps David will use it to build that merchantman for his brother to captain. I am more than happy to invest in such a venture."

"Perhaps." Shaking, heart racing, she turned toward his door, raised her hand to knock, then lifted the latch and simply walked in so he couldn't refuse her entrance.

He was seated at the desk, pencil in hand, with the design spread out before him. At the click of the latch, he dropped the pencil and shoved to his feet. "Morwenna — um — Lady Pen—"

"Morwenna will do." She closed the door and glided toward him, her hands outstretched. "David, I needed to come see you . . . I want to tell you . . ." She swallowed. She licked her dry lips. She raised her eyes to meet his gaze and knew exactly what she needed to tell him. "I am not returning to Penmara. If the lands are sold, the mines can be reopened, but that is Mihal's future, not mine. I'll leave Penmara behind for the plovers and gorse and follow you to Cape Town or around the Horn of Good Hope or the Sandwich Islands to be with you."

His eyebrows arched and a smile tugged at his lips. "Are you proposing to me?"

"Yes, I do believe I am." She dropped her gaze and her hands. "I'm still a brazen wanton. Probably not good enough for you and your family."

"You not good enough, my dear?" He stepped closer and nudged her chin up with his thumbs. "I am a poor boatbuilder with a Somerset accent. I wanted to offer to live with you at Penmara and help rebuild it —"

"But you build boats, not houses."

"I'll give up the boats for you. Perhaps, in time, I can learn to be the squire of an estate with a lord for a stepson."

"You would do that for me?" She gazed at him in awe, her heart no harder than melted wax.

He caressed her cheeks with his fingertips, callused and scarred from his labor. "I'd do that for you."

"You'd be bored."

"Not with you for a bride."

"You'd miss your family."

"We'll make one of our own."

Her knees went limp and she grasped his lapels for support. "Penmara will be sold so you need not be a squire. You are a boat-builder. And Mihal will do well having cousins — if your mother can bear to see a Trelawny around."

"Mama told me we're not leaving here without you." He grinned. "And several cuttings from your grandmother's garden. Of course, if she wants to expand the garden, we can't expand the house."

"Grandfather wants to invest in a brig for you to build and your brother to sail. With that and my dowry, we can build our own house." Sobering, she lowered her lashes. "I want to start afresh without my past around to plague us. I want a future with —"

He drew her against him and kissed her before she got out the "you." She gasped, then laughed, then opened her mouth under his, nestling against him as though she would never be parted from him starting that moment.

The door clicked open behind them, and before they could pull away from one another, Tasik said, "I do hope this means you have asked her to marry you."

"I believe," David said, "she asked me first."

"And you haven't in truth answered,"

Morwenna reminded him.

"I'd say he has," Tasik said.

"Do you truly think I would say anything other than yes?" David asked. Then he kissed her again.

"And here I thought I would never plan my daughter's wedding," Mammik said over Tasik's shoulder.

Morwenna turned to see her parents both in the doorway smiling at her, looking a little bemused. "I would like to have you there."

"And then I'll need to stay here long enough to attend my next grandchild's birth," Mammik continued.

"Considering the chaos you've wrought in the two months you've been in England, Mammik," Morwenna said, "another year might cause a revolution."

"Chastain," Tasik said with mock severity, "you will have to teach her how to be a good daughter, as you are a good son."

David coughed, then chuckled. "I'll do my best to be a good husband." He held Morwenna against his chest. "I love her more than I knew possible."

"And I love you." Morwenna turned in his arms to lay her head against his shoulder and circle her arms around him.

"Then you have our blessing," Tasik said.

"But I'm not closing this door."

Morwenna hid her hot cheeks in the front of David's coat and joined him in joyous laughter.

DISCUSSION QUESTIONS

1. At the beginning of the book, Morwenna saves a stranger from drowning. Why is she determined to keep him close at hand?
2. Morwenna fears several things. What are they and why does she fear them?
3. Morwenna holds considerable resentment toward her grandparents. How do you think her past drives her present actions?
4. Which of these actions are justified? Which are not?
5. How do Morwenna's actions affect her spiritually? In her relationships?
6. How can you relate to Morwenna — or not?
7. How does David's relationship with his family affect his ability to cope with everything he endures?
8. How does he justify not telling

Morwenna about her parents?

9. David is of a vastly different social class than Morwenna in a class-conscious society. What insecurities about his rank does David show — if any — and how do they affect his actions?

10. How are David and Morwenna alike despite their different backgrounds? How are they similar?

11. Morwenna is determined to succeed on her own. In what ways have you acted with a similar actor and what were the outcomes — positive or negative?

12. How does the romance between David and Morwenna help them both grow spiritually and emotionally?

ACKNOWLEDGMENTS

Writing this book shortly after the death of my mother has been one of the most difficult tasks of my career, as Mom was one of my biggest fans. Thanks to many people, I got through it and have even found joy in my craft once more. Mere mention of names cannot express a fraction of the gratitude I feel towards these ladies, and that is what I have space to do here. My agent, Natasha Kern, made sure I got the time I needed to grieve and still turn in my book. Becky Monds, my editor, took on an author she didn't know and helped me find the story I wanted to tell. My Facebook accountability group kept me on the straight and narrow when I wanted to lose my sadness in someone else's book. And, as always, Debbie Lynne, Louise, Marylu, Patty, and Ramona prayed me through. And so did a group of people new in my life — the ladies from my community group at church: Emily, Kathryn, Whitney, Kayla, and Krystal. My life is so much richer with all of you in it.

ABOUT THE AUTHOR

"Eakes has a charming way of making her novels come to life without being over the top," writes *Romantic Times* of bestselling, award-winning author **Laurie Alice Eakes.** Since she lay in bed as a child telling herself stories, she has fulfilled her dream of becoming a published author, with a degree in English and French from Asbury University and a master's degree in writing fiction from Seton Hill University contributing to her career path. Now she has nearly two dozen books in print.

After enough moves in the past five years to make U-Haul's stock rise, she now lives in Houston, Texas, where she and her husband are newly minted church leaders. Although they haven't been blessed with children — yet — they have sundry lovable dogs and cats. If the carpet is relatively free of animal fur, then she is either frustrated with the current manuscript, or brainstorming another — the only two times she genuinely enjoys housekeeping.